Praise for *A Duke to Die For*

"Intriguing danger, sharp humor, and plenty of simmering sexual chemistry."

—*Booklist*

"Sweeps readers along at a lively pace in a lusciously spicy romp."

—*Library Journal*

"Amelia Grey's writing style is fresh and expressive, bringing you right into the minds of the characters she so obviously built with love."

—Blog Critics

"Deliciously sensual… storyteller extraordinaire Amelia Grey grabs you by the heart, draws you in, and does not let go."

—Romance Junkies

"Bewitching, beguiling, and unbelievably funny… Amelia Grey starts off her new trilogy, The Rogues' Dynasty, with an absolutely enchanting and addictive tale."

—Fresh Fiction

Praise for *A Marquis to Marry*

"The second in Grey's elegantly written Rogues' Dynasty Regency trilogy delivers a captivating mix of discreet intrigue and potent passion."

—*Booklist*

"The combination of a gripping plot, scorching love scenes and well drawn characters make this book impossible to put down."

—The Romance Studio

THE ROGUES' DYNASTY

AN *Earl* TO *Enchant*

AMELIA GREY

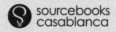

sourcebooks
casablanca

Published by Sourcebooks Casablanca, an imprint of Sourcebooks,
Inc.
P.O. Box 4410, Naperville, Illinois 60567-4410
(630) 961-3900
FAX: (630) 961-2168
www.sourcebooks.com

Printed and bound in the United States of America.
QW 10 9 8 7 6 5 4 3 2 1

This book is dedicated with grateful appreciation to Usha Rao Palep for so willingly sharing her knowledge of India and its beautiful people with me. And always to Floyd, for his constant support and love.

One

My Dearest Grandson Lucas,

No one can put matters more succinctly than my dear friend Lord Chesterfield. Read what he says here and remember it well. "The wisest man sometimes acts weakly, and the weakest man sometimes acts wisely."

Your loving Grandmother,
Lady Elder

WAS SHE LATE OR SIMPLY NOT COMING?

Lucas Randolph Morgandale, the ninth Earl of Morgandale, sat in his book room with his booted feet propped on the Louis XIV writing desk. He sipped brandy from a glass that had been warmed by his hand and listened to the rain gently beat against the windowpane. The foul weather, the indulgent amount of drink he'd consumed, and the fact that the woman hadn't arrived had him feeling restless, much to his irritation.

But it was more than the weather and the absent

courtesan that had him in an ill humor. Morgan had watched both his cousins, Blake and Race, fall in love and marry during the London Season, and he had no intentions of falling prey to the same trap, despite their clever machinations over the past few weeks. In order to avoid any such confining pitfalls, he'd decided to quit the city early and spend the entire summer at his Valleydale estate in Dorset.

The first couple of weeks, it had been easy for him to fill his days with endless paperwork, hunting, and working with his thoroughbred horses. Later in the summer he had taken the time to ride over the vast lands of all his holdings, visiting with each of his tenants and thanking them for their hard work and dedication. In the evenings, he had enjoyed gaming at the local tavern or attending one of the many house parties that were scheduled at various estates around the area.

Still there was a void, an inexplicable feeling that something was missing in his life. Since a young lad, he had always enjoyed his stays at Valleydale, and he couldn't put his finger on what made this time different.

Perhaps he had simply grown tired of the slower pace of country life. But every time he thought about going back to London, he remembered the knot of frustration over Blake's and Race's scheming in trying to show him how wonderful married life could be. He had told them on more than one occasion that he had no desire to be tied down by the bonds of matrimony.

Gambling, drinking, riding, and all the other things he'd done had not completely distracted him from the fact that his two best friends, cousins at that, had married. And while both of them had done the proper thing and invited him to dinner often, it hadn't taken him long to realize that was half the problem. Every time he turned around, one of them was having him to dinner at their home with their wives and very conveniently happened to invite a string of uninspiring young ladies as well.

He was tired of being entangled in their schemes.

Morgan huffed under his breath and took another sip of the brandy, letting it settle on his tongue a few seconds before swallowing. They were mollycoddling him as if he couldn't find feminine companionship for himself.

He had to get away. He had to get away from them. London Society was fueled by gossip, and all the scandalmongers were laying bets he'd be married by the end of summer. Morgan had scoffed at that ridiculous notion as utterly preposterous. But it hadn't kept White's from making it an official wager, much to his consternation.

Morgan would rather pay for his women so there would be no strings attached. But finding a suitable bedmate was obviously more easily planned than carried out so far from the City.

It wasn't that there weren't plenty of women around willing to share their beds or to give him a few minutes of pleasure, but Morgan had realized a few months ago, when he was at Valleydale with his cousins, that a quick romp with an upstairs wench at the local tavern no longer held any appeal for him. And unlike his cousins, Blake and Race, Morgan had never cared for the idea of setting up a paid mistress in Town to be at his beck and call. Mistresses demanded time and attention that he wasn't willing to give.

So in desperation, he supposed, he had come up with a grand plan to hire a woman never destined to be a wife to come and spend a couple of days with him at his estate; a beautiful, willing woman he could sink his flesh into with no strings attached, only relief.

With the help of his solicitor, Buford Saint, Morgan had gone to great lengths to arrange for an exclusive and quite expensive lady of the evening to travel out via a private coach to see him. Saint had assured him she was highly sought after, and even Prinny himself had been known to enjoy her services from time to time.

Morgan had a letter from Saint saying she would arrive this afternoon, but afternoon had turned to evening, and evening had become late night, and there still was no sign of Miss Francine Goodbody. When she hadn't made it by nine o'clock, and it was clear she wouldn't be taking supper with him, Morgan had sent his two house servants to bed. Since then, he had been in his book room drinking too much, as was evidenced by the pounding in his temples and the roar in his ears.

He hated the feeling of not being quite in control of himself. That and the cursed headaches the next day were the reasons he'd fallen out of favor with drunkenness years ago. But tonight, for some damned reason, he had uncharacteristically given in to frustration and ended up feeling justified for overindulging in the fine brandy his cousin Blake had given him before he left London.

While continuing to grumble over his unfortunate plight, Morgan heard a noise. A sharp sense of warning shimmied up his back for a second, and he regained control of himself instantly. Did he hear the sound of a carriage coming up the tree-lined drive that led to his house? Had the much-anticipated Miss Francine Goodbody finally arrived? As quietly as possible, he lowered his feet to the floor and placed the brandy glass on the edge of the desk. He rose, walked to the opposite side of the room, parted the sheers that covered the window, and looked out into the darkness.

A dense fog had settled over the landscape, and rain fell in a steady stream. No one should be out in this downpour, but he was certain that he saw the lights from a coach coming up the lonely road that led to the front of his house.

She had made it at last.

Morgan threw a glance at the brass-encased clock on the mantel. Almost midnight.

"It was probably Lord Chesterfield who said 'better late than never,'" Morgan mumbled softly. And for once, he agreed with the pompous earl. Though he doubted Chesterfield had said half the stuff his grandmother attributed to the man.

If Morgan met Miss Goodbody at the door, perhaps he could get her above stairs and settled into her room without waking the servants. It wasn't that he felt as if he had to sneak around in his own house or censure his conduct around his staff, but he would just as soon not have to deal with his butler, Post, or the man's wife until tomorrow morning.

Three days ago, when he received the letter from his solicitor saying that all had been arranged and Miss Goodbody would be arriving today, Morgan had given most of the staff a week off. At first he had had no feelings for the servants' sensibilities concerning this matter, but later, he wisely decided it was best to take precautions and be discreet. Why let his entire household of servants know about his dalliance with the courtesan?

The fewer eyebrows he raised with his aberrant behavior of inviting a woman to entertain him in his home, the better. Most of the servants at Valleydale had been with his grandmother for many years and were reluctant to leave, feeling they would be neglecting their duties to him to take a full week off. Morgan finally had to insist they take the holiday.

Miss Goodbody would be gone by the time the staff returned, and hopefully, because Morgan had complete trust in Post and his wife, no one else would be the wiser about Morgan's rendezvous with the delectable-sounding woman Saint had selected for him.

Morgan grabbed the low-burning lamp from his desk and walked toward the front of the house. As he strode by the drawing room, he saw lights from the lanterns on the coach pass by the window. He picked up his pace, wanting to get to the door before Miss Goodbody hit the large brass knocker that was fashioned in the shape of a magnificent horse. The clang from that thing could wake the hounds of hell. He placed the lamp on a vestibule table, and then as quietly as possible, he threw the latch and opened the heavy door. It creaked, but he hoped not enough to wake the servants who slept on the second floor and off the main section of the house.

As he stepped onto the porch, the wet, chilling air filled his lungs and helped clear his head. In the distance, behind the coach and through the trees, he saw a break in the clouds. The moon shone down, giving an eerie cast to the whorls of fog that lingered and hovered close to the ground.

Through the rain, he watched the driver jump down and open the door to the coach. A lady covered head to toe in a black hooded cape stepped out. In the gray light from the lanterns attached to the outside of the coach, he saw another woman who looked to be wearing what he would consider a servant's headpiece start to step down, too, but the lady on the ground turned and spoke to her.

Morgan couldn't hear what they were saying, but it seemed to him that they were having a heated discussion. He assumed that the maid wanted to follow Miss Goodbody to the door, but she wasn't having any of that. It struck him as odd that Miss Goodbody's maid would take her to task over anything, especially considering the fact her employer was getting drenched from the cascading rain while she was doing it. After a few moments, the maid disappeared back inside the coach, and the driver shut the door.

It hadn't dawned on Morgan that his courtesan would bring her maid, but it should have. He had intimate knowledge of how difficult it was to get a woman out of her clothing or back into it for that matter. That thought sent a wave of anticipation shooting through him. He could more than adequately handle that job for Miss Goodbody while she was at Valleydale. In fact, he was looking forward to it. There were times when unlacing stays could be quite titillating. He would find a place for the maid on the servants' floor. Her services wouldn't be needed tonight.

Miss Goodbody turned and headed his way. Though the rain pelted her, she remained unfazed by the downpour and calmly walked up the steps toward him, shrouded in a drenched, hooded cape that was lavishly trimmed along the edge in a brightly colored braid. She was tall and walked with a graceful, regal air that made his lower stomach clench in anticipation. Saint had said she was as cultured and polished as she was skilled, and Morgan was looking forward to finding out all about her talents.

Beneath her heavy cloak, he could see that she was slender and not as voluptuous a woman as Saint had promised, but that didn't bother him. Morgan had learned many years ago that a woman's prowess had nothing to do with her size. She stopped before him, and though he couldn't see much of her face in the gloomy light, he was instantly struck by her ivory complexion and searching eyes. Was that uncertainty he saw in their sparkling green depths?

"Sir," she said rather breathlessly as she took a quick, fervent look behind her before fastening her gaze on him. "I'm sorry to disturb you this late in the evening, but I've been traveling all day to get here."

She had a beautiful lilt to her soft voice that surprised and intrigued him immediately. She was British, of that he was certain, but he heard a hint of a foreign accent as well that he could only identify as perhaps from a mid-Eastern country. He was certain it wasn't French or Italian.

"Never mind all that," he said. "The only thing that matters is that you are here now. Come in where it's dry."

He opened the door wider and allowed her to walk past him and into the front hall. Once inside, she folded back the dripping hood, exposing the most beautiful light auburn hair he'd ever seen, flowing over her shoulders in a cluster of rich-looking curls. As she untied the braided cord at her neck, the movements of her slender fingers and delicate hands were equally prim and sensual.

Morgan's heart started beating a little faster.

With her hood off and in the light from the lamp he'd left on the entrance table, he could see she was quite a bit younger than he'd expected for a courtesan with the experience Saint had assured him she possessed. Morgan would trust that the man had thoroughly checked her out and knew what he was talking about.

Her soft-looking skin was uncommonly pale. He was surprised that her full lips had little color, and dark circles lay under her large, expressive green eyes as if she had recently been gravely ill or hadn't had proper rest for several days.

In spite of her wan appearance, she was beautiful, enticing in a dreamy, exotic way that caused a sudden surge of heat in him that settled low. Already he wanted to reach out and caress her cheek. He wanted to bring her into the circle of his arms and pull her close to his chest. He wanted to bury his nose in the crook of her neck and breathe in her soft, womanly scent.

Saint had certainly done well for him as far as beauty and allure were concerned. From the heavy rise Morgan felt between his legs, there was no doubt he was physically attracted to her. That alone told him she would be worth every pound he was paying her.

"What delayed you?" he asked, simply to make conversation. "It must have been the weather—or perhaps your driver was a laggard."

Her dark, fan-shaped brows rose slightly as if to question him. "We didn't let anything delay us. I came straight here," she countered.

Morgan looked closer at the young woman. He couldn't see her dress, but the fabric and trim of her cape were of fine, expensive materials that couldn't be bought in ordinary shops in London. She had definitely piqued his interest.

"I suppose it rained all the way from London. But no worry, you are here now. I have your room ready. Let me help you with your cape, and then I'll go tell your driver how to get to the carriage house. Your maid, of course, will be given a room as well."

As he reached for her, she stepped away from him. Her eyes challenged him with a high-handedness he hadn't expected from a woman he was paying.

"Excuse me, sir. You didn't know I was coming. How could you have a room prepared for me?"

Morgan paused, confused for a moment, but quickly remembered that Saint had told him Miss Goodbody was excellent at role playing. She could be any type of woman he wanted. Morgan wasn't really into masquerades and mystique, even though it was the current rage in London Society. He was much too conventional to find pleasure in hiding behind a mask or pretending to be someone he was not. But if it made Miss Goodbody happy, he supposed he could play along with her for a little while, even though his head was throbbing, and playing games at this hour of the night was the last thing he wanted to do.

"Madame, surely you know that I always have a room ready in case an unexpected guest arrives at my house in the middle of the night."

Her darkly fringed gaze searched his face, and her uneasiness became more noticeable as she threw another furtive glance toward the front door. For a moment Morgan thought she was going to bolt out of it.

"This is your house? Sir, I think I should leave immediately. Because of the fog and rain, I believe my driver has brought me to the wrong door."

Another snag of concern caught in Morgan's head, but he immediately dismissed it. Did she think to arouse him by acting the part of a skittish, innocent waif who had lost her way and ended up at his mercy? If so, she should have been on time. It was far too damned late in the evening for her antics of the damsel in distress to work for him.

"Don't be coy," he said, wanting to end her ruse and get on with the matter for which he'd hired her. "I'm afraid your acting abilities, while really quite good, are wasted on me. Now allow me to take your cloak so we can retire."

Her eyes widened in alarm. She took another step back, and her foot landed against the closed door.

Morgan gave into the worrisome feeling that something wasn't quite right, even though there was something infinitely compelling and mysterious about her.

Keeping her gaze riveted on him, she looked suspiciously at him and seemed to struggle for words. "I fear you have mistaken me for someone else."

"Don't be silly. I knew you were coming. I had Mr. Saint arrange your visit for me, though it is true I was expecting you earlier in the afternoon."

She looked at him from eyes sparkling hot from outrage and surprise. "How dare you, sir! I don't know what you are talking about. I have never heard of anyone by the name of Saint."

More doubt about her stirred around Morgan. If she was acting, she was damn good. Could what he was thinking be possible? No, he didn't want to believe that.

He tensed and allowed the silence between them to lengthen. He wasn't sure he really wanted to know the answer, but finally he calmly asked, "Are you Miss Francine Goodbody?"

Her chin lifted defiantly as if an inner confidence surfaced, fortifying her. "Sir, I am not."

Morgan groaned as the realization that he would not be enjoying the pleasure of this soft, alluring woman in his bed tonight seeped through him.

But another thought suddenly struck him as well, and he said, "My cousins sent you here, didn't they?"

"What?"

"They somehow found out about my arrangements, and this is their idea of a humorous trick. I suppose they waylaid Miss Goodbody and sent you in her place. No doubt they are having a laughing good time at my expense as we speak."

The young woman bristled perceptibly. "I have no knowledge of Miss Goodbody, the cousins you speak of, or anyone else you might know." She looked straight at him and very confidently said, "I am Miss Arianna Sweet."

He eyed her skeptically at first, but the longer he stared at her the more he wondered what her role in this debacle really was. Could she possibly be telling the truth? She certainly looked like she was. A stab of disappointment struck him, and it instantly turned to anger.

Morgan swore softly under his breath.

Her assertion that she was not the courtesan he expected sobered him more than he liked. A sardonic chuckle passed his lips, and he shook his head. This situation would be laughable if it wasn't so annoyingly unbelievable. A beautiful, tempting woman finally arrives at his door, but now quite obviously not the one he was expecting. What were the chances of that ever happening?

Spending his summer at Valleydale was not turning out to be one of his better ideas. Perhaps life in London wasn't so bad after all.

Morgan fought to quell his frustration over the realization that this delectable young lady was not Miss Goodbody, and she would not be spending the night beneath him.

He stared at her, unable to look away from the intensity of her gaze. She was so indignant at his accusations that he felt forced to believe her.

"Obviously, I was anticipating someone else, Miss Sweet," he said, unable to hide his frustration or his impatience. "So if you are not here by way of my cousins' conniving or at Mr. Saint's behest, by all means, tell me what is it that brings you to my door on this rainy, late evening? If it was directions you wanted, I could easily have spoken to your driver."

His brusque tone didn't seem to faze her as she took a commanding step toward him and said, "I came to speak to Lady Elder. I realize she is not receiving at this unbelievably late hour, but do you think she would mind if I waited until she's available to see me?"

Morgan grunted another laugh. What madness was this woman up to?

"Lady Elder is not here," he said, unable to keep the sarcasm he was feeling out of his voice.

Miss Sweet stared at him with guarded surprise. Morgan got the distinct impression she didn't believe him.

"But she must be," the young lady challenged him in a stiff voice. "This is Valleydale, is it not, or am I, indeed, at the wrong estate?"

"Yes, Miss Sweet, it is," he said derisively. "You are here, but she is not."

Her hand flew to her forehead in contemplation, and Morgan thought he saw her fingers tremble. He noticed vulnerability in her that he hadn't seen before, and he was certain now she wasn't acting.

Something troubled her, but what and why had she brought it to his door?

She looked up at him with imploring eyes, and in a

soft voice said, "I came all this way to see Lady Elder. Tell me where she is at once, and I shall go there."

The throbbing in Morgan's temples increased. Just who the hell did this chit think she was?

Unable to keep a hint of accusation out of his voice, he stepped closer to her and said, "Excuse me, Miss Sweet, but are you issuing a demand to me?"

Morgan realized he'd spoken more sharply than he intended, but this encounter had gone beyond being a dreadful farce. It was more than comical or frustrating, it was damned maddening, and he was ready for it to end.

She seemed unruffled by his gruff behavior and looked straight into his eyes.

"No, of course not." She took in a quick, deep breath and then slowly exhaled before adding, "All right, maybe it was a demand. But you don't understand. It's imperative that I speak to her as soon as possible."

Miss Sweet was nothing if not direct; he would give her that.

Morgan shook his head and laughed softly under his breath. Of Lady Elder's three grandsons, Morgan was the levelheaded one. He had always been rational, sensible, and clear-minded no matter the situation. He was a planner and never did anything without thinking through the consequences, and he never lost control. He was determined this intriguing young lady's allure was not going to get the best of him.

He watched as she moistened her lips, giving them a little shine and color. Though she remained quiet, he could tell by her rigid stance and rapidly blinking eyes that she struggled to keep her composure. She lightly shook her head as if to clear her thoughts and to renew some inner strength that was weakening. There was a determined edge to the set of her jaw, and sudden fear that he hadn't seen before shimmered in the depths of her beautiful green eyes that gave him a moment's pause.

But only a moment.

Another time, Morgan might have been more indulgent with this captivating lady standing before him and enjoyed the conversation, but not tonight. She had picked the wrong evening to arrive at his door with her odd request to see his grandmother. His head pounded from the drink, and his stomach had begun to roil.

"I can tell you that it won't be possible to see her or speak to her, and I should know. I'm her grandson."

Alarm flashed in her eyes. Her gaze swept down his body as she took in his attire.

"Oh, my lord, or is it Your Grace?" She immediately curtsied. "I apologize for mistaking you for one of Lady Elder's staff. I shouldn't have jumped to conclusions. I know that she has three grandsons, an Earl, a Marquis, and a Duke. Forgive me, but I don't know which you are."

Morgan glanced down at his clothing and silently cursed. Sometime during the long evening in his book room, he had not only discarded his neckcloth and collar but his waistcoat and coat as well. She had no way of knowing he was the master of the house. It was no wonder she thought him a servant, and a damned sloppy one at that, giving the state of his rumpled shirt that was more than half pulled from the band of his riding breeches.

He cleared his throat and said, "There is no need for an apology. I am the Earl of Morgandale and Lady Elder's oldest grandson."

"My lord, if your grandmother won't be away for a long time, do you mind if I wait for her to return? I really must speak to—"

Morgan held up his hand to stop her from further discussion of his grandmother. For a moment, he thought he saw her body tremble.

Did she think him such a scoundrel that he wouldn't offer her the hospitality of his house for the night before sending her on her way in the morning? That angered him. Damnation, he wasn't an ogre, but his patience was already on a short tether before she had arrived. And it was damned frustrating that he was immensely attracted to her, since clearly he couldn't do anything about that. Given the lateness of the hour and the foul weather, he really had no choice but to offer her shelter for the evening.

Still, he wasn't in a mood to be kind along with having to be accommodating. "You will be waiting a long time to see her, Miss Sweet," he said grimly. "My grandmother died over a year ago."

A soft, anguished gasp fluttered past her lips. "No," she whispered, shaking her head. "That can't be."

"I'm afraid it is," he said, thinking it was rather odd that she seemed to be taking the news of his grandmother's death so hard. Morgan watched the last shade of color drain from her beautiful face. Her green eyes blinked rapidly and then slowly.

"Miss Sweet?"

But she didn't respond.

Her head tilted back as her eyes fluttered closed, and despite a long night of drinking, he leaped forward just in time and somehow managed to catch her as her body collapsed and she fainted into his arms.

Two

My Dearest Lucas,

I thought this quote from Lord Chesterfield very wise. Take heed to this lesson. "A man of sense soon discovers, because he carefully observes, where, and how long, he is welcome; and takes care to leave the company, at least as soon as he is wished out of it. Fools never perceive where they are either ill-timed or ill placed."

Your loving Grandmother,
Lady Elder

ARIANNA'S LASHES FLUTTERED, AND HER FIRST CONSCIOUS thought was that she was a little girl again being carried in her father's strong arms and held protectively against his powerful chest. She snuggled deeper into the protective embrace, slipping her hand around a firm neck and letting the languid warmth settle over her. She couldn't remember why she had felt fearful for so long, but now she felt safe. Safe, for the first time in months. She could sleep peacefully. She breathed in deeply and relaxed into the secure hold.

However, Arianna's disoriented mind would not let her have the tranquility and comfort her body craved. Niggling doubts disturbed her rest. Something wasn't right. She wasn't a little girl anymore, so why was she being carried? Her eyes opened to swirling darkness as her mind tried to sort out what was happening. She felt lethargic, dizzy. Her eyes closed again, and for a few seconds she snuggled once more into the depths of the powerful arms that carried her. She didn't want anything to spoil the feeling of being safe.

But an inner strength that had served Arianna so well in the past rose up inside her. She blinked several times, willing the vertigo to pass, letting her eyes adjust to the darkness, forcing her mind to wake up and think. She saw a masculine neck and commanding jawline. She was definitely cradled in a man's strong arms, but it couldn't be her father.

In whose arms was she?

The earl!

Startled, Arianna kicked and pushed against his chest, trying to dislodge herself from him. Her weak arms and legs protested her hasty movements. She felt as if they were disjointed from her body. Fatigue consumed her; still she fought. Her feeble effort caused the earl's strong arms to tighten around her again.

"Be still and stop struggling," he grumbled. "I don't want to drop you."

"What you are doing?" she commanded.

"I thought it was quite clear that I am carrying you," he said in an annoyed tone.

"Of course that is clear," she answered tersely. "Why are you carrying me?"

"You fainted."

Arianna stiffened in his arms. "I certainly did not. I have never fainted in my life."

"Until now," he mumbled caustically under his breath and kept walking through the darkness.

She opened her mouth to deny his claim but quickly saw the folly in that and refrained from going that route again.

Bapre! She hadn't really fainted, had she? How could she have let that happen?

Arianna was mortified that the earl was carrying her, holding her so closely she felt her hip pressed tightly against his firm, lower stomach. The intimacy of the contact sent a rush of heat to her cheeks and a slow roll of something wonderful cascading through her abdomen.

In response to her unusual reaction to the man, in her most authoritative voice she said, "My lord, I must insist that you put me down immediately."

"Not yet, Miss Sweet, but I assure you, just as soon as I get you to the settee in the drawing room I will. You may be light as a feather under normal circumstances, but trust me, with your soggy cape and my pounding head, you are, indeed, quite heavy. I shall be happy to be rid of you."

Shocked by his gruff complaint, she protested, "There is no reason for you to sound so grumpy."

He heaved a deep, exasperated sigh, and she felt his chest move against her side.

"Oh, but there is, Miss Sweet, but I will refrain from telling you my reasons and keep them to myself."

She pushed at his muscled chest again, though she already knew that trying to get out of his arms was a hopeless endeavor. The man was strong as iron.

"I don't know why you are in such an agitated state," she argued to mask just how uncomfortable she was cradled in his arms.

She felt him take another deep breath, as if to gain control of his temper before speaking.

He glanced down at her, but it was too dark to see anything other than the whites of his eyes. "Me, in a state? Just who do you think you are talking to, Miss Sweet?"

"You, of course. You have been disconcerted since shortly after I arrived and you discovered I am not the person you were expecting."

"Your impertinence is unbelievable."

"And so is your arrogance. It's not like I asked you to pick me up and carry me."

"You know, most young ladies would be thankful, if not indebted, that I had kept them from landing on the floor and knocking a goose egg on their head, but no, not you. There doesn't seem to be an ounce of gratitude in you."

Arianna studied over his words. He made a very good point. She didn't know why she challenged him when she was in such an untenable position. It must be the remnants of the fever causing her to be so bold.

"Perhaps I have been a bit rash and maybe too forthright in the way I spoke to you."

"Perhaps?" he questioned on a broken breath. "You won't give an inch, will you?"

"I don't mean to sound unappreciative, my lord."

"Then you certainly fooled me."

She scoffed at his mumbled comment. "I'm trying my best to make you understand that I don't need to be carried; I can walk."

"Yes, I know you can," he said dryly. "I've seen you do it, and nothing would please me more at the moment than to let you. But I don't trust your feet to hold you."

"Nonsense. You are treating me like a child."

"Did you stop to think that might be because you are acting like one? Now stop wiggling and be still for a few more steps, and I will gladly put you down."

Arianna huffed. "All right, my lord, if you most know, the truth is that I have never been in a man's arms before, and I find it quite disturbing and highly improper to be held so close to your body."

He grunted a laugh. "I find it quite disturbing, too, Miss Sweet, but I'm sure for a far different reason than you find it so."

She gasped. "You are a shameless scoundrel, my lord; now put me down. I would rather crawl on my hands and knees than be carried another step by you."

As the last word left her lips, the earl unceremoniously plopped her onto the small sofa with a groan and then stood staring down at her.

"Happy now?" he asked sardonically.

Arianna gasped at his rudeness. "Immensely," she answered, quite thankful he couldn't see much of her face for the darkness of the room. Her cheeks were burning with embarrassment.

But not to be outdone, Arianna took a deep breath and started to rise.

Lord Morgandale pointed a finger at her and said, "If you get up, I will pick you up again and put you back on that settee."

She gasped. "How dare you expect me to simply obey you without question!"

"I find it very easy."

"Probably because you are an earl and no doubt used to everyone jumping like a grasshopper to your every wish, and you think that I am to meekly comply with your every command, as well."

"Precisely. You are in my home by my permission, and as long as you are, you will abide by my wishes. Is that clear, Miss Sweet?"

"Perfectly," she said tightly.

"Good. Isn't it more pleasant between us now that you are beginning to understand exactly who is in charge around this house?"

"You are the most infuriating man I have ever had the displeasure of meeting. And you are stubborn, too," she added as an afterthought.

"How odd, I was just thinking the same thing about you."

"Unlike you, I have a reason. It's because you bring out the worst of me."

"Why is it not surprising to me that your ungrateful attitude is my fault? I fear someone misnamed you. Are you sure you are not Miss Sweet but instead Miss Tart?"

"Oh, you are an impossible man." She could have added fascinating and invigorating but held her tongue on those attributes. "I don't even know why I'm continuing to speak to you."

"At this point, you have no choice. So tell me, is your clothing wet, or only the cape?"

"My clothing is dry."

"All right," he said and turned away from her and walked to a nearby table. "It is best you take that garment off immediately. I would just as soon you not take consumption right here in my house."

"So would I," she mumbled, suddenly feeling terribly weak and shaky once again.

The only thing Arianna could see in the dark room was the earl's white shirt as he prepared to light a lamp. She must have awakened him from a deep sleep for him to be in such a rumpled state and disagreeable mood.

For some reason she couldn't just dismiss the earl's appalling attitude toward her. Her father had always teased her by saying that she always had to have the last word in any discussion, and he was right.

"You certainly are in a foul temper, my lord. I realize I interrupted your evening, quite possibly your late night nap, but you are acting as if I took your most prized possession from you, and you are in a temper about it."

She was sure she heard the earl chuckle under his breath, but he said nothing.

Arianna stood to remove her cape and was surprised at how shaky her legs were. She quickly sat back down for fear of fainting again. Thankfully the earlier dizziness she had experienced was gone. She closed her eyes and took in a deep, steadying breath, silently hoping the debilitating fever she'd caught on the ship wasn't returning.

She should have stopped at an inn and taken a few days to rest before trying to find Lady Elder. Why had she been so impatient to find the woman her father had told her about that her common sense failed her? Her impatience usually landed her in trouble, and this was no exception.

The wick caught fire but wouldn't flame, adding only a faint yellow glow to the room. She could see just enough to know the earl was as imposing from the back as he was from the front. Straight, dark brown hair fell just past his nape. She saw muscles in his wide shoulders and back ripple beneath his collarless shirt as he fiddled with the lamp. His slim-legged trousers fit perfectly across lean hips, firm buttocks, and long, powerful looking legs.

Bapre!

What was she thinking? She shouldn't be looking at the earl's backside or anything else about him. What was wrong with her? Obviously the fever *was* back. What else could have her thinking such improper things, especially about a man she had just met?

The earl seemed to be having trouble making the light brighter. A silent half laugh passed her lips at his seeming ineptness. He was, indeed, a man of privilege if he didn't even know how to turn up the flame on a wick. The earl obviously was not used to doing anything for himself—other than give orders. He was exceptional at that.

As she watched him, she wondered where all his servants were. She had been away from England for a long time, but surely things had not changed so much that an earl answered his own door, and inappropriately dressed at that, even if it was the middle of the night.

Lord Morgandale mumbled something that Arianna didn't quite understand, but it sounded very much like he was damning the lamp. She smiled. She didn't know why, but his struggles with the light amused her greatly, and tired and lethargic as she was, it felt good to have a reason to smile. There had been far too few of them recently.

Knowing she was at risk of his ire but unable to stop herself, she asked, "Do you need help with the lamp, my lord? I'll be happy to show you—"

"No, Miss Sweet," he said gruffly, cutting off her sentence as, suddenly, greater light filled the room. "I do not need your help with anything. If you must know, one of the servants trimmed the wick too blasted short."

"That is exactly what I was thinking must be the problem," she answered, unable to hide the humor in her voice.

"I'm beginning to believe you are a vixen rather than a waif, and something tells me you often rush in where fools dare to tread."

His comment made it obvious that it hadn't taken him very long to assess her. The earl turned and started back toward her, and she quickly averted her eyes.

"I can build a fire if you are chilled."

"No, that won't be necessary. I assure you I am fine, and contrary to my earlier mishap, I am not given to fits of the vapors."

He walked closer to her, stopped and reached for the wet cape she held, and said, "Really?"

Arianna opened her mouth to speak as she held the cloak up to him, but once again her words were silenced when she stared into the earl's magnificent eyes. They were the bluest eyes she had ever seen. When she looked at him, strange sensations curled in her stomach, tightened her chest, and did confounding things to the rhythm of her heart.

Now she understood why she had such a strong reaction to the earl. She was attracted to him the way a woman was to a man she wanted to pay her attention. That struck her as odd, considering the fact the man was an ill-tempered ogre. She had felt that way about a man only once before when, a couple of years ago, a young viscount visiting from England had caught her fancy, but never with such physical reactions that had her blushing like a schoolgirl putting on her first stays. And the feelings for the man had faded when he left Bombay.

The earl's straight, dark hair fell attractively across his broad forehead. The bridge of his nose was narrow and his cheekbones high and angular, making him easily the most handsome man she'd ever seen. Not even the wrinkle of agitation that furrowed his broad brow took away from the fact that this man was devastatingly attractive. And judging by the way he stood and looked at her with arrogant self-confidence, she had no doubts that he knew just how handsome he was to her.

Arianna's shoulders relaxed a little, even though looking at the earl made her breaths come short and choppy. "All right, I suppose I will have to agree that I might have fainted."

His brows lifted. "You might have?"

The infuriating man wouldn't give her an inch. "Oh, all right, just to please you I will say yes, I fainted."

"About time you admitted it," he said and hung her cloak over the back of a side chair that stood near the unlit fireplace. "No matter how grudgingly."

Arianna huffed at his last remark. "I assure you I have never done anything like that in my life."

"Then perhaps, Miss Sweet, as Lord Chesterfield once said: 'There is always a first time for everything.'"

"I have never heard of Lord Chesterfield, but I believe that as well."

The earl's bright blue eyes searched her face, and a strange calm settled over her. She didn't understand it, but just being in the same room with him made Arianna feel better, safe. Suddenly a contented peace like she hadn't experienced since her father had died spread through her. She didn't know why she felt all these different emotions, because Lord Morgandale was surely the most contrary and brusque man she had ever met.

He walked closer to her again and said, "You have never heard of Phillip Dormer Stanhope, the fourth Earl of Chesterfield?"

"No, I've been away from England for a number of years. I'm afraid I really don't know very many people at all."

He seemed to study over her words and said, "Hmm, someone who has never heard of Chesterfield. That's refreshing."

"Is he quite famous?"

"Not anymore. So tell me, you say you've been away. Where have you been?"

"India."

"Good lord! That's halfway around the world. What were you doing there?"

Arianna moistened her lips and carefully chose her words. "My *pitaji* was doing—"

"Your what?" he interrupted.

"I'm sorry. My father. Sometimes I forget and use words I learned in India. My father was doing research for the Royal Apothecary Scientific Academy for the Study of Herbs, Plants, and Spices in India in hopes of finding cures for a variety of different ailments."

The earl grimaced. "And he allowed you to travel back to England alone?"

Not wanting to meet his blue gaze, Arianna looked down at her hands as a somber mood washed over her. "I'm not alone. My maid is with me."

"Hardly a proper companion for someone as young as you, Miss Sweet."

The last time Arianna saw her father flashed through her troubled mind, and she winced. It always caused a pain in her chest when she was reminded of that afternoon. She and her maid had returned home to find her father lying in a pool of blood with his Indian *bhagidar* standing over him. When she screamed, Mr. Rajaratnum quickly stuffed her father's research journal into his pocket and fled. The British and Indian authorities had searched for him, but when she left Bombay, her father's associate still had not been captured.

"I know it's not what my father would have wished for me. I'm sorry to say I didn't have much choice in the matter." Arianna paused. She was going to say a few weeks ago but suddenly realized it had been much longer than that. Time had passed so quickly.

She inhaled deeply, looked at the earl's searching eyes, and continued by saying in as strong a voice as she could muster, "My father died several months ago."

For the first time since she'd arrived, Arianna saw a change in Lord Morgandale's features. His brow relaxed, his eyes softened, and his mouth lost its tightness.

"That couldn't have been easy for you. I'm sorry about your father."

Arianna didn't know why, but those few words meant the world to her. Their friends, associates, and servants in India had all offered their condolences, but none of their words meant as much to her as hearing the few words spoken from the earl.

She swallowed hard and then said, "Thank you, and no, it wasn't."

"You had no other family there?"

"Neither there nor anywhere, which was one of the reasons I stayed with my father in India when he very much wanted me to come back to England and live what he considered a normal life. I had many things to keep me busy during the first months of my mourning. I had to write letters about his death to his colleague and friend in London, Mr. Robert Warburton, and to the Royal Apothecary Scientific Academy. I had to pack and arrange the shipment to London of all of our personal possessions. I have some of his papers and books with me, but my father had a tremendous amount of research documents, vials and potions, notes and books, and other items. I packed most everything and sent them on to London so that

I could sort through his private possessions when I get there."

Suddenly Arianna realized she was rambling about things she was sure the earl had no interest in. "Sometimes I find it difficult to believe he's been gone so long now."

Lord Morgandale sat down in the chair opposite her. "I'm sure it is. And it doesn't look to me as if you fared well on the voyage. You are pale as a ghost, and you have dark circles under your eyes. You look as if you haven't slept well or eaten properly in days."

Arianna's hands flew to her hair, and she brushed it away from her face. She hadn't looked in a mirror in months, as there wasn't one available to her on the ship, but she had done the best she could to make herself presentable before she disembarked.

Obviously she hadn't done enough.

"My apologies, my lord, I didn't realize I looked so dreadful."

His eyes narrowed, and he rubbed his temples with the tips of his fingers again. She remembered him saying something about his head pounding. Perhaps he wasn't well either.

"Don't put words in my mouth, Miss Sweet. I didn't say you looked dreadful, and you don't. I said you look as if you have been unwell for a long time. There is a difference."

"You're right," she admitted, no longer feeling the need to hide the fact. "I have been sick, but I had never been sick a day in my life until I boarded the ship for England. There was a horrible fever going around the passengers and, unfortunately, I caught it. I'm afraid I was very ill for most of the journey. In fact, the captain forced those of us who were sick to disembark at port in Alexandria, Egypt, when we stopped for supplies."

"Good Lord. That must have been a hellish time." *You have no idea!*

"My maid and I stayed there until I was well enough to continue the long journey, which was more than a month, I believe, and then it was a couple of weeks before we could book passage on another ship."

Arianna couldn't help but shiver as she finished her sentence, knowing she still had lingering effects of the fever she hadn't been able to shake. She came down with the illness on the third day of the voyage, and the constant rocking of the ship was sheer torture for her. She couldn't keep anything down. If it hadn't been for the excellent care Beabe gave her and the medicinal potions her father had made that she brought with her, Arianna was certain she wouldn't be alive today.

She watched Lord Morgandale's brow crease again and his lips tighten in concern, so she quickly added, "But there is no need for you to worry that I have brought the fever to your house, my lord. I assure you I'm well now."

"I'm not at all concerned about the fever, Miss Sweet, and I can see that you are so healthy that you fainted after you'd been on your feet for just a few minutes. Yes, I'd say that would make you completely fit."

"You are being condescending, my lord."

"And you can stretch the truth farther than anyone I know, and certainly much farther than I'm willing to believe. Now tell me, did you say you've only recently returned?"

She nodded.

"How recently?"

Arianna really didn't want to answer that, but after his terse remark about her stretching the truth, she felt she had to be a little more forthcoming with him.

Finally she said, "Today. When the ship docked at Southampton, as soon as we disembarked, I hired a coach and came straight here."

His blue eyes widened. "And it didn't dawn on you that you might need a few days to rest before coming here?"

She shook her head. "Not at the time, no. I was in a hurry."

"To see my grandmother?"

"Yes."

His brow wrinkled again. "Why?"

Understandably, he was curious as to why she would step off the ship and immediately head for his grandmother's home. She looked down at her hands. "I do have an impulsive steak, as my father called it. But I think perhaps it was just that I was so grateful to be back on English soil. Perhaps I was simply too exhausted to think clearly. I'm not sure what exactly I was thinking at the time. I only knew I had to get here."

"So you came straight to Valleydale because you knew my grandmother?"

"Yes. No, I mean yes, I came straight here, but I didn't know your grandmother personally. My father met her on several occasions when he came to visit his cousin. He always spoke very highly of her. I'm sorry she is no longer with you."

"Thank you. Perhaps you should start at the beginning of your story, Miss Sweet, and tell me exactly why you wanted to see my grandmother."

Arianna hesitated again. How much should she tell him? She was quite prepared to tell Lady Elder everything, but she wasn't sure she wanted to tell the imposing grandson about her father's murder and the stolen journal with the formula in it. The thought of telling him everything chilled her, and she knew she had to keep the whole truth from him.

"My father was a cousin of Lady Elder's husband."

"Which one? My grandmother had four husbands."

Was that humor she finally saw lurking in the blue depths of his eyes? Was he, at last, turning from the scowling earl to a more approachable person? Just that small glimmer of friendliness lifted her spirits.

"Yes, of course, I do remember hearing that. Sir Walter Hennessy was his name. My father, Albert Sweet, was his first cousin."

The earl nodded. "I remember Sir Walter. I was already a young lad by the time she married him. He is the man who gave my grandmother the legendary Talbot pearls, which now belong to my cousin."

"I can tell I've been away from England for a long time. I've never heard of the Lord Chesterfield you mentioned, and I'm afraid I don't know the significance of the Talbot pearls."

"Both require long stories that I'm not prepared to go into tonight. So tell me exactly what were you going to ask my grandmother to do for you?"

A wave of dizziness struck Arianna again, but she fought it and said, "My father had always told me that if anything ever happened to him, I was to contact Lady Elder. He said because of our distant relationship to Lady Elder, that she would be willing to help me find an appropriate place to live in London and suitable companion who could help me reestablish a life in London. I don't need monetary assistance. I'm far from destitute, and I don't want you to think that. My father had his associate in London, Mr. Warburton whom I mentioned earlier, set up an account for me years ago. I have more than an adequate income from my father to sustain me."

"I can look at you and your clothing and tell that, Miss Sweet."

Arianna watched his gaze feather down her face, neck, and to her breasts, and then glide over to her hands and back up to her eyes. She knew without him saying a word that, even though she was disheveled from more than two months of traveling, she had found favor with him, and that same curling feeling of something wonderful that she had experienced earlier started flowing in the pit of her stomach again.

The only thing she could figure was that she was much too tired and weary to fight the fanciful notions that kept occurring. She cleared her throat and tried to focus on the discussion at hand.

"Even before he died, it was his desire for me to return to England, but I resisted."

"That does not surprise me, but please go on."

"He thought a gentle, older woman would help reintroduce me to Society and help fill me in on what

I've missed these years I've been away. Of course, he also hoped that would lead to introductions of eligible gentlemen that I might allow to court me."

"I see."

Arianna cleared her throat once again. "I am well-schooled in world history, mathematics, and, of course, I'm quite proficient in the sciences. I believe I would be an excellent asset for someone who enjoys a lively discussion."

"I can attest to that," he said quietly.

"I'm sorry, my lord, I did not intend to burden you with my life's story. I should have left immediately when I heard the news about Lady Elder. I'll get my cape and be gone." She started to rise, but the scowl that formed between his eyes made her quickly sit back down.

"Don't be ridiculous, Miss Sweet. I will not allow you or your driver to go back out in this foul weather tonight."

"But—"

"But this time for you, there is no but. You are staying here. My grandmother would roll over in her grave if I allowed you to leave at this hour of the night, and believe me, she has done enough of that already because of my cousins' recent antics. Now tell me, when is the last time you had food?"

"This morning—" were the only words she managed to say as they both turned toward the drawing room door. Loud, hurried footsteps sounded on the stairs, and then down the corridor. An older man and woman hurried in, both holding a lamp and both impeccably dressed in clothing befitting servants of the manor.

"My lord," the man said, "We heard voices and came at once. I see the guest you were expecting has arrived."

"Should I light a fire in her room, my lord?" the woman said eagerly. "It's such a nasty night, or perhaps she'd like a cup of tea?"

Lord Morgandale slowly rose and said, "No, she is not the lady I was expecting but someone else. This is Miss Sweet. Miss Sweet, my butler, Post, and his wife, Mrs. Post."

Arianna started to rise, but saw Lord Morgandale lift his masculine brow, and she quickly sat back down and said, "How do you do?"

Post was a small, thin man with big brown eyes and a sharp nose. His wife was a buxom woman a head taller than her husband. Her dark hair was pulled severely away from her face and knotted at her nape. Arianna assumed they had heard her when she was trying to get the earl to put her down and had taken the time to make themselves presentable before coming downstairs.

"Now that you are here, Mrs. Post, would you go to the kitchen and get Miss Sweet something to eat?"

"Yes, my lord."

"But I'm not hungry," Arianna offered quickly. "There is no reason for her to go to any trouble for me."

The earl looked at her and said, "You also told me you didn't faint. I learn fast, Miss Sweet."

"A proper gentleman would not remind a lady that she had misspoken, especially when she had already corrected that mistake."

"And I have no fear that you will correct this one once you eat." He turned back to Mrs. Post. "Make it a simple plate of bread and butter, and preserves and milk. See that she eats it all, and help her get settled in a room. The one you had prepared for my other guest will do fine. See to her servants, as well."

"Right away, my lord," she said and hurried away.

"Post, go out to the carriage and bring in Miss Sweet's maid and their trunks. Tell the driver where the carriage house is and to make himself comfortable there."

"Yes, my lord," he said and turned away.

Lord Morgandale walked over to a table that sat between two beautifully upholstered wingback chairs. She watched him pour amber liquid in a glass and bring it back over to her.

Arianna hesitated.

"You are very intriguing, Miss Sweet. At times, you seem very skittish, almost suspicious for someone who came to a stranger's house in the middle of the night."

She hoped her gaze remained steady, but her heart flipped at his words. She had good reason to be wary, but she didn't want him to know that.

"When I arrived, I wasn't aware this was your house."

"And if you had?"

"I would have thought twice before stopping."

Lord Morgandale smiled and then laughed. He extended the glass closer to her.

"What is it?" she asked, taking the glass from him.

"Brandy. Have you ever had it?"

She shook her head. "Wine, but not brandy. Why do you want me to drink it?"

"Don't look so frightened, I am not trying to get

you drunk so I can have my way with you. This will make you sleep as soundly as a newborn babe, and I think one thing you desperately need right now, Miss Sweet, is rest. So drink every drop."

She started to put it to her lips.

"Wait," he said and closed his hand over hers to stop her.

Their eyes met and held. Arianna felt a tingle that started at her breasts and flew all the way down to her toes. She wondered if the earl felt the same shocking feelings she felt when he touched her.

"Not now. Wait until you have eaten. It will be much easier on your stomach. But drink every drop."

With his hand covering hers, she didn't trust herself to speak, so she nodded.

"Mrs. Post will take over from here. If you need anything, just ask her. I'll see you sometime tomorrow, and we'll talk further."

He slowly removed his hand, letting his fingertips glide ever so slightly over her skin. His gaze wafted down her face to her lips and lingered there for a moment before lifting to her eyes once again.

She felt a sudden tightness between her legs, and to cover the sudden awkwardness, she said, "Thank you for allowing me to stay the night."

"Good night, Miss Sweet."

He turned and walked out of the room. She heard his footsteps going up the stairs. She heard a door open and close. Only then did she let out a tired, moaning sigh and fall against the back of the settee.

"*Bapre*," she whispered.

So much for thinking she could handle anything

and everything that came her way. She never expected to meet a man as imposing as Lord Morgandale. It took every ounce of her strength just to talk to the man.

Her gaze fell on a large painting of a regal-looking woman hanging over the fireplace. She couldn't see it well with only one lamp lit in the room, but she assumed it was of Lady Elder. Arianna stared at the woman. She would never have come to Valleydale if she'd known Lady Elder had died.

When she arrived in London, perhaps Mr. Warburton would offer to help her find a place to live as well as help her find or reconstruct her father's formula. They needed to do that quickly. It could even be too late if Mr. Rajaratnum had already sold the formula to someone else or to another country's Apothecary Research Academy.

Suddenly Arianna felt weak and shaky again, and that angered her. She couldn't accomplish anything in her current physical condition. The encounter with the earl had made her realize just how weak she was. She must find an inn or some place to stay so she could rest and regain her strength before she contacted Mr. Warburton. The earl was right. Only a few minutes on her feet, and she was completely exhausted.

Arianna swirled the amber liquid in the glass and watched it twinkle and glimmer in the light from the lamp. She didn't understand why, but she felt safe in Lord Morgandale's house. But that was no matter; she had to leave tomorrow. She must get her strength back, get to London, contact Mr. Warburton and convince him to help her fulfill her father's dream, and establish his legacy to the world before Mr. Rajaratnum sold the formula to someone else and they took the credit that was due her father.

Three

My Dearest Grandson Lucas,

I think one of the reasons I always enjoyed the company of Lord Chesterfield was because he had such a wealth of knowledge and was never embarrassed to show it. Read this: "I am convinced that a light supper, a good night's sleep, and a fine morning, have sometimes made a hero of the same man, who, by an indigestion, a restless night and a rainy morning, would have proved a coward."

Your loving Grandmother,
Lady Elder

MORGAN CHUCKLED AS HE SPLASHED COLD WATER ON his face and neck, washing away the residue of shaving soap. He was up early, which was unusual for him. And by some miracle, he wasn't jug bitten. There was no doubt he had too much to drink last night, something he hadn't done in years and didn't want to do again anytime soon. He had gone to bed with a pounding head and roiling stomach, but thankfully, in the bright light of day, he felt fine.

While he shaved, he had studied over the tart-tongued Miss Sweet and the unusual events of the evening. After drying his face, he tossed his crisp white shirt over his head and then fit his collar around his neck. He had expected a delectable courtesan skilled in ways that were sure to make a man forget all other women he'd ever been with. Instead, he got a very different young lady at his door, an innocent, unwell lady of quality who was obviously in desperate need of his help, though he was sure she'd rather swallow her tongue than ask for it.

Stepping into his riding breeches, Morgan realized he'd been thinking about Miss Sweet since his eyes opened half an hour ago. He kept seeing her troubled, bright green eyes and her luxurious, light auburn hair spilling around her shoulders and down her back. He should have been able to tell that Miss Sweet was a lady of quality and innocence the moment she took the hood off her head. As Lord Chesterfield was so fond of saying: there were two things a woman just couldn't fake, no matter how skilled she was at acting—innocence and quality.

Morgan chuckled lightly again as he remembered thinking, at first, Miss Sweet was Miss Goodbody and that she was simply playing a part for him in order to heighten his arousal. Making mistakes like that should be enough to compel him to swear off ever drinking brandy again and just stick to ale and wine, but it probably wouldn't.

There were a lot of clues he'd missed that he shouldn't have, and wouldn't have, had he not been brooding, and he wouldn't have been brooding had he not had too much to drink. He wouldn't have been so confounded if he had not been so brandy-faced by the time Miss Sweet arrived that his powers of observation had all but vanished. But in the bright light of day and with a clear head, he was remembering little things. Was there something more than just her illness and exhaustion that caused her to get off that ship in Southampton and make such a hasty journey to Valleydale? She had seemed to be in a hurry when she first arrived.

In any case, Morgan woke with the realization he must assume responsibility for Miss Sweet, since she had traveled all the way to Valleydale hoping to receive assistance from his grandmother. Even if he didn't want to help her, which, of course, he did, he would be obligated to simply for the reason that she was distantly related to his grandmother's second husband.

Miss Sweet had told him a little about herself last night, but he wanted to know more about her. She intrigued him. Not just because she had lived in India for a time and had that alluring lilt to her soft voice. Not just because she engaged him in one of the liveliest conversations he'd had in years. There was something about her that drew him to her, and because of that he had made a few decisions concerning her welfare.

Morgan swiped his neckcloth off his bed. Long ago he had learned how to quickly wrap the three feet of cloth around his neck and under his collar to efficiently tie his neckcloth into a simple bow without the help of a valet or looking in a mirror.

He walked to his window and looked out over the spacious gardens and grounds at the back of his house.

The late summer rains had been good for the flowers, roses, and shrubs. The trees were full of dark green leaves, and the yew hedge was thick and solid as a wall. The knot garden, with its intricate design built around a three-tiered fountain, was the masterpiece of the formal gardens, and it had been his grandmother's pride and joy when she had walked the grounds.

The rain had stopped sometime during the night, and the clouds were scattering. It appeared as if there might be a glimmer of sun trying to shine from behind the gray skies. It would be a good day to spend at the stables to watch and help with the training of his thoroughbred horses. If the weather continued to improve, he would exercise Redmond in the afternoon. The young bay loved the opportunity to go for a long, fast run. But because of Miss Sweet, Morgan had a few things he wanted to accomplish before he headed to the stables.

He turned away from the window and grabbed his camel-colored waistcoat off the bed, slipped it on, and fastened the leather-covered buttons. He sat down on his slipper chair and tugged on his knee-high boots. He picked up his black coat and walked out of his bedchamber, stuffing his arms into the sleeves as he went.

When he made it to the bottom of the stairs, he went in search of Post but instead found the man's wife. She was in the breakfast room preparing the table for his morning meal.

She looked up at him in astonishment. "My lord, I didn't expect you up so early. I'll have everything ready for you shortly."

"There is no hurry, Mrs. Post. I have some things to do in my book room. Tell me, have you seen Miss Sweet's maid this morning?"

"Yes, my lord, I left her just a few minutes ago. She was in the kitchen, preparing a tray of hot chocolate and toast to take up to Miss Sweet."

"That won't do. Miss Sweet needs to eat more than toast if she's going to regain her strength. As soon as you've finished what you're doing, prepare her a plate as you would for me, with eggs, quail, and scones with plenty of butter and preserves. See that she eats everything you put on her plate."

The woman blinked rapidly and twisted the napkin she held in her hand. "But, my lord, but... but..."

"Stop stammering, Mrs. Post, and tell me what is wrong."

"The maid said her mistress told her last night that she wanted to be on her way to London as soon as possible this morning. I'll prepare her food right away, but she may not be willing to wait that long."

Morgan frowned. He should have expected as much from the headstrong lady. The last thing she needed right now was more traveling.

"Go up to Miss Sweet's room and tell her I insist she spend the entire day in bed, resting. She is not well enough to leave this house, and until I am satisfied that she is healthy enough to travel, she will remain here under my care."

"Yes, my lord," Mrs. Post said nervously and turned away from the table.

"And, Mrs. Post, I'm sure Miss Sweet would like a tub of hot water sometime today. She's been on a ship for only God knows how long. Until the rest of the staff returns, help her maid with whatever needs to be done to make her mistress comfortable."

"Yes, my lord."

Mrs. Post turned again to leave but stopped when Morgan said, "The first thing I want you to do is to find Post. Tell him to go immediately and pay Miss Sweet's driver and send him on his way. We will no longer require his services."

"Right away, my lord," she said, but this time she made no effort to move.

"And one thing more, Mrs. Post, if Miss Sweet has any questions about my instructions, which after my conversation with her last night I feel sure she will have, tell her I will be available to speak to her in the drawing room before dinner. Make that tomorrow evening, as I've already promised to ride over to Lord Hastings's house tonight and must leave early."

Morgan turned and headed toward his book room. He supposed he was minding Miss Sweet's business, but obviously someone needed to. She wouldn't be happy once she heard he'd sent her driver away. If she had no way to travel, it would ensure that she would be forced to stay under his care and get proper rest. When she was well enough to travel, he would see to it that she had a safe, comfortable coach to take her to London. Until then, she would have to accept his hospitality whether she wanted it or not.

Morgan whistled as he continued down the wide hallway to his book room. He paused at the door and shook his head in wonder. Why was he whistling? What had gotten into him? He couldn't remember the last time he'd whistled like a carefree school boy walking along the coastline on a hot summer afternoon.

Was it because of Miss Sweet? He didn't know why, but having her to take care of seemed to have evaporated all the restless feelings he'd had the past few weeks. For some reason, just having her in his house made him feel good.

Damn good, in fact.

He sauntered over to his desk and sat down. He pulled a sheet of foolscap out of his desk drawer, uncapped the ink jar, and picked up the quill. He thought for a few moments and then dipped the quill into the black liquid and wrote:

My Dearest Constance,

I find that I am in urgent need of your help with an important matter.

He sat back and studied on that sentence. That wouldn't do. It made him sound needy, and Morgan certainly didn't want her getting that idea. He laid down the quill, crumpled the paper, threw it aside, and retrieved another sheet.

He thought again and then wrote:

Constance,

I have a favor to ask of you.

"Good lord," he mumbled to himself as he wadded the second sheet and threw it on top of the other discarded note. He didn't like the sound of the second one any better than the first. The truth was that he had seldom asked anyone for help, and he wasn't exactly sure how to go about it.

But the fact remained that Miss Sweet was too weak to travel elsewhere, and that was the only thing that made it acceptable for her to remain under his roof without a proper companion. She needed another lady in the house other than servants. He wouldn't want a hint of anything sullying her reputation.

There was also the fact that he couldn't help Miss Sweet with the things she needed once she arrived in London. Constance had stepped in and helped Blake with Henrietta, so perhaps she would help him with Miss Sweet. But, Morgan realized as he drummed his fingers on the edge of his fine Louis XIV desk, Constance and Blake had been lovers for a short time, so maybe she had felt she owed him. And Blake was a duke. Few people turned down the request of a favor when asked by a duke.

But he had more than that going against him. Constance was in London, in her own home when she helped Blake with Henrietta. It was during the Season when Constance would be going out to parties every evening anyway. In order to help Morgan, she would have to first make the day-and-a-half journey from London to Valleydale. And while there were endless house parties scheduled throughout the area, Miss Sweet was not in good enough health to attend any of them. But with excellent care, there was hope she would be well enough to travel by the time Constance could arrive.

Morgan tapped the feather end of the quill on his chin and studied on what he needed to say. Surely he could think of a damn good reason to entice Constance to make the journey to Valleydale and assist him. He thought of offering her payment but quickly dismissed that idea. Not only would it probably offend her, but her husband had adored her and left her well taken care of in his will. She wasn't in need of monetary assistance.

So what could he say to persuade her to quit the city for a spell in the country? What would tempt an unmarried woman to do something she might not really want to do?

He glared at the blank sheet of paper. What the hell was the matter with him? Why did it matter how he wrote the letter to Constance?

"Because I don't want her to tell me no," he whispered.

He just needed to state the facts, get it written, and get the damned thing on its way to London.

Frustrated, he took out another sheet of the foolscap, dipped the quill into the ink, and tried again:

My Lovely Constance,

My hope is that your carefree summer in London has been exceptional. But if for some reason that might not be the case, I have a special request that concerns a delicate matter, and I am certain only you have the skills and the countenance to manage this intriguing situation for me.

Morgan sat back in his chair, looked at the sentence, and smiled.

Was he really trying flattery? What happened to just stating the facts?

"They aren't nearly as persuasive," he said and then chuckled.

Yes, flattery always worked on a woman. And what he had written should work very well and get him the answer he wanted. He dipped the quill back into the ink and continued.

Four

My Dearest Grandson Lucas,

Read with interest this tidbit of philosophy from Lord Chesterfield: "You will say perhaps, one cannot change one's nature; and that, if a person is born of a very sensible gloomy temper, and apt to see things in the worst light, they cannot make-new themselves. I will admit it to a certain degree, for though we cannot totally change our nature, we may in a great measure correct it."

Your loving Grandmother,
Lady Elder

ARIANNA HEARD HER MAID CALLING HER NAME, BUT she didn't want to wake up. Her dream was too alluring. She was in a room where bright sunlight streamed in through an open window and thin sheers billowed hypnotically from a gentle wind. She lay on crisp, clean sheets that felt heavenly to her tired body. The scent of summer flowers permeated the air all around her, and a soft breeze stirred across her face.

No, she didn't want to wake from the dream that took her back to her childhood home in the Cotswolds. If she woke, she'd find herself lying on damp sheets, in a small room, on the cold, drafty ship. She would feel the swaying and rocking, the constant movement that tortured her day and night. She would hear the howling wind and the creaking of the hull as the ship tossed about on the swelling waves. If she opened her eyes, the scent of flowers would be gone, and in its place would be the stale, pungent smell of wet wood, salty air, and stale food.

"Miss Ari, I have your breakfast."

With a jerk, Arianna's eyes flew open. She rose up on her elbows and quickly glanced around the swirling bright, spacious room. The dizziness was back. She squeezed her eyes closed and willed the room to stop spinning. She breathed in deeply three times and slowly opened her eyes again. By concentration she was able to focus on her maid who stood at the foot of her bed, holding a tray.

Arianna's gaze strayed to a small bud vase on the tray that held a single flower that was the exact shade of blue as Lord Morgandale's eyes. Her stomach tightened. She wasn't dreaming. She was no longer on the ship. She had finally made it to England and she was safe at Valleydale, and the handsome Lord Morgandale was in residence.

Arianna went limp with relief.

"I didn't mean to startle you," her maid said.

"No, Beabe, you didn't," Arianna said, swallowing

past a dry throat. "I'm afraid I was sleeping so hard I didn't want to wake up."

"You asked me to rouse you early, but you looked so weary last night that I waited until mid-morning. I hope you won't be cross with me for delaying."

"No, no, it's all right," Arianna said, wishing she didn't feel so blurry-headed, so lethargic that all she really wanted to do was go back to sleep. "I obviously needed the extra time this morning."

When would she start feeling the way she had before the fever? She was eager for her strength and good health to return so she could accomplish what she had to do for her father.

Thankful that the dizziness had passed, she sat up in bed and stuffed pillows behind her.

"I think last night was the first night in months that I've slept all night without waking."

"To tell you the truth, Miss Ari, the same goes for me. Though I haven't been sick with the fever like you, I didn't take well to the sea voyage, either." She placed the tray across Arianna's lap.

Arianna looked at Beabe and for the first time realized she looked tired, too. There were sagging, dark circles under her eyes, and she was thinner than she used to be, too. The strain of the journey and taking care of Arianna had taken its toll on her maid as well. They both needed a place to rest and recover.

"I know, Beabe. I appreciate all you have done for me. You've taken such good care of me all these weeks. I wouldn't be alive today if not for your kind attention, and I will see to it that you are handsomely rewarded when we finally get to London, and that you have at least a month or longer to visit with your family."

Beabe smiled at her. "Don't you worry about me, Miss Ari. I promised your papa I would take care of you. I couldn't let him down, now could I? But this is a mighty fine place we've come to. It's a shame we won't be staying for a little while longer."

"Yes, it is," Arianna agreed, realizing she wasn't in a hurry to leave Valleydale either but knew she must.

A worry wrinkle formed between Beabe's eyes, and she asked, "Do you think they've found that man who killed your father, Miss Ari?"

Arianna swallowed past a dry throat. "I hope so, Beabe," she said, trying to sound a lot more cheerful than she felt. "I choose to believe there will be a letter waiting for me when we get to London, telling me that."

"You don't think Mr. Rajaratnum followed us to London, do you?"

Arianna smiled affectionately at her. "Of course not. Why would he? He wanted the formula, not us."

"But he knows we saw him."

"He also knows we have already reported him to the authorities, and they are looking for him. He has what he wanted, Beabe."

Beabe smiled, nodded, and turned to look through one of the trunks that sat on the floor. "I know you're right. It's just that every time I see a gentleman from India, like yesterday when we got off the ship, I think it's him."

"But it couldn't have been him, as you know. Mr. Rajaratnum had no way of knowing we would be waylaid in Egypt for weeks or that we would have booked passage to Southampton rather than London."

Arianna looked at the woman who'd been her maid for the ten years she'd been in India. Beabe was a sturdy, robust woman in her early forties. Her light brown hair had only recently begun to show signs of gray, but Arianna seldom saw it, as most of the time it was completely covered by her mobcap. Beabe's wide brown eyes were always sparkling. Her thin lips often lifted in a smile for Arianna.

Most of the people she and her father had associated with in India had Indian servants, but her father had insisted she have a British maid so that Arianna would constantly have the influence of her homeland in her life.

Arianna took a sip of the warm chocolate and slowly swallowed. It had been months since she'd had any to drink, and it was delicious. Beabe started humming, and Arianna settled against the soft pillows with her thoughts. They went immediately to the earl. She remembered how strong his arms were when he'd carried her last night and how tightly he'd held her. She remembered how warm and firm his body had been when her hip was pressed so close to him that she felt the rise and fall of his chest. She remembered his strong neck, his masculine lips, his wide shoulders, his...

Arianna shook her head and took another quick sip of chocolate, thankful her maid could not read her thoughts. What was wrong with her? She had to stop that nonsense of thinking about the earl's physique. It was maddening.

She looked around the room and was at first puzzled by the lack of color. The walls, the draperies, and even the bed where she sat were in varying shades of white.

Although Arianna found the room very restful, she wondered why the only colors in the room, other than the dark wood furniture, were the flowers sitting on the dressing table that stood between two windows. A tall, oval mirror was attached the table. A large wardrobe stood on one wall, and a fireplace and sitting area with the chairs upholstered in white brocade were on the other side of the room.

Her bedchamber in India had been decorated with fabrics dyed in rich, vivid tints of orange, red, gold, green, and purple. The people of India adored bright colors and used them liberally. Arianna had come to love every shade and variation of all the primary colors. Now she couldn't imagine living without vivid color in her life.

After living in India for a couple of years, her father had relented and allowed her to have some of her dresses and a few saris made in the brighter fabrics of India rather than the pastels that she had always worn as a child. Though he had remained strict and never allowed her to wear the sari and matching *cholis* out of their house.

"I know that all your trunks were brought up last night, Miss Ari, so what would you like for me to pick out for you to travel in today?"

"It doesn't matter to me, Beabe, as long as it is bright and cheerful. I will let you decide. But go ahead and work on that now, as I would like for us to be on our way to London by noon."

"I'll have to hurry to make that happen. I've been a slugabed today."

"Nonsense, Beabe, you deserved the extra rest. When we get to London, I will find us a suitable place, and we will hole up until we are both over this journey that has taken us so long."

Beabe smiled at her as a soft knock sounded at the door. Arianna knew it had to be Mrs. Post, the woman she'd met last night, because the housekeeper had told her all the other servants had been given a few days off.

Beabe walked over and opened the door. Arianna heard Mrs. Post ask if she could come in, and Beabe stepped aside and allowed her to enter.

Mrs. Post was once again impeccably dressed in a pale gray, high-waisted dress that was covered by a neatly pressed apron.

"Good morning, Miss Sweet. I trust you had a restful night."

"Yes, thank you."

"Good. I'm sorry to disturb your breakfast, but I just spoke to Lord Morgandale, and he asked that I give you a message."

Arianna's breath kicked up a notch. Perhaps the surly man was unhappy she wasn't out of his house fast enough. Though she hardly felt like moving, she'd remedy that soon enough. And she didn't know why but she didn't want this to be the last time she saw the earl. The thought of never seeing him again made her chest feel heavy. Considering the man had such a prickly temper, it was all very odd to her that he caused her heartbeat to race and her breath to grow short.

"You aren't disturbing me, Mrs. Post. What did the earl have to say?"

"That I am to bring you more food to eat than toast and chocolate. He wants you to have a hearty breakfast, and that I should see that you eat all of it."

Arianna looked down at the toast, butter, and jam that she hadn't even touched. Her appetite hadn't returned since the fever. And the earl wanted her to eat more? So, it appeared the earl was not through ordering her around as of yet.

"Just who does he think he is?" Arianna said as much to herself as to the women in the room.

Mrs. Post remained stiff and unflustered as she offered, "He is the master of this house, Miss Sweet."

That was difficult to argue with. "Yes, that is true, but I should think he'd have better things to do than concern himself with what I eat."

"I'm sure he looks at his instructions as for your benefit, Miss Ari," Beabe offered.

"Lord Morgandale also said that you should spend the entire day in bed."

Surprised, Arianna looked at Mrs. Post and said, "You mean he is going to allow me to stay here today? He's not rushing me off?"

"Quite the contrary, Miss Sweet. Lord Morgandale told me to inform you that he has paid your driver and sent him away."

Arianna gasped. "No!" she whispered. "What am I to do? I can't believe he did that! How am I to get to London?"

"I'm sure he will arrange that for you at the proper time. For now, he intends for you to stay here at

Valleydale while you recuperate from whatever it is that ails you."

Arianna didn't know what to say. She looked at Beabe. The woman couldn't hide the hopeful expression on her weary face. Arianna felt a twinge of anger at herself for not realizing sooner that her maid needed the rest the earl had mandated, too; Arianna just didn't like it that the man hadn't given her a say in the matter.

"Lord Morgandale said if you wished to speak to him about this or any other matter, he would be available to see you in the drawing room tomorrow evening before dinner."

"Tomorrow?"

"That is his first opportunity to be available."

Arianna supposed, being an earl, he was busy. At least the overbearing man had granted her the opportunity to speak to him later.

Mrs. Post continued. "He said I should arrange for hot water to be brought up to you whenever you are ready for it so that you can wash away the traveling dust, so to speak."

How had the earl known exactly what she needed and wanted? A tub of hot water to wash in sounded divine. The earl might have the temperament of a grouchy bear, but without his knowing, he was not only giving her the comforts of his home, he was giving her what she desperately needed right now; a place to rest so that she could renew herself and be ready to accomplish her goals as soon as she reached London.

"All right, please tell Lord Morgandale I will accept his hospitality for a few days."

Mrs. Post nodded and looked as if a weight had been lifted off her shoulders.

"Tell me, Mrs. Post, what time does the earl have dinner?"

"He usually dines around seven-thirty."

"In that case, I'll be down at six tomorrow evening so I won't miss him. You may tell him to expect me."

"Yes, Miss Sweet," she said and exited the room.

Arianna relaxed against the pillows once again.

"Can you believe that, Miss Ari?" Beabe said excitedly as soon as the housekeeper's footfalls could be heard on the stairs. "Hallelujah, we can stay here for a few days. I can put this dress away, because you aren't going anywhere today."

Arianna smiled, knowing she'd made the right decision for herself and for Beabe.

She sipped the warm chocolate. She couldn't help but feel a twinge of eager expectancy because she would get to see the earl one more time and look into his enthralling blue eyes once again before she left his home.

Five

My Dearest Grandson Lucas,

What do you think of these wise words of Chesterfield? "Always take care to keep the best company in the place where you are. And the pleasures of a gentleman are only to be found in the best of company; for that riot which low company most falsely and impudently call pleasure, is only the sensuality of a swine."

Your loving Grandmother,
Lady Elder

AFTER MORE THAN TWO MONTHS OF FEELING AS IF SHE couldn't lift her head off a pillow without the room spinning, Arianna woke for the first time without feeling dizzy. It was amazing what a tub of hot, soapy water, a fresh night rail, and two days of uninterrupted rest could do for a person. Though she hated to admit it, even to herself, the voyage and the fever had taken a lot out of her. She had been weak-kneed when she first arrived at Valleydale, but now she was feeling stronger.

After waking from the nap, she donned a bright melon-colored dress with long, sheer sleeves that were banded at the cuff with a bright multicolored trim. The same trim bordered the hemline and high waist of her skirt.

She supposed in England that most people would frown on her for not still wearing black, as it wasn't yet a year past her father's death. But in India, there were only twelve days of mourning, and *kala* was not a color that was worn often and not at all for mourning.

She sat at the dressing table and fashioned her long, freshly-washed hair into a chignon at the back of her head. She then clasped around her neck a choker necklace of four strands of light green beads, that had been woven together, and clipped matching earrings to her ears.

By the time she finished dressing, she was feeling weak again. It frustrated her that her body gave out on her with the least exertion. Arianna looked at the barely touched tray that sat on the dressing table. Her appetite had not returned to normal yet, but hopefully that would come back soon. She had found it difficult even to look at the tray laden with a bowl of steaming chicken, potato, and onion soup, with a large piece of bread covered with butter and a side dish of cooked figs. She asked Beabe to find a nice way to explain to Mrs. Post that she would rather not have so much food on her tray at one time. Arianna had received word back that her tray was prepared the way Lord Morgandale had requested. That didn't surprise her.

It wasn't quite six o'clock, the time she had told Mrs. Post she would be down to see the earl. Arianna wanted to satisfy her curiosity about the house and hopefully build some strength in her legs, strolling around the house. Because it was so dark, she hadn't seen much of it the night she arrived.

Taking her time and holding onto the banister, she walked slowly down the wide, curved stairs. She could see just how grand and large the front hall was. The entrance alone looked as if it could hold more than fifty people. Now she knew why it took the earl so long to get her from the door to the drawing room after she fainted.

On one wall hung the most magnificent floor-to-ceiling mirror she had ever seen. It was framed in the baroque style and painted in shiny gilt. On another wall in the entrance area was draped a huge tapestry of a colorful garden that almost reached to the floor. The centerpiece of the garden scene was a three-tiered fountain that was held up by three winged cherubs. A side table with an oval crystal platter sitting on a highly polished silver stand was filled with calling cards. Arianna couldn't help but wonder if the earl ever looked at them. She was tempted to pick up one and read it but decided that though snooping around the rooms was acceptable, reading his calling cards was not. Besides, she hadn't spent any time in England since she was sixteen, and she probably wouldn't recognize any of the names.

She made her way over to the open double doors on the left of the wide corridor and peeked inside. It was the loveliest room she had ever seen. It was painted in a soothing shade of pale blue. All the trim and fretwork had been painted in gold leaf. A handsome pianoforte was positioned in the middle of the room, and a violin had been propped on a tall gilt stand beside it. Settees, side chairs, and window seats, all upholstered in varying shades of blue and gold patterns, dotted the room. Exquisite blue velvet draperies were held back with large gold tassels and framed the two tall windows in the room. Late afternoon shadows filtered through the glass and danced around the room and glinted off the gold tones.

Arianna wondered if the earl played either of the instruments, or did he perhaps have them available for his guests to play. She walked over to the pianoforte and let her fingers glide softly over the cool, smooth, dark mahogany wood. She closed her eyes and imagined the room filled with beautifully gowned ladies and handsomely dressed gentlemen. She imagined the earl standing before her in his evening coat, smiling, bowing, and then taking her hand and leading her to the dance floor.

Shaking her head, Arianna opened her eyes and smiled. Why was she having these fanciful notions about the earl? It was absolutely ridiculous. He was arrogant, maddening, and ill-tempered. He was quite the master at giving orders and expecting them to be obeyed without question. But she also knew he looked like the paintings she'd seen of Apollo, Adonis, and the statue of David. She realized that thinking that kind of nonsense was just another indication of how weak her mind and body still were from the fever.

Strolling down the corridor, Arianna stopped at the double doors just behind the staircase and saw immediately that it was the drawing room where the earl had taken her after she had fainted. When she entered, the most prominent item in the room was the life-sized painting of a tall, regal lady dressed in a formal black gown and standing by a chair, with a smug expression on her face. She had briefly noticed the oil a couple of nights ago.

Arianna walked closer to get a better look. One hand rested on the chair and the other on her hip. But what most caught Arianna's immediate attention was the necklace she wore. There had to be at least five strands of the exquisite pearls draped around her neck. Each strand fell to just below her waist.

After a closer look at the woman's face, Arianna saw that the woman and Lord Morgandale had the same color of extraordinary blue eyes. The painter had perfectly captured the shade she remembered. This had to be his grandmother, Lady Elder.

Arianna recalled the earl saying something about the Talbot pearls, and she couldn't help but wonder if those were the ones the lady wore.

Glancing around the room, Arianna saw that all the chintz, velvets, and watered silk in the room were in pastel colors and either floral or stripes in design. None of the fabrics were bold or intense. She was once again reminded of the differences in the shades of dyes of Indian and British people. Indians loved to use rich, vibrant colors in their homes and in their clothing, while it appeared that most of the English people preferred pale, subdued shades.

She had enjoyed her time in that faraway land, but her short stay in the earl's home helped her realize that

England was where she belonged. Her father had told her before his death that they would be leaving India to return to England. He wanted to present his extraordinary findings to the Royal Apothecary Scientific Academy, and then he would put his research aside until she was properly wed to a suitable and worthy gentleman. Only then did he plan to return to India to continue his work.

A pang of sorrow sliced through her.

Arianna took a deep breath and refused to let the melancholy take hold. She looked at the brass-encased clock on the mantel and saw that it was after six. The earl had not arrived, and although she was growing tired, she decided to continue her perusal of the house.

The next room she came to drew an audible gasp from her. The spacious, elaborately mirrored dining room held a table set with thirty chairs and five evenly spaced silver candelabras, each holding twelve candles. She pulled out one of the chairs padded with light blue cushions and sat down, pretending she was a guest at a lavish affair.

After leaving the dining room, she took a quick peek into the breakfast room, where she saw a round table circled by eight ladder-back chairs. A corner china cabinet displayed a lovely china pattern. The white plate had a pink rose in the center with three colorful butterflies surrounding it.

Astounded by the opulence of the rooms, Arianna moved down to a door at the end of the corridor and walked inside.

Startled, she gasped. "Oh, excuse me, my lord, I apologize for intruding. I had no idea you would be in here."

Lord Morgandale rose from his chair behind the desk, and Arianna's heart skipped a beat. What she saw of him two nights ago hadn't done him justice. She swallowed the lump of appreciation that clogged her throat.

The earl was tall and powerful-looking in his black coat cut perfectly to fit across his straight shoulders and broad chest, which tapered to a slim waist and lean hips that were hidden beneath buff-colored breeches. The fabric of his camel-colored waistcoat and expertly tied neckcloth spoke of prosperity and privilege, and he wore both of them well. The style of his fine, dark brown hair was straight and attractive, hanging longer at his nape. Feathery wisps fell across his thick eyebrows, making him look a little roguish, a little daring, but also breathtakingly handsome.

Arianna's chest tightened, and her stomach quickened deliciously when she realized Lord Morgandale was looking her over as carefully as she was perusing him. She watched his gaze skim down her face, over her breasts, before he glanced back up to meet her eyes once again. His deliberate scrutiny made her tingle with expectancy all the way down to her toes.

After what she must have looked like when she arrived, after her more than two months journey, she couldn't help but feel a twinge of satisfaction when she saw in his eyes that he approved of the way she looked now.

Clearing her throat, she said, "I was walking around your home. It's lovely."

He acknowledged her compliment with a nod. "I heard you."

"You did?"

"I've been waiting for you. I knew you would eventually make your way into my book room."

"You were so quiet, I didn't know you were in the house. I thought you would be in the drawing room." Arianna stopped talking when she saw humor in his eyes. Much to her consternation, she had amused him once again.

"I don't usually make a noise when I go over my account books. Would you have been happier if I had been running around my house as if I were a nincompoop?"

He smiled at her, and Arianna's heart started beating faster. She couldn't have kept herself from returning his smile and a breath or two of a chuckle even if she had wanted to. He was so engaging that she was powerless to control the new and intriguing sensations that she felt whenever he was near.

"No, of course not, my lord. I can't imagine you ever being that silly. I only meant that I wouldn't have ventured into your private domain if I had known you were working."

"But now that you are here, I must say that you look as though you are feeling a little better today."

"I am. So, as much as I would like to take issue with you for sending my driver away, I cannot. I know that it would serve me and my maid well to stay put for a few days to rest."

He cocked his head to one side and said, "Was there a thank you in what you just said, Miss Sweet? If so it was unrecognizable as one to me."

His tone, the shimmer of humor in his eyes, made her stomach quicken excitedly.

She nodded, smiled, and then said, "Yes. Thank you for taking me into your home and allowing me to stay here while I regain my strength before continuing my journey."

"You are welcome. I see no reason to hurry your recuperation, so I took the liberty of sending a letter to a friend of mine who resides in London in hopes that she can come to Valleydale, as long as you need to be here, and escort you to London. Perhaps she can even be your companion while you search for one."

Arianna pursed her lips. She was grateful for his shelter for a few days but couldn't allow him to take charge of her life.

"My lord, I am twenty-seven."

"That old?" He gave her a look of feigned horror, which she chose to ignore.

"Yes, and I have been on my own for several months now. I have my maid with me, and you have Mrs. Post. Surely, you don't need to go to the trouble for the short time I will be here. As soon as I can I must travel on to London."

"I agree that you may not need a companion with you, Miss Sweet, but I do."

She searched his face, trying to decide if he were serious or finding his amusement at her expense once again. His eyes were so disarming, she couldn't tell.

"What do you mean?" she asked.

He walked from behind his desk and over to where she stood. "Imagine what it would do to my spotless reputation in London if someone found out that I had a young lady staying in my home and did nothing to secure her a proper companion. Why, I would be the talk of London."

His horrified expression was so exaggerated, Arianna smiled. He could be an engaging rogue when he wanted to be. No doubt with those eyes, that smile, and his teasing conversation, he had broken hearts all over London.

"Spotless reputation?" she questioned with a knowing smile.

His heavenly blue eyes sparkled. "Odd as it sounds, do you doubt that?"

"Yes, my lord. And my usual good sense, which I admit leaves me at times, tells me that you are already the talk of London."

He chuckled. "Perhaps I am. But on the odd chance that I am not, you don't want to ruin my good reputation, do you?"

"That is an impossible notion."

"So is the notion of you arriving in London without a proper companion. Propriety can be overlooked here for a time because of your illness, but London Society is unforgiving." He moved closer to her and in a low voice said, "You know, your laughter is quite fetching. You should do it more often."

Arianna was amazed at how quickly his tall, powerful body seemed to fill up the space around her. A shivery awareness of him stole over her, stirring up her womanly senses. It was so unlike her to be attracted to a man in this way, and especially to a man who frustrated her as much as this one did. She didn't know what to do about it.

She lifted her lashes and looked into his eyes. Taking a calming breath, she said, "It felt good to laugh, my lord. I haven't had much reason to lately."

The earl leaned in nearer to her. She sensed his strength, and she felt the heat of his body as pleasing warmth flooded her, though he never touched her.

"Perhaps your luck is about to change for the better."

"It would be welcomed," she managed to say without sounding as breathless as she felt.

"There is another reason it will be good for Mrs. Constance Pepperfield to come to Valleydale and accompany you to London should she accept my invitation."

"What is that, my lord?"

His face moved a little closer to hers. Her gaze met his and held. The fresh-washed scent of shaving soap stirred the air and teased her nose.

"She can guide you as to who in London might be seeking employment as a companion."

"I can see the value in that."

"She can make introductions, will know addresses, and if necessary, can help you write letters to the appropriate people."

With him so close, Arianna didn't know how she was managing to continue the conversation. Her legs suddenly seemed weak, and she knew the feeling didn't come from her recent illness but from her body's unusual reaction to the earl's nearness.

"That would, indeed, be most helpful."

"Good."

"Though I'm not sure how I can ever repay you."

"Perhaps you can by simply accepting my hospitality graciously."

Teasing sensations skittered across her breasts, down her stomach, and settled low. She sensed a quickening between her legs. She stared into his eyes again and suddenly felt hot, breathless, and eager for something, but she didn't know what. She didn't understand why the earl caused her to have all these delicious and wonderful feelings when she wasn't even sure she liked him.

She was barely breathing but managed to say, "That I can do. Thank you, my lord."

"See, that wasn't so difficult, was it?"

Arianna shook her head.

Lord Morgandale bent his head to the crook of her neck and breathed in deeply. She stood perfectly still and was certain she felt his lips, or maybe it was the tip of his nose, that lightly touched her skin as he whispered in a husky voice, "What is that exotic scent that I smell?"

Suddenly, the same glorious sensations she'd felt earlier rushed through her once again.

He kept his face hovering so close to her neck that she tingled all over. "It's a blend of oils from various plants in India. My father made it into perfumed water for me. If it bothers you, I can refrain from using it while I'm here."

"It bothers me," he said softly, "but don't stop using it."

He lifted his head slowly. She felt his breath fanning her heated skin as it skimmed over her jawline, up her cheek, past her eye, until he looked down at her again.

A small puff of air was all that escaped her lips. She knew she should step away, but she had no desire to do so. She stood there, barely breathing, and allowed him to mesmerize her with his assault on her senses.

Morgan swallowed hard, and his chest heaved. His lips were so close to hers he could almost feel them. He wanted to feel them beneath his own. He had been attracted to her when she first arrived at his door and, if possible, he was even more attracted to her now. Propriety and the devil be damned, he wanted to kiss her. He bent his head closer to hers, but just a second before his lips touched hers, Morgan heard his butler's familiar footsteps coming down the corridor.

Perfect timing.

Morgan stepped away from Miss Sweet and turned toward the doorway as the servant stepped into view. "Yes, Post."

"Excuse me, my lord," the servant said from the doorway. "May I have a private word with you?"

"Certainly."

Thanking his lucky stars, Morgan walked over to where the butler stood. Kissing Miss Sweet was the last thing he needed to do.

"Miss Francine Goodbody has arrived," Post whispered, "and would like to speak to you."

Morgan swore softly. "This is not good news, Post."

"I didn't think so, my lord."

Damnation, she was two days late. In truth, he had forgotten all about the woman. He had assumed she had found something better to do than keep her appointment with him. He hadn't even heard a carriage drive up the lane, but that might have been because he was so busy engaging Miss Sweet in mindless conversation and trying his best to keep his hands and his lips off her.

What an uncomfortable position to be in. He found no humor in the current situation fate had sprung on him, but he had the urge to laugh at the improbability of it.

Instead, Morgan quickly considered his few options and said, "Show her into the drawing room, and tell her I will join her shortly."

"Yes, my lord," Post said and turned away.

Morgan took his time walking back to Miss Sweet. With luck he could get Miss Goodbody out of the house without Miss Sweet ever knowing the courtesan was there.

"Something has come up that needs my attention, Miss Sweet. But since you are in my book room, why don't you take your time and browse through the titles and pick out several books to read? Assuming Mrs. Pepperfield is available to come to Valleydale, it will be a few days before she will arrive. I think you should spend most of that time in your bedchamber, resting. Reading will help you pass the time."

"Thank you, my lord. I would love the opportunity to look over your books. I'm sure there are many here that I haven't read."

Morgan nodded and said, "Good. And remember, take your time. There's no hurry."

She smiled at him, and his stomach clenched. Damnation, what was wrong with him? He was feeling like a schoolboy with his first romantic crush.

"I will."

"Good evening, Miss Sweet."

Morgan derided himself as he walked down the corridor to the drawing room.

What a hell of a mess he'd gotten himself into! Two nights ago he'd convinced himself that Miss Goodbody had decided not to come. But now that she had, there was no way he could allow her to stay overnight with Miss Sweet in the house. Not that anyone would ever know except him, but still he couldn't bring himself to do it.

Fate had a wickedly odd sense of humor.

This situation had almost become laughable. How could it be that the one time he had invited a woman of the evening into his home, a lady of quality arrived, as well?

Morgan strode confidently into the drawing room, and Miss Goodbody rose from the settee and curtseyed graciously.

Morgan swallowed hard. It would be sheer hell sending her away. She was as beautiful, as enticing, and as voluptuous as his solicitor had promised. Golden blonde hair was piled high on top of her head, with a few wispy curls framing her delicate face. Her dark brown eyes were full of expression, and her smile was alluring. Her pale pink dress was cut temptingly low, showing the full swell of her lovely breasts.

It had been weeks since he had been with a woman, and looking at her, he couldn't help but question if he really wanted to send her away.

Morgan took a deep, steadying breath and said, "Good-evening, Miss Goodbody. I'm afraid I had given up on your arrival."

She took a step toward him, smiling seductively, leaving him no doubt that she would be all that his solicitor had promised. But of course, Morgan had no choice but to send Miss Goodbody back to London without so much as a taste of her alluring body.

Suddenly he had two desirable women in his house, and he couldn't touch either one of them. Society would be unforgiving if anyone ever found out that he had a woman of Miss Goodbody's ilk in his home at the same time he had a lady like Miss Sweet as his guest. No, he couldn't take the chance, no matter that his body clawed at him to do otherwise.

And if he should ever find out that his cousins were somehow behind this maddening situation that he found himself in at present, he would throttle them both until they begged for mercy, and then he would throttle them some more.

"My lord, I beg your forgiveness. I'm sorry I have been delayed by more than a day. There were problems with rain making traveling slow on the first day, and then there was a problem with one of the wheels of the coach the next. We were forced to stay at an inn and wait until the coach could be repaired. I tried to hire another coach, but all were already in use."

"I understand that those kinds of things can happen, and we have had nasty weather."

She smiled sweetly at him. "I do hope you will forgive my tardiness and welcome me. I promise that I will make up for lost time by staying longer than originally anticipated, if that would please you."

He was loathe to say it, but he must. "I'm afraid my plans have changed."

"What do you mean?"

"I must pass on your visit and send you back to London without so much as a rest."

Her eyes widened, her lips parted, and she took a step toward him. "But I don't understand. Because I was late, you no longer want me here?"

"No, no, this has nothing to do with your tardiness. That was obviously not your fault. It's just that—"

Morgan stopped. Did he really have to explain himself to a woman he was paying?

No.

That was why he preferred women he paid. No strings and no explanations needed.

"I know it has put an undue burden on you to make this trip for naught, and now to have to immediately turn around and leave. Naturally I will make arrangements for you to receive a handsome bonus for your trouble."

With an understanding smile on her face, Miss Goodbody walked up to him and laid her hand on the lapel of his coat. "If I must go, I must, but why be so hasty? We don't have to be in that big of a hurry, do we, my lord?"

Her hand slipped from his lapel down to the hardness beneath his riding breeches and she cupped him. He was instantly aroused. His body stiffened, and his breath caught in his throat.

She stood on her toes and lifted her face to his. Her lips were full and inviting; her breasts touched just enough of his chest to tease him. He inhaled, and the womanly scent of lavender filled him. He couldn't help but contrast the familiar perfume to the exotic scent of Miss Sweet. No, he had never encountered a woman who had the enchanting scent of Miss Sweet.

"I would never pressure you to do anything you don't want to do, but I assure you I will do anything you want. I'm well trained in what gentlemen want and need. And judging from what I feel in my hand, I do believe you need me."

Oh yes!

Morgan remained silent while his body made war with his brain, and his gaze searched her face. There was no doubt that she was a beauty and her touch was skilled.

Miss Goodbody applied the merest of pressure to his hardness, and he stiffened. Oh, yes, he had no doubt she was very good at her job. Just her touch had him ready to make use of the settee.

"I came all this way, my lord. Surely before I go there is something I can do for you."

If only!

Morgan didn't know where he found the control, but he managed to say, "Your offer is tempting, but I don't think so, Miss Goodbody."

She smiled, obviously not ready or willing to take no for an answer. With the ease of long-practiced art, she lifted her mouth up to his ear and whispered in slow, warming breaths that fanned the flaming arc of his desire, "I promise you it won't take long for me to ease the heavy burden you are carrying here."

With the merest hint of pressure, she closed her hand over him. Morgan sucked in a deep, ragged breath, and a curse passed his lips.

She moved to look into his eyes. "Now, are you sure you don't want me to step over and close the drawing room doors before I go, my lord?"

No, he wasn't sure at all that he didn't want her to do exactly what she was doing and much more.

He had longed for this. He had paid for this. He deserved this.

But...

Suddenly he remembered sparkling, innocent green eyes and tempting lips and propriety. Morgan dug down deep and found the courage to take hold of Miss Goodbody's hand and, reluctantly, he did the right thing and stepped away from her.

Once the deed was done, he let out a long, calming breath. He agreed with Saint. Few could match Miss Goodbody's appeal, and the woman would have been perfect—if Miss Sweet hadn't arrived first.

He looked into the courtesan's soft brown eyes, and he knew she was as disappointed as he. After all, she wasn't the kind of woman men usually declined.

"I don't doubt that you can deliver what you promise, Miss Goodbody, but you must accept that at this time your services are no longer needed."

Morgan saw something out of the corner of his eye and turned in time to see Miss Sweet hurrying by with her arms full of books.

Damnation! How much had she heard or seen?

"I understand now," Miss Goodbody said as she took a step away from him. "She's lovely."

He cleared his throat. "As I said, you will be well compensated for the change in plans."

She nodded once. "Thank you. I don't ever burn bridges, my lord. You are a handsome, powerful man." She paused, lowering her lashes and dropping her gaze to where her hand had recently held him. "A very big man." Her gaze popped back up to his. "Perhaps you will have reason to call on my services in the future."

Obviously, along with her other expertise, Miss Goodbody was a professional business woman. She had wisely decided not to give him any trouble. A trustworthy name in her business was as valuable as a good name in Polite Society.

"Not far down the road at the village you passed is The Weary Traveler's Inn. I think it best you stay there for the evening. The proprietor is Mr. Harrisburg. Tell him I sent you, and he will give you his best room. He knows that I will take care of him later."

"Thank you, my lord. I will do as you suggest."

Morgan nodded once. "I'll get Post to show you to the door."

Six

My Dearest Grandson Lucas,

Over the years I've had many gentlemen steal my heart, but the great Lord Chesterfield was the only one to steal my mind. Read this: "Though men are all of one composition, the several ingredients are so differently proportioned in each individual that no two are exactly alike; and no one at all times like himself. The ablest man will sometime do weak things; the proudest man, mean things, the honestest man, ill things; and the wickedest man, good things."

Your loving Grandmother,
Lady Elder

ARIANNA STOOD AT ONE OF THE WINDOWS IN HER bedchamber and watched two horses grazing in a paddock. Earlier in the day she had watched several men working with different horses, first walking them and later riding them, but the workers seemed to have left for the day. The stables looked quite large and were situated not far from the main estate, on a grassy knoll dotted with trees. There was a field of colorful wild flowers to one side of the stone structure that housed the animals and another larger paddock with more horses situated just beyond the field of tall light blue blooms.

She didn't know if it was the fourth or fifth afternoon of her stay at Lord Morgandale's manor. She had spent so much time reading through some of the many journals of her father's that she'd brought with her, sleeping, and eating that the days had run together. Her bouts of dizziness were less frequent, and she had started eating a little more. Once she accepted that what she needed to do was stay put and regain her strength, she was determined to do everything possible to get strong enough to continue her journey to London.

And she was getting stronger. Just that morning, for the first time, she felt strong enough to do movements and steps of one of the dances she'd learned in India. Losing herself in the Indian dances had always been a way for her to relax and clear her mind of any troubles or concerns. Her room was quite large, and she had plenty of space to maneuver around without bumping into the furniture. But it hadn't taken her more than a minute or two to become out of breath and feel weak and shaky once again.

When not searching through her father's journals, she studied on her plan of all she needed to do when she reached London. The first thing was to lease a house and get her belongings from the freight company. Once she had the rest of her father's papers and books safely in her possession, she would see Mr. Warburton and ask his assistance in finding and reconstructing her father's formula from his notes. Once that was accomplished, he could present it to the Royal Apothecary Scientific Academy in her father's name. After they approved it, the medicine could be widely distributed.

But more often than Arianna wanted, her thoughts drifted to the handsome earl. She hadn't seen him since she had walked past the drawing room and saw him standing close to the woman. Arianna couldn't hear what they were saying, but they both seemed intent on each other.

Arianna assumed the lady must have been the person he had been expecting the night Arianna arrived. She only got a glimpse of her face, but it was enough to know she was a beautiful woman. For some reason she hadn't stayed long, but Lord Morgandale must have had some tender affection for her, for they were holding hands.

Though Arianna had tried to keep the incident from her thoughts, she had spent more than a little time the past couple of days wondering why she had felt a tight curl of something similar to envy in her chest when she saw them so intimately together. Surely it was none of her concern. Besides, not only did she not really know the earl, she repeatedly reminded herself that she didn't even approve of him. He was much too forceful and arrogant for her tastes.

She realized that at twenty-seven, she was fast approaching the age of becoming a spinster, if not already there. But she had always thought that if she ever caught a gentleman's eye, he would be a soft-spoken, scholarly man like her father. She didn't want to be enamored of such a worldly and enchantingly handsome gentleman as Lord Morgandale.

And she would have to keep telling herself that until she believed it.

The longer Arianna stood and watched the horses, the more she wanted to go out and enjoy the beautiful afternoon. There wasn't a cloud in the hazy blue sky. The temperature was warm and inviting. A gentle breeze blew through the open window. It was as if the outside world beckoned her to come out and play.

And why shouldn't she? The stables looked to be a reasonable walk from the main house, and she hadn't seen anyone coming or going from them in at least an hour. Now seemed as good a time as any to test her legs and see how strong she was. She couldn't stay under the hospitality of the earl's house one day more than necessary, no matter how much she would like to. She needed to get to London and meet with Mr. Warburton. Maybe walking and dancing a little each day would rebuild her constitution faster.

Arianna glanced down at the bright pink sari that she wore with its vivid yellow and green trim. She had donned the Indian dress that morning and spent all of a couple of minutes dancing. The short-sleeve tunic she wore with the skirt had a low, scooped neckline and was cropped more than two inches above her natural waistline.

Since all of her clothing had been made in India, even her English-style clothing was of brighter and more vivid colors than would be allowed for unmarried young ladies in England. After she had spent more than three years in India, her father had finally relented and allowed her to wear dresses made from the bright colors, styles, and fabrics of the Indian people, but he had always insisted that when she returned to England, she would have to wear the colors and styles that were fashionable in her homeland.

Even in India she had never been allowed to wear a sari outside the house. Except for the end of the fabric which was thrown over the shoulder, it left her midriff bare. She looked at the wardrobe that held her English clothing and back out the window again. She had no idea where Beabe was or how long it would take to go below stairs, find her maid to help her change her clothing, and then pull up her hair into a chignon as would be proper for walking about the estate.

Arianna's desire to get out of the house was too great to waste all that time. And she wanted to get out to the paddock and see the horses before someone came to put them back inside for the night. The easiest thing to do would be to simply throw on a lightweight cape over the sari and not take time to change.

Once she settled that in her mind, she grabbed a straw bonnet with a wide, bright green ribbon and a dark brown cape from the wardrobe. Seconds later, she was out her bedchamber door. As she walked down the wide staircase to the entrance hall, she made a bow under her chin with the ribbon on her hat and then tied the braided cord of her cape around her neck. As quietly as possible, she opened the heavy front door and stepped out, closing it gently behind her.

Arianna stood for a moment and breathed in deeply, stretching her arms above her head and then out to her sides. It was heavenly to finally feel better. She must come up with a suitable way to thank the earl for allowing her this much needed rest to improve her health.

Knowing the stables were to the left of the house, she headed that way. It didn't take her long to realize that the stables and paddock were farther from the main house than she realized and that what looked like a gentle rise up to the grassy knoll was, in her weakened condition, actually a very steep hill. She took her time but was still out of breath and weak-kneed by the time she made it to the paddock and leaned on the fence.

The horses' ears had pricked forward as she neared, and the animals watched her with big, deep brown eyes. Both animals were dark chestnut. Their healthy coats gleamed in the late afternoon sun.

One horse was taller and more powerfully built than the other. In some places, his coat was so dark it looked black, reminding her of Lord Morgandale's thick hair. The big stallion watched her closely with a suspicious eye as she leaned heavily upon the fence and calmed her breathing. He whinnied and threw his proud-looking head in the air as if he were asking her to explain her presence in his domain. The smaller horse had a gentle-eyed stare and seemed more curious than outraged or agitated by her being there.

Arianna smiled and watched both with interest while she rested.

"Good afternoon," she called and waved to the stallion who hadn't taken his penetrating gaze off her.

Much to her amazement, he trotted over to her with his head held high, his mane gently flapping in the breeze. He came right up to her, snorting. She reached out to touch him, but he backed away, snorted at her again, and tossed his head belligerently. He then turned his back on her and trotted off to the other side of the paddock as if she wasn't worth his time.

Arianna laughed. She had never been snubbed by a horse before. The stallion's behavior reminded her very much of Lord Morgandale the night she arrived unannounced at his house.

She lifted her straight skirt several inches above her ankles and climbed up on the first rung of the wooden fence. Her soft-soled slippers were not ideal for the long walk or climbing a fence, but she managed to find a comfortable, stable way to stand by putting most of her weight on the center of her feet.

Leaning over the fence, she kept her voice soft but loud enough for him to hear as she said, "You are arrogant, just like your master. Mind your manners. Come over here and greet me properly."

The horse whinnied, snorted, and pawed at the earth again as if to remind her of his power and to warn her away from him.

"You do not frighten me. Come here and let me rub you. I will prove to you that you are really as gentle as a baby lamb."

His dark eyes stared at her. He twitched his ears and then turned away, but just as quickly he changed direction, acquiesced, and raced toward her in a charging manner. He stopped short of reaching her, snorted, and continued his watchful stare.

Arianna remained calmly on the fence and spoke firmly to the horse. "Stop that. You are not a menace."

His nostrils flared excitedly, and he moved restlessly, kicking up clumps of the soft dirt beneath his hooves.

"You are trying to intimidate me, aren't you? Well your bestial attitude won't work on me, Master Brute. I have ridden atop elephants in India and have not been frightened. They are bigger and stronger than you. And I have walked beside a tiger that was un-tethered, and they are more ferocious than you. So stop your snorting and pawing. You cannot scare me away. Now, be a good *ghoda* and come here and let me rub you."

Lifting her skirt even higher so she could bend her knee, Arianna slowly climbed up to the second rung of the fence, making her as tall as the horse. She reached out her hand and waited until he relented, walked up to her, and sniffed her palm. He tossed his head again, whinnied, and backed up, but he didn't run off as he had the other two times.

She smiled. She was winning him over.

"Oh, I see that it is not friendship you want from me but only a treat, and my hand was empty. Very well, I will bring you something delicious the next time I come."

His ears twitched as if he were listening to every word she spoke.

"Yes, yes, you drive a hard bargain. I promise," she told the horse. "Let's be friends. Come closer, I want to rub your shiny coat."

He walked closer and then stood still and let her rub down the hard bridge of his long nose. She raked her hand down his firm neck, and gently patted him. His taut muscles shuddered beneath her touch. His coat was smooth and warm.

"You are a fine, powerful animal," she said, rubbing him. "I am not afraid of you any more than I am afraid of your powerful master."

"Is that so?" came a voice from behind her.

Startled, Arianna gasped and jerked. At her sudden motion, the horse reared up, knocking her wide-brimmed hat to her shoulders. Arianna lurched back and lost her footing. She felt herself falling backward, but suddenly she was caught up in strong, familiar arms. Once again, she found herself pressed against Lord Morgandale's wide, muscular chest, looking up and staring into his magnificent blue eyes.

The quickening sensations she felt last time he held her so close surfaced, only much stronger than before. This time, she didn't fight him or struggle to be released. One reason was that she couldn't have even if she had wanted to. In her fall and his catching her, her arms became wrapped inside her cape, thankfully covering her sari. But more importantly, she didn't struggle because, strangely, she felt as if she was where she belonged.

His body was warm, and she felt strength in his embrace. The scent of horse, leather, and shaving soap teased her nose. She stared up at him with no embarrassment and no feeling that being in his arms was the wrong place to be.

"I have several questions," he said calmly, "but maybe just asking what you are doing out here will answer most of them."

Her gaze darted up and down his face. "I wanted to see the horses."

He gently set her on her feet and removed his arms from around her, but didn't step away. She grabbed hold of her cape with her fingers and held it together so he would not see what she was wearing underneath. She rolled her shoulders and lifted her chin. The sun was in her eyes, and the breeze blew strands of hair across her face, but she couldn't turn loose of her cape to put her hat back on her head; so much to her consternation, she left it hanging on the back of her shoulders.

"Could you not see them from your bedroom window?" Lord Morgandale asked.

She nodded and then moistened her lips before answering, "Of course. But I have rested for several days now, and I felt the need to get out and stretch my legs. I wanted to see how strong I am. I must leave soon."

He nodded. "But that doesn't explain why you were rubbing that horse. He is not yet completely broken, Miss Sweet. He is a dangerous animal. And you should be very much afraid of him, and of me."

She gave the earl a curious stare, much like the one the smaller horse had given her when she first approached the paddock.

"You worry too much, my lord. I have been around big animals before. They don't frighten me."

"Is that so?"

"Yes, and it's been my experience that most brutes are eventually tamed."

His eyebrows rose, and slowly his masculine lips formed a smile. Suddenly he was laughing softly. The sound was sensuous and entrancing and seductive.

There was something wonderful about seeing his handsome face glowing with genuine laughter. It set her heart to fluttering.

"Do you ride, Miss Sweet?"

"Yes, but not horses."

He regarded her curiously. "I am going to assume that does not mean what I'm thinking at this moment. Perhaps you should explain yourself."

"I have no idea what you might be thinking."

"Thank God for small favors," he mumbled softly.

"I have ridden on top of elephants many times in India."

His eyes narrowed again, and he smiled as the breeze scattered his thick dark hair away from his forehead. "You amuse me, Miss Sweet. You have ridden an elephant?"

"Well, I didn't control him, you understand, as it takes years to learn how to handle a *hathi*, an elephant; the *mahout* does that, but yes, in India it's quite common to ride them. Elephants have been quite domesticated there and are used for a variety of things, including transportation, leisure riding, and work camps. I became quite efficient in climbing on an elephant's back without the aid of a ladder."

"And your father knew this?"

There was always a twinge of pain in her chest when her father was mentioned. And she knew there always would be until she either found or reconstructed his formula and delivered it to the Royal Apothecary Scientific Academy.

"Ah, no," she said softly. "He would not have approved."

"I believe you. The next time a carnival or fair brings an elephant to London I shall have you prove to me that you can, indeed, climb on top and ride one."

"I will be most happy to if the *mahout* or whoever owns the elephant will allow it. And just so you know, my lord, I wouldn't have fallen off the fence had you not walked up so quietly that I couldn't hear you. There was no reason for such stealth."

His brow furrowed, and his lips formed a grim line. "Stealth? Surely you jest." Without turning around, he pointed his thumb over his shoulder and asked, "Is there a big bay behind me?"

She looked at the reddish-brown horse that stood obediently behind the earl. "Yes."

"Even if you did not hear my light tread, Miss Sweet, surely you heard Redmond's heavy footfall."

She moistened her lips, realizing there was no way to get out of this situation. "No, I'm afraid I didn't," she admitted reluctantly. She looked over her shoulder to the big chestnut in the paddock behind her. "I believe I was much too interested in the conversation I was having with Master Brute to pay attention to other sounds around me."

"Obviously, but tell me, did you take it upon yourself to name my newest stallion?"

Her eyes widened. "Absolutely not," she replied. "I would never be so presumptuous."

"Good."

She felt a smile teasing her lips, and she added, "However, you may feel free to use the name for him if you feel it suits."

He seemed to reflect on her words for a moment

and then nodded. "Now before I completely forget, I must warn you again not to climb on the fence. You could have fallen over it. And if you had, that horse, which you were so sweetly conversing with, might have trampled you."

"Nonsense. Master Brute is no more dangerous than you are, my lord."

Lord Morgandale folded his arms across his chest, and his gaze burned hotly on hers. "I can be a very dangerous man, Miss Sweet."

Her first thought was to ask him to prove it, but instead, she lifted her chin defiantly and said, "Obviously, you like to think so, my lord, but I think not. Like the horse, you snort, paw, and—"

"Paw," he interrupted, moving in closer to her. "Did you say I paw?"

Her stomach jumped excitedly when his face came close to hers. "Well, perhaps that was going a bit far."

"Perhaps so. I believe you are deliberately issuing a challenge for me to prove you wrong."

Was she?

"Am I?"

And if so, what on God's green earth was making her behave so foolishly?

Because he challenged her in ways she'd never been challenged before, and she enjoyed the banter with him. She looked forward to it. Besides, she had never minded a challenge.

The tightness in his features suddenly evaporated, and she saw nothing but a desirable man who set her pulse to racing.

He lowered his head as well as his voice and calmly said, "Yes, and if you insist, I'm sure I can prove that you are wrong."

A shiver of expectation raced through her and settled low in her stomach. For some reason this conversation had peppered her with anticipation.

"Can you?"

He nodded. "The question is, should I?"

Arianna didn't know why, but his words thrilled her so much that she wanted to whisper, "Yes, please," but instead, at the last moment, for once she resisted her impulsive urge and came to her senses and said, "Perhaps not at this time."

His eyes swept up and down her face so intimately that her stomach quivered with wanting like she had never experienced before.

"You know that answer leaves the door open for another time, don't you?"

She nodded.

"Are you sure?"

He was standing so close she could feel the power of his body and the warmth of his breath. She was completely immersed in him.

She shook her head. Right now, with the speed her heart was beating and the way her stomach was jumping, she wasn't sure of anything.

Slowly he reached out, gently took hold of her shoulders, and pulled her to him. Without saying a word, he dipped his head low and placed his warm, soft lips on her forehead, and then without lifting them off her skin, he lightly kissed between her eyes, down the bridge of her nose, and over the tip until his lips rested so close to hers she could feel them but was certain he didn't touch them.

"You know, Arianna is a lovely name."

His lips remained just above hers, yet he didn't kiss her. It was maddening.

"Thank you," she managed in a whispery voice.

Arianna felt as if he were weaving a sensuous spell around her, and she didn't want him to stop. If he lowered his head just a fraction of an inch, their lips would touch. Yet he teased her unmercifully and didn't let that happen.

She was tempted to make him finish what he started and kiss her, yet she held off, too, and they remained so close their breaths mingled.

He whispered, "Frightened, Arianna?"

"Not yet," she murmured.

Seven

My Dearest Grandson Lucas,

Though some may disagree with me, they are all wrong. Lord Chesterfield was right when he said: "I would have you very well dressed, by which I mean dressed as the generality of people of fashion are; that is, not to be taken notice of for being either more or less fine than other people; it is by being well dressed, not finely dressed, that a gentleman is distinguished."

Your loving Grandmother,
Lady Elder

WILLPOWER. THAT'S WHAT MORGAN NEEDED RIGHT now and in the worst way, but he was struggling to find it. Miss Sweet was not helping him. Instead of pushing him away, as he thought she would do, she was encouraging him to kiss her.

He hadn't expected that.

In fact, he was sure that she was silently begging him to kiss her.

She smelled good, she felt good, and she tasted good when his lips had brushed her soft skin. But, with the way he was feeling right now, the last thing he needed to do was kiss her, even though he was aching to do so.

He closed his eyes and swallowed hard. It took every ounce of resolve he had, but Morgan turned her loose and stepped away.

Morgan immediately reached for Redmond's reins and swung into the saddle. He looked down at Miss Sweet as he pulled his brown leather riding gloves from his coat pocket and put them on. He could see by the questioning look in her bright green eyes that she was stunned by his abrupt withdrawal. It gave him some comfort to know that she was as aroused as he and wanted him to kiss her as much as he'd wanted it.

It was clear she felt bereft, though she tried to hide it by asking, "Are you going for a ride?"

"Yes."

"May I come with you?"

That was not what he wanted to hear. He shook his head. "That would be as improper as my kissing you, Miss Sweet."

"Yes, of course," she said as her courage renewed, and the sparkle returned to her eyes and a smile to her lips. "How could I have forgotten? Should it get out in the halls of London that you had let me ride with you, your reputation would be ruined beyond repair, and I don't believe you would ever be welcomed in anyone's home ever again."

Morgan grinned. She was so tempting. The rules of Society be damned.

"You know, it's times like this that I think your name should be Miss Tart rather than Miss Sweet."

"You have told me that before, my lord."

"I know," he said and blew out an audible breath. "All right, come here, I'm going to lift you onto my horse in front of me. We're going for a ride together."

She stepped toward the large horse with an eagerness that sent a long spear of desire shooting through his abdomen and straight to heaviness between his legs.

She asked, "Are you sure, my lord?"

Oh, yes!

"No, I'm not sure at all. But, even as highly improper as it is, I find I don't want to deny you this small joy. If the thought of a kiss from me doesn't frighten you, maybe a fast run along the Dorset coastline on Redmond will scare the devil out of you."

She laughed as she pulled her bonnet back on top of her head. "You will have to come up with something bigger than a horse to frighten me, and I welcome your trying."

"I do not need you issuing challenges like that, Arianna. Now turn your back to me before I change my mind. I'm going to reach under your arms, and on the count of three I want you to jump high. I will lift you up and onto the saddle so that you will sit sidesaddle in front of me, all right?"

She nodded and did as he asked. Morgan reached down and took hold of her, counted and lifted her as if she weighed no more than a feather, and seated her sidesaddle in front of him. The instant she landed, he realized he should have positioned her behind him, not in front. His lower body reacted immediately to the warmth of her hip as it nestled right between his legs.

And if that wasn't enough to take him right up to the edge of his control, somehow while lifting her, her cape and skirt were caught up underneath her buttocks, exposing her shapely legs almost up to her knees. Her cape had fallen open, revealing that she wore some kind of bright pink cloth that was wrapped around her waist and then thrown across one shoulder. The bodice she wore was some kind of short tunic that was cut low at the neckline, showing the perfect swell of her breasts. Her midriff was completely bare, and the skirt fell at least an inch below the indention of her bare waist.

Trying his best to calm his soaring arousal, in astonishment, Morgan asked, "What the devil do you have on?"

Arianna glanced down at her gaping cape, and at last she looked frightened. That gave him a moment's satisfaction.

"I have on a dress." She started squirming from side to side as she tried to pull the cape from underneath her so that she could close it.

"That is not a dress, Miss Sweet."

"Actually, it is called a sari. The top is called a *cholis,* or in English, a tunic. This is the style of dress for the women of India."

"I do know that much, Miss Sweet. But is there a particular reason why you have that on rather than the kind of clothing ladies wear in England?"

She looked over her shoulder at him. Her eyes searched his. "No reason other than comfort."

"And you thought it would be perfectly fine to wear that outside of the house, in public where anyone around the estate might see you?"

"No, of course not," she argued. "I didn't act as impulsively as you might think. I did consider changing before I came outside, but I had watched from the window in my bedchamber for the better part of an hour and saw no one come or go from the paddock. Besides, I meant to be out here only a short time, but then you arrived and, well, you know what happened."

"Miss Sweet?"

"Oh, all right, you are correct again. I should have taken the time to find my maid, changed my clothing, put up my hair before coming out of my bedchamber; but once again, as my father so often reminded me, I let my impatience rule my common sense."

"Undoubtedly."

"My father always said it would be my downfall."

"He was a wise man."

"Yes, but I want you to know that I have been completely covered by my cape until you picked me up just now and it tangled underneath me."

"You aren't saying this is my fault because I picked you up, are you?"

She pursed her beautiful lips and seemed to think over her answer.

He felt a smile tugging at the edges of his mouth. "Miss Sweet?"

"No, of course not. So does this mean that I can't go for the ride on Redmond?"

She looked so disappointed that he had to chuckle. He didn't think he had ever met anyone quite like

Miss Sweet. He couldn't imagine that any other lady would want to ride on a horse with him, and he was quite sure none of the ladies he knew would ever be caught wearing a sari.

"No. I will keep my word, and we will ride to the coast together as I promised."

"Thank you, my lord," she said and smiled gratefully.

She immediately started moving from side to side once again, trying to pull her cape from underneath her so that she could close it over her legs and the sari. Morgan groaned inwardly with every swipe of her hip and buttocks against him. Apparently she didn't realize that her bottom was pressing right between his legs, causing him immense but gratifying pain with every move she made. All the while, he was finding it most difficult to keep his eyes off the tempting swell of her breasts, the beautiful indention of her waist, and the smooth shapeliness of her legs.

The wide brim of her bonnet knocked his chin, and he grunted.

"Oh, I'm sorry. I hope that didn't hurt."

"No, but perhaps we could push the hat to the back of your shoulders again."

"Yes, that would work," she agreed.

They both reached up at the same time, and their hands collided. She smiled sweetly at him and slowly lowered her hands, allowing him to shove the bonnet off her head to hang on her shoulders. The fresh-washed scent of her hair filled his nostrils, and Morgan had the urge to take the length of it and crush its softness in his hands. It felt so damn good to have her so close to him that Morgan's lower body swelled with desire for her.

He didn't know why he was putting himself through such delicious pain just to give her a ride.

While he straightened her hat, she continued to concentrate on trying to pull her cape out from under her bottom, pressing her hip farther and farther into the juncture of his legs.

When he could no longer take the sweet torture of her movements, he took hold of her arms and said, "Leave it, and be still. You are not accomplishing anything but torturing me."

She looked down and saw where her hip was jammed against him and gasped. "Oh, why didn't you tell me I was so close to you... of course," she said and fell still.

"Never mind, Miss Sweet, you've done all you can do to cover yourself. Besides that, I believe the time for modesty has already past. Slide your arms around my waist and hold on. Redmond is young, and he likes to run fast and stop short."

She turned toward her side and slipped one of her arms around his back and slightly above his waist. Though she held him lightly, Morgan was so attuned to her body next to his, he was sure he could feel her breasts pressed against him, and it was heavenly. He hadn't been with a woman since before he left London, and being alone with the charming, half-dressed Miss Sweet was playing havoc with the tenuous rein he had on his self-control.

The exotic scent of her wafted past his nose, and he wanted to reach up and bury his face in her glorious, light auburn hair. He wanted to nuzzle the warm, soft skin behind her ear, and only God knew how he restrained himself.

Morgan settled in the saddle as far away from her body as he could and kicked Redmond's flanks. The bay took off at a fast canter. Morgan might live to regret it someday, but for now, he was going to enjoy the ride with Miss Sweet's desirable body, showing more than any proper lady ever should, nestled warmly, firmly, and naturally between his legs.

Arianna felt freer than she had since her father died. She loved the feel of the wind in her face, the power of the animal beneath her, and the warmth of the man she held so close. It was exhilarating to be riding with the earl on his magnificent, fast horse. The movement of the horse seemed to feel more like rocking back and forth rather than the up and down motion that she had expected. She wanted to move her hips and sway as she would if she were dancing the Indian dance but knew the danger in that and remained still.

She didn't know why she had desperately wanted to ride with the earl other than the fact that he could be so charming at times, and as much as she hated to admit it, she had wanted him to kiss her. Perhaps she felt this way simply because she had spent so much time inside that small room on the ship and then in her bedchamber at his house, that she wasn't ready to go back into her room.

At the top of the first rise, Lord Morgandale pulled back on the reins and stopped Redmond. The horse snorted and pranced around, pulling against the earl's tight hold. But finally he obeyed his master and turned back toward the house.

Arianna gasped in pleasure. She could see everything in the valley below. "Oh, my lord, this is an exceptional view of the house and grounds of Valleydale."

"I thought you would like the landscape from up here."

From on top of the hill, she could see how the estate was situated in a lush, green valley. A long, tree-lined lane led up to the main house that had a large, three-story center building with matching wings that jutted out at an angle on each side. The carriage house was opposite the stables, and what looked to be a small summer house stood just past the carriage house.

A small plot of land had been dedicated to the kitchen garden on the east side of the house, but the vast, formal garden that made up the entire back lawn of the house looked like a beautiful oil painting in which the artist had used every color and shade in the world. In the Cotswolds, where she grew up, everyone had a garden, and some were very large and beautiful to behold, but none that she had seen compared to Valleydale.

The grounds were completely outlined with tall, perfectly trimmed topiary trees. Just inside the border of trees were rows upon rows of colorful flowers, stretching the length of the garden. It was the most color Arianna had seen since she arrived in England. Inside the borders of the topiary trees and flowers, she saw crushed stone pathways that led to separate inner plots of knot and rose gardens, each one enclosed by a short yew hedge.

In the center of the garden was a large reflection pool, and in the middle of the pool stood a tall, three-tiered fountain held up by three cherubs, just like the one that was on the large tapestry in the front hall.

"I'm seldom lost for words, my lord, but I don't

know what to, say. The beauty of the house, the gardens, and the stables simply takes my breath away."

"My grandmother deserves all the credit for the gardens. They were almost nonexistent when her third husband purchased this place for her. She had a master plan drawn up shortly after she acquired the house. It took years of constant attention to detail and dedication on her part to get the grounds the way she wanted them."

"Once it was finished, she must have ridden to the top of this ridge every day just to look at the grandeur of it all."

The earl laughed. "I doubt she did that, though I remember that she often walked in the garden in the early morning. In the summer, when no guests were in residence, she liked to walk barefoot while the dew was still on the grass. She said it made her feel very free."

Arianna turned toward him and said, "Oh, I'm sure it did. I should like to do that sometime, to feel the wet grass under my feet."

She obviously saw his eyes darken with disapproval, because she quickly added, "But of course, I wouldn't do anything like that here. I'll wait until I have my own house in London and do it in the privacy of my own garden, and only on the gardener's day off."

One side of his mouth lifted in a smile. "That would probably be best. I don't think it would be proper for the gardeners to look at your bare feet."

She smiled too. "I'm delighted to see so many shades of flowers; light and dark reds, pale and bright blues, simple yellows, and I'm amazed at all the pinks. I didn't know there were so many different shades of pink. They are so beautiful that I want to cut them all and place them in my room."

Lord Morgandale laughed. "That would be a lot of flowers, Arianna."

"I know, but I would love it to be surrounded by such magnificent color."

"You do have fresh flowers put in your room each day, don't you?"

"Yes. Mrs. Post is very conscientious, and I enjoy looking at the flowers and touching their soft petals." Arianna stopped and glanced up into Lord Morgandale's eyes once again. A breeze fluttered his hair across his forehead, making him roguishly handsome.

"I'm sorry to be carrying on so," she continued. "It's just that I'm so happy to be outside for the first time in such a long time. I seldom left my room on the ship, and this is the first time I've been out of your house. Everything looks fresh and new."

His expression softened. "That is understandable. Sea journeys are tiresome without being sick. The reason I'm not fond of long voyages is because the ship is so confining."

His gaze feathered down her face, and she had such an urge to reach up and kiss his lips, but she resisted it, and instead turned her face back toward the garden and said, "Tell me, isn't that fountain just like the one in the tapestry that hangs in your front hall?"

"Yes, that's right. You are very observant, Miss Sweet."

"So now, of course, I'm wondering, did your grandmother have the fountain built to match the tapestry, or did she have the tapestry woven to match the garden?"

"Since the tapestry is somewhere in the range of over two hundred years old, I'd say it definitely came first. My grandmother always loved it, so she commissioned the fountain to be built and the center of the garden to look as much like the tapestry as possible."

"I hope she had many years to enjoy it once it was finished."

He nodded. "She did."

"This is so lovely and peaceful; I could spend the rest of the afternoon right here."

"Ah, but you haven't seen the coast yet. Hold on, you are about to have the ride of your life."

Arianna turned to her side and slipped her arms around the earl once again, and the horse took off. Lord Morgandale gave Redmond all the free rein he needed, and within moments, he was running at a fast gallop.

She looked in every direction as the horse ate up the ground quickly. There were many different landscapes to catch her eye and fill her mind with memories. As they continued to climb, the terrain changed often. She saw gentle grassy slopes, fields with tall grass, and low-lying bogs. In the far distance, she saw a rise that was dotted with sheep and another that was blanketed by a vast expanse of blue and white wildflowers. As they rode, she saw fens, ridges, hollows and, of course, valleys as far as her eyes could see.

It was easy to tell when they neared the coast. The wind kicked up, and the air became heavier. In the distance, she saw gulls flying overhead. When the terrain quickly changed from hard, flat earth to rocky soil, Lord Morgandale slowed the horse to a walk.

The low hills around them were peppered with craggy peaks, jagged cliffs, and age-old rock walls that must have been built hundreds of years ago when the first settlers came to the area.

As they made their way to the top of a short rise, Lord Morgandale put his mouth very close to her ear and said, "The Channel is straight ahead of us."

Arianna turned and saw the dark blue, rushing water and suddenly shivered. Memories flooded back to her, and she felt the rocking of the ship, heard the constant flap of the sails in the wind, and smelled the dank odor of wet wood. Reflexively, she hugged the earl tighter and turned and buried her face in his chest, wanting to banish the memories from her mind and absorb his warmth.

He pulled the horse up short and stopped him. His arms went around her, and she breathed a sigh of contentment.

"Are you cold?" he asked.

"A little," she said but knew it was more than just the chill of the wind and the graying skies that made her tremble.

After the miserable weeks she had spent on the ship, she didn't think she would ever look at the sea again with enjoyment, but she would always be impressed with its beauty.

"Come on; let's get down so you can wrap your cape around you."

She hated to give up his warmth but allowed the earl to help her slide down the side of the horse. She quickly wrapped her cape tightly about her. Lord Morgandale jumped down beside her and then tied Redmond's leather reins to a scrub bush.

"Let's walk a little closer to the edge," he said as he stuffed his gloves into the pocket of his coat. "Will it bother you to look down? It's only about a ten meter drop."

"I don't think so," she answered, taking a deep breath.

Standing on the cliff, looking at the water below, was very different from being on the ship, and her fears faded. She stepped closer to the edge to peek over the rim of the jagged cliff to the stony coastline below.

She stared at the churning water of the English Channel as it washed over large, black, slippery-looking rocks. A few birds scuttled among the rocks, looking for sea urchins and plankton left by the crashing waves. She could make out the sails of a ship far out across the sea. It looked so tiny on the big ocean of water. She saw a white cottage with a small flower garden in the distance across the land.

"Does anyone live in that house?" she asked.

"Not for a long time. It was originally built for one of the caretakers, but my grandmother always used it as a guest house. She discovered early on that her guests enjoyed staying up on the coast because of the views of the water. In fact, it's very possible that your father could have slept there on one of his visits."

Her heartbeat sped up at the mention of her father. Thinking of him reminded her of seeing him lying on the floor in a pool of blood, his Indian partner, Mr. Rajaratnum, bent over his body. Arianna shivered again and closed her eyes.

"You're still cold, and it looks like a storm is blowing in. We should go."

She looked up and saw the skies darkening and

remembered how quickly fierce storms could rise up over the water.

She swallowed hard. "No, I'm fine, and it's so beautiful here. Let's stay a little longer. Tell me, do you really think my father might have slept in that house?"

"It's possible, Arianna."

"May I be allowed to come back here sometime before I leave for London and see inside the cottage?"

He seemed to question her with his expression, but he said, "I don't see why not."

"Thank you. I would like to see where my father might have stayed the night when he was here."

He nodded. "One of the many things my grand-mother was famous for was her house parties. Even though the main house of Valleydale is quite large, there were times she couldn't accommodate everyone, and she would always end up relegating some of the guests to the cottage. I'm told that once she started using it, everyone wanted to stay here because it's always so peaceful on the coast."

"Did you ever stay here?"

"Too many times to count. When my cousins and I were younger, we spent many nights here over the years. Come closer and look down at the large rocks at the base of that cliff. A little farther along the edge there's a pathway that leads down to the water. We made it years ago. When the tide was out, we would go exploring down on the rocks and find spider crabs, oysters, and sometimes we would catch fish and take them back to the cook. We always found it quite satisfying to eat at night what we had caught that day."

"That must have been an enjoyable way to spend your visits here."

"It was. Sometimes we would hunt. It didn't matter to us what we shot—pheasant, partridge, or pigeon—we simply enjoyed practicing our skills, and we wanted whatever we killed or caught that day to be on our dinner plate that night."

Arianna looked up into his eyes. She was enjoying him more than she ever had. Talking with him about the past like this, it was easy to forget he was at times surly, testy, and authoritative with her.

This man before her now was charming, approachable, and desirable. He seemed more real, and even a little vulnerable. This was the man who, minutes ago, made her body tremble with wanting just from his touch and made her eager for the kiss that never came, just by looking at her. This was the man who enchanted her and had her dreaming of being held in his arms, pressed against his chest with his lips on hers. And this was the man who was too worried about propriety to do it.

She sighed and then whispered, "I can tell you really love this place."

His gazed shifted from her face to the sea. "I think my grandmother knew that, as well. I always enjoyed coming here and working with her horses more than my cousins Blake and Race. I think that's why my grandmother left this place to me."

His eyes swept up and down her so intimately that her stomach quivered with anticipation. She wanted to kiss him. More than anything, she wanted to kiss him right now. She knew that one day soon she would leave for London and never see him again. She wanted to be kissed by him before that happened, and she wanted it to be here on the bluff by the water, the place that he loved.

"Call me Arianna," she said.

"Miss Sweet, we have done far too many things that are not proper as it is. I don't think we need to add one more thing to the growing list of impropriety shared between us, do you?"

Bapre! She didn't care about his list. She wanted to kiss him.

Without further thought, Arianna put her hands on his wide shoulders, lifted on to her toes, and placed her lips on his. They were warm, moist, and soft. She didn't know much about kissing, so she quickly stepped away and looked into his stunned blue eyes and waited.

Whatever it was she was feeling that made her so bold, he must have been feeling the same thing, because he gently took hold of her shoulders and pulled her to him. Without saying a word, he dipped his head low and placed his lips on hers. He added the merest amount of pressure to the kiss and gently moved his lips back and forth across hers.

Arianna caught on fast about how to kiss. Her stomach started jumping with pleasure, and she stepped in closer to him.

With every movement his lips made over hers, her breaths grew shorter. Her breasts, stomach, and between her legs tightened. His kiss lingered, and she responded by instinct and parted her lips. His tongue slid slowly between her teeth. He explored the roof and the sides of her mouth with slow, sensual movements that left her breathless.

She lifted her arms and circled his back. He was broad, powerful. Lord Morgandale moaned his approval, and his kiss deepened and became more urgent. She stretched her arms farther around his wide, muscular back and hugged him closer to her. She felt safe and protected in his embrace.

Arianna pressed her body tightly against his, and her abdomen caressed the hardness of his lower body. It filled her with an anticipation she didn't quite understand but wanted to. She only knew that no matter how close she got to him, it wasn't close enough.

His lips left hers and kissed their way down her chin, over her jawline, and then he brought his tongue down the long sweep of her neck to where the ribbon of her bonnet lay at the base of her throat. With his teeth, he grabbed the ribbon and, with two or three quick pulls, the bonnet fluttered to the ground, and his lips found hers once more in a deep, satisfying kiss.

His hands slid beneath her cape. Arianna tingled deliciously when his hands touched her bare skin, and she trembled. He hesitated at first, but then his hands moved to the bare part of her back and then quickly around to her front again, where his thumb nestled in her navel and gently stroked back and forth, sending little shivers of desire spiraling through her.

"If you continue to do that, I think I might stop breathing, my lord."

He chuckled quietly and continued his caresses. With his other hand, he brushed her cape away from her body.

He looked at her and smiled. "My name is Morgan, Arianna. Call me Morgan."

She easily returned his smile. "Should we add my calling you Morgan to that long list of improprieties we talked about earlier?"

A half grin lifted one corner of his mouth. "Sometimes I think you know how much you tempt me, and then other times I feel you are a complete innocent and have no idea what you are doing."

Arianna smiled and eased her head back. He kissed and tasted the hollow of her throat before letting his moist lips slip farther down to the swell of her breasts. Arianna gasped from surprise and pleasure. Her heartbeat jumped erratically, and her knees went weak. He brushed the fabric of the sari off her shoulder and let his hands skim across her chest.

The continued pleasure caused a clenching tightness low in her abdomen. She didn't understand why she felt this way about this man. She only knew that being in his arms felt right, natural, and she didn't want the feelings he was creating inside her to disappear.

His other hand slowly moved up her rib cage until his palm completely covered her breast. A small, involuntary moan slipped past her lips. With little effort, he found her nipple beneath the fine fabric of her tunic and rubbed it between his thumb and finger. She closed her eyes and gave herself up to the mind-numbing feeling of enjoying and being enjoyed by a man.

A tremor shook the earl's body, and she realized he was as affected by these wonderful sensations as she was. That thrilled her as much as his touch.

"You should be wearing stays, Arianna, not this tempting sari."

"They are very uncomfortable," she whispered.

Arianna's breaths became tiny gasps, and her arms tightened around him. As he continued the easy, unhurried stroking of her breast with one hand and her navel with the other, her fingers kneaded his back. He kissed his way from her chest up to her lips and back down her neck to her chest again.

She was dizzy with wanting more when, suddenly, she felt something wet and cold on her face. It was the first sprinkling of gentle rain. It cooled her heated skin and invaded her senses. She wanted the rain to go away. She wanted the heat of Morgan's body, not the cooling drops to dampen what she was feeling.

The earl kissed the droplets of rain from her lips, from her cheeks, and from the hollow of her throat. She wanted to go on feeling forever what he was making her feel, but slowly, he withdrew from her.

He looked at her with regret shining in his startling blue eyes. He took hold of her arms and gently pulled them from around his back and stepped away from her.

Rejection stung, and her heartbeat slowed.

"The storm is coming in fast, Arianna," he said. "We have to go now."

"Why?" she asked, too dizzy from desire to comprehend. "Do you not like the way I kiss?"

"I assure you, kisses have nothing to do with our leaving. Getting drenched in a rainstorm is the last thing you need. I don't want to do anything that could make your fever come back."

She moistened her lips and swallowed hard. "Yes,

of course you are right," she said. "I wasn't thinking clearly for a moment. I can't get sick again and further delay my journey to London."

"Arianna, you seem at times eager to get to London. Are you sure there isn't something you aren't telling me?" he asked while he took his gloves out of his pocket and put them on.

"Yes. No." She blinked rapidly and quickly pulled her cape around her body. "I mean, about what?"

"About you. About London. Sometimes I get the feeling you aren't telling me everything about yourself."

"I'm sure it's just that you have a curious nature about yourself," she said, wiping raindrops from her cheek.

"Maybe." He reached down and picked up her bonnet, placed it back on her head, and tied the ribbon under her chin for her. "And maybe not."

Arianna remained silent. Did she owe him the whole truth? Perhaps. After all, he had taken her in and given her time to regain her strength. Maybe she owed him some of the truth. If he asked specific questions, she knew she wouldn't lie to him.

Morgan untied Redmond and then swung into the saddle. She turned, and he picked her up and lifted her onto the front of the saddle in front of him the same as they rode before, but he said nothing else as he kicked Redmond in the sides and the horse took off at a canter.

Eight

My Dearest Grandson Lucas,

If you don't remember anything else that I have sent you from Lord Chesterfield, remember this: "It is only the strength of our passions and the weakness of our reason that makes us so fond of life."

Your loving Grandmother,
Lady Elder

IT WAS A GLOOMY LATE AFTERNOON, BUT MORGAN hadn't let the soggy air and gray skies dampen his spirits. Ever since he had kissed Arianna yesterday afternoon, he had been feeling like a young boy who couldn't wait for a new day to begin so he could experience it. Before Arianna arrived, he was feeling unsettled, restless, but now he felt contented to be at Valleydale.

Had she caused this sudden change in him? And if so, how?

Morgan climbed onto the fence at the paddock and waited for his groom to saddle Master Brute and lead the animal over to him. If Arianna could get the high-strung stallion to let her rub him, then he could damn sure ride the rogue without being thrown off. Besides, the animal had seemed to be a bit calmer today as he had worked with the other horses, and he couldn't help but wonder if Arianna's soothing voice and gentle touch had anything to do with the change in the thoroughbred.

Perhaps she had precipitated the changes in the horse as well as Morgan's better attitude.

He hadn't seen Arianna since their fast ride back to the house in the rain. He had sent her immediately up to her room to get out of her wet clothing, and she never came back down. He had remained in the drawing room the rest of the evening, hoping she might venture below stairs again, but that hadn't happened. Before he headed to the stables earlier in the day, he had inquired of her to Mrs. Post. His housekeeper said she was well, and the fever had not returned.

She had looked healthier than she had the last time he saw her, which must have been at least three days before. The circles under her eyes weren't nearly so large or so dark. He couldn't tell that she had put on any weight yet, but Mrs. Post had assured him she was eating a little.

But just because he hadn't seen her again last night, it didn't mean he hadn't thought about her. Sleep had been almost impossible. He kept seeing her long, beautiful legs as they rode the horse, the pressing of her firm hip against his hardness on the wild ride to the house. He loved the feel of her arms around his waist and the caress of her hair as the wind blew a strand across his face. He didn't know why he hadn't considered, sitting as they were, that her hip would be jammed tight against him.

And when he had held her so close, caressed her bare skin, kissed her soft lips, it had been sweet torture not to continue and take his pleasure.

But what he couldn't figure out was what she was doing wearing such clothing, especially outside her bedchamber, where anyone in the house or on the grounds of the estate could see her. Didn't she know the appeal she had without adding the revealing sari or whatever the hell it was she called the fabric she had draped about her body? And what was he doing trying to be so circumspect around a young lady who obviously didn't mind flaunting convention?

What confounded him more than anything was the fact that since she had been at Valleydale, he had not had that restless feeling of needing to go back to the busy streets of London. He had been quite satisfied here. And it wasn't even that he'd seen that much of her. She spent most of the time in her room, but he knew she was in his house, and that made all the difference.

No doubt the reason Arianna was so tempting to him was because it had been weeks since he'd been with a woman, and his body was so eager. More than once he had chided himself for sending Miss Goodbody away. He should have set her up in the guest cottage on the hill that overlooked the sea and visited her there for what he had so dearly paid for.

Why had he felt the need to send her away? Yes, it was the proper thing to do, but why had he felt compelled to protect Arianna's sensibilities? Obviously, she felt no compunction at scandal. She had accepted his kisses and caresses with eagerness and melted into his arms like she belonged there. She was a mystery to him, and the more time he spent with her, the more he wanted to spend time with her.

But he was wise enough to know that Miss Sweet was an innocent. She was untouched—of that he was sure. A woman couldn't fake her first taste of desire. She had to experience it first in order to know how to replicate it.

He smiled just thinking about the soft, feminine sounds she made when he kissed her neck, throat, and chest. It pleased him that he had shown her how a few simple kisses could make her feel, but he would have to make sure he never did it again. And that shouldn't be too difficult. The morning's mail had brought a note from Constance, saying that she should reach Valleydale within a day or two. Once she arrived, the plans would be set to take Arianna to London, but for some reason that thought didn't bring him the peace of mind that it should.

But until Constance arrived, Morgan would have Arianna all to himself, and already he had convinced himself to ask her to have dinner with him tonight. It was improper to say the least, but what the hell did propriety matter after their intimate encounter yesterday? He had kissed her so thoroughly that if that hadn't compromised her reputation beyond repair at that point, sitting across the dinner table from each other for an evening meal surely wouldn't.

The snort and whinny of the stallion brought Morgan out of his reverie, and he turned his attention to the horse. As the groom led the horse up to the fence where Morgan waited, the animal tossed his head, snorted, and tried to back up.

"I hear your warning, Master Brute, and I'm ignoring it," Morgan said to the jittery horse. "I'm riding you today."

Morgan stood up on the second rung of the fence and took the reins. He threw his leg over the horse and quickly settled his weight into the saddle. The chestnut started bucking, snorting, and stomping. He reared back on his hind legs, twisted, and changed direction. A second later, Morgan landed on the ground with a swoosh and a grunt.

The groom caught the bucking horse and led him away. Morgan moaned and stood up, brushing dirt from his breeches. Suddenly, out of the quietness, he heard clapping, whistling, and cheers. He glanced in the direction of the commotion and saw his two cousins, Race and Blake, sitting on their horses a short distance away, laughing.

His first thought was one of exhilaration. He was damned glad to see them, but his second thought was "bloody hell." What the devil were they doing riding up to Valleydale without letting him know they were coming? Under normal circumstances he would welcome them, but Arianna was with him. And he didn't want them here while she was in his house.

Would they understand that she was ill and he had to offer her shelter? Probably not, especially now that she no longer looked as unwell as she had the night she arrived.

Was there a chance they had heard about Arianna? Maybe Saint had talked to Miss Goodbody, and she had mentioned there was a lady with him.

No, his solicitor would never tell anyone, including his cousins, anything about his business. So what were they doing here, and if they hadn't heard about Miss Sweet, how was he going to keep them from knowing there was a tempting young lady living in his house?

There was a catch in his hip from where he fell as he walked up to the fence and leaned his forearms on the top rung.

Morgan grinned at his cousins and asked, "What the devil are you two blackguards doing here?"

"We came to see you, of course," Blake said as he dismounted.

"Yes," Race added, jumping down from his horse. "It was good of you to put on an excellent show for us. I think that stallion just convinced you that you will not sit atop his back until he is ready."

Morgan watched the two tall, impressive-looking men walking their horses toward him. Arianna aside, he was happy to see them. He'd always gotten along well with them. They all had their strengths and weaknesses, and when necessary, they were always united. In their younger years, there were times rivalries surfaced when one would try to best the others in shooting, racing, fencing, or the attention of a young miss, but they never forgot they were family.

For a moment, Morgan wondered if they had come because something was wrong, but he quickly dismissed that idea. They wouldn't have been clapping and acting so jovial if that were the case.

Could it possibly be that they had come just to see him? It had been more than two months since he'd been in London. But no, he concluded. They had a reason for coming, and it must be a damned good reason to have persuaded them to leave their wives to make the long ride to Valleydale.

Despite the pain in his hip, with the ease of having done it many times, Morgan climbed the first two rungs of the fence and then jumped over it to land in front of his cousins, stifling a grunt as his feet hit the ground. He hugged first Blake, the taller of the two by maybe an inch, and then Race, who had the darker hair and eyes.

"Tell me," Morgan asked as he took off his riding hat and tossed it over a fence post. "How are Henrietta and Susannah?"

"Henrietta is beautiful, happy, and getting ready for a holiday," Blake said. "We're going up to Blakewell for a couple of months."

"That sounds like the thing to do. Suffolk is nice this time of year, and I'm told that traveling usually makes wives happy."

"Yes. Henrietta hasn't seen our home there, so this seemed a good time to make the journey."

Morgan looked at Race and started peeling off his brown riding gloves. "How about you and Susannah?"

"Couldn't be better. Henrietta is helping Susannah get to know everyone in Town, and she is fitting in quite well."

"Good, and her mother?"

"Much better than when you left London. With the help of a new tonic, her mother's health has improved enough that she will be leaving London at the end of the week. Susannah has tried to persuade her to say she'll eventually move back to London, but there's been no commitment from her as of yet. And, we will be accompanying Blake and Henrietta on the trip up to Blakewell. We leave sometime next week."

Morgan stuffed his gloves into his coat pocket and looked from one to the other, still trying to figure out why they had come. They could have told him by letter or messenger that they were going away. He hoped they were not going to try to persuade him into going with them to Blakewell. There was no way in hell that was going to happen.

"Splendid," Morgan said. "I'm sure you will both enjoy the time and your wives, as well. I'll look forward to hearing all about it when you return from Suffolk and I return to London."

"Well, that is sort of what we wanted to talk to you about," Blake said, taking off his gloves.

"No," Morgan answered.

"No?" Race said. "What's this? We haven't asked you anything yet. How can you say no?"

"You don't have to ask. Whatever the reason you are here, the answer is no."

"Morgan, don't be devilish about this. At least let us ask the question before you answer."

"No," he said again. "I'm not going with you to Blakewell. No, I'm not going to meet anyone's daughter or cousin or niece. No, I don't care that she's the most beautiful young lady in all of England. The answer is still no, no, and hell no."

Race and Blake looked at each other and laughed.

Morgan's irritation grew. This was the first time he could ever remember not wanting his cousins around. It was an odd feeling. Since he'd received the letter from Constance, he realized he had at most two more days with Arianna before Constance arrived. And he didn't like the fact that he would now be having dinner with his cousins tonight rather than Arianna.

"All right," Blake said. "We'll accept your answers to all of the questions we had no intention of asking."

That gave Morgan an uneasy feeling. His gaze darted from Race's eyes to Blake's. His cousins were suddenly too quiet as they stuffed their riding gloves into the leather pouches on their saddles.

Morgan combed his hair back with his hand, willing himself to ease the jittery feeling in his stomach and relax.

"Something is telling me that the two of you did not ride all the way out here just to say hello or to tell me you are heading to Blakewell; so what is going on?"

"What's this?" Blake asked, holding out his hands as if he didn't understand. "You don't think we would come out here just to see you?"

"With no other purpose in mind?" Race added.

"That's right, I don't," Morgan said honestly as he rubbed the back of his neck, trying to ease the tension that had settled there.

"What's this you're saying? We've done it plenty of times," Blake said.

"Not since you married."

"That's not a fair assessment. We haven't either of us been married very long," Blake said. "Besides, you would be wrong. We would come all the way to Valleydale just to spend time with you. However…"

"We didn't this time," Race finished for him.

"Right, and unfortunately we can only stay the night. We'll leave at first light."

Morgan's mind started whirling with thoughts, and he motioned for the groom to take their horses and stable them. If Race and Blake were leaving at first light, he might be able to arrange it so they wouldn't even know Arianna was in the house. He would start by giving them rooms in the opposite wing of the house. The fewer explanations he had to give these two, the better. They would be like hounds after pheasant if they found out about her.

When he got back to the house, he would write Arianna a note asking that she not leave her room tonight.

"Morgan, what are you thinking about?" Blake asked.

"Hmm? Oh, Gibby," he lied without guilt. "If it's not your wives who brought you here, I know something is going on with him; so tell me, what kind of trouble has Gibby gotten himself into this time?"

"How did you know it was Gibby who brought us out here?" Blake asked.

"Because your wives and Gibby are the only people you care enough about to make this journey. And you just told me Henrietta and Susannah are doing quite well, and we've already established that you didn't come all the way out here just to say hello to me."

"But Gib hasn't exactly done anything this time," Race said and then looked at Blake.

"Well, he hasn't done anything since Morgan left London," Blake qualified.

"That is that we know of right now," Race added with a half laugh.

"So what's the problem?" Morgan asked absently as he watched the groom take the saddle off Master Brute. His mind suddenly drifted back to Arianna. How had she quieted the stallion?

Thoughts of her triggered his memory of how desirable she had been yesterday afternoon dressed in that Indian sari. He had vivid memories of her exotic scent, the sweet taste of her mouth, and how smooth, beautiful, and soft her skin was. Just thinking about her small waist and gently flared hips had him almost to the point of arousal.

Morgan cleared his throat and shifted his stance. Somehow, he had to keep his mind off his house guest.

Realizing he had no idea what Blake had said, Morgan said, "Sorry, what was that?"

"You heard me."

"Actually, I didn't, so could you humor me and repeat it?"

"What's wrong with you?" Race asked. "You've seemed distracted ever since we arrived."

With good reason, but Morgan was going to have to keep his thoughts away from Arianna.

"Cousins, I'm fine. I'm glad you have come, but could you just get to the point and tell me, why are you here?"

"We think you need to come back to London so you will be near Gibby if he needs you for anything."

Concern flashed through Morgan. "Is he ill?"

"No, nothing as serious as that."

"What kind of double-talk is that, Race? Did he do

something or didn't he? And if he did, what the devil did he do?"

"Gibby may have fathered twins," Blake said.

Nine

MORGAN SWALLOWED HIS INITIAL SHOCK AT BLAKE'S words, thinking his cousins were having a little fun at his expense, and he wasn't going to fall for it. "So what else is new?"

"We're serious," Blake said.

A nervous laugh started low in Morgan's throat. His gaze darted from Blake to Race. Neither of them was laughing. They weren't even smiling, and suddenly neither was Morgan.

"You'd best have a good foundation for what you are saying," he growled.

"We do," they said in unison.

Morgan watched the humid breeze blow through their hair and the ends of their neckcloths flutter. He knew Race and Blake well. They had played plenty of tricks on him in their time, but this wasn't one.

They *were* serious.

Morgan was worried.

Doing his best to remain skeptical of their claim, Morgan said, "Please don't tell me that Miss Prattle was with child when she accused Gibby of dishonoring her and has now had twins?"

"Bloody hell, we hope not," Blake said on a whispery breath.

Race's eyes narrowed and he rubbed the back of his neck. "I haven't heard from Miss Prattle's brother since his boxing match with Gibby. Last I heard, Miss Prattle and her brother had left London, and as far as I know, no one has heard from them since."

"And hopefully we'll never hear from either of them again," Blake added. "I'm glad Gibby made it out of that uncomfortable situation without losing any money or any of his teeth in his boxing match with Miss Prattle's brother."

Morgan's ire quickened again. "So if Miss Prattle was not with child, what the hell are you two jacka-napes talking about? What do you mean he may have fathered twins? He may have fathered an elephant, too, but I can assure you, he didn't."

"We'll tell you what we know so far," Blake said. "A week or so ago, three gentlemen came to Town.

The oldest is Viscount Brentwood. Do you know of him?"

"Seems we've met a few times," Morgan answered, struggling to bring the man's face to mind. "He came for some of the parties during the Season a year or two ago, and maybe even this year. He doesn't usually spend too much time in London. I have no idea why."

"Now that man is in a hell of a bind, isn't he?" Race said to Blake.

"For sure," Race agreed. "I wouldn't want to be in his boots."

"Me either," Blake offered. "I guess there's something to Lord Chesterfield's words about 'not letting your shoes get caught under the wrong woman's bed.'"

"Did Chesterfield say that?" Race asked.

"According to our grandmother, he said everything, and he said it first. I guess if there is anything good about Viscount Brentwood's situation it's that Lady Gabrielle is a beautiful young lady."

"There's no doubting that," Race agreed.

"Hold it right there, you two," Morgan grumbled, breaking into their conversation. "I don't know what the devil you blasted ninnies are talking about. What do Viscount Brentwood and Lady Gabrielle have to do with Gibby?"

"Them?" Blake said innocently. "Nothing."

Morgan threw up his hands in frustration.

"Morgan, the viscount figures into this," Race countered.

"How? Get to the point quickly about all this, including Brentwood."

"Don't be so fidgety. We have to fill you in on some of the details, so you'll know what we're talking about," Blake said.

"All I want to know is who is accusing Gibby of being the father of her twins?"

"No one," Blake said.

A frustrated chuckle blew past Morgan's lips, as much from his cousins' stalling as to hide the pain in his hip. "Why do I suddenly feel like I am at a poorly acted farce at the Lyceum? Did you or did you not tell me Gibby may have fathered twins?"

"We did," Race said.

Morgan inhaled slowly, trying his best to hang on to his patience and keep control of his rising temper. The gray afternoon grew darker, and the tepid breeze was feeling damp. He wondered if his cousins had always been this exasperating, or was his irritation on a short tether because they had barged in, apparently for no good reason, and upset his plans to ask Arianna to dine with him.

Yes, that's the reason.

"Obviously there is still more for you to tell me, but let's go down to the house. Night is falling, and I feel in need of a glass of wine."

"It's about time you asked us," Blake said. "I was beginning to think we were going to have to stand out here by the stables the rest of the evening."

"Would you two please get this conversation back to Gibby and not on gossip about people I really don't care to hear about?"

"Oh, yes, right. Anyway, back to the twins," Blake said as they started down the slope toward the house, flanking Morgan as they went.

"Yes, please back to the twins, and tell me who had the babes."

"They aren't babes."

"Not by a long shot," Race added.

Morgan held up his hands with his palms flat. "I'm going to strangle both of you and leave your carcasses out here for the vultures if one of you doesn't get to the heart of the matter right now."

"It seems Viscount Brentwood has younger, twin brothers, and they came to London with him last week," Race said.

Morgan frowned. "I still have no idea what the viscount and his brothers have to do with Gibby."

"You will," Race offered and looked at Blake.

Blake nodded and took in a deep breath. On his exhale, he said, "The twins are the spitting image of a much younger Sir Randolph Gibson."

"Bloody hell," Morgan whispered and stumbled to a halt.

The cousins stopped, too. Morgan swallowed hard, not wanting to believe what Blake had said. The implications were damaging to too many people for this to be some kind of trick his cousins were playing.

Cautiously, he asked, "What do you mean spitting image?"

"You know what we mean, Morgan, don't be a masher," Blake said, looking him directly in the eyes. "They are tall like him, built like him, their eyes are like his, and they have his thick hair, his nose, and his smile."

"It appears one has his charm and the other his strict sense of honor," Race added.

Blake said, "From what we can tell, they have everything about him but his name."

"That privilege, of course, belongs to Viscount Brentwood's deceased father," Race finished.

"Have either of you seen these gentlemen? Have you met them?"

"Both of us," Blake said.

Morgan's eyes narrowed with tension. "And what did you think?"

"That they look just like Gibby," Race said.

"Why have we never seen them before?" Morgan asked.

"Well, of course we think it's clear now what the real reason was that they never came to London, but of course the *on dit* is because they each spent time in the military," he answered.

Blake started walking again, and the other two fell into step beside him. "Rumor also has it that more recently, they've been abroad, touring the far reaches of the world. As you know, some young men enjoy doing that sort of thing before they settle down for a look around the marriage mart—which we can only assume is the reason they have now taken up residence in Town."

Race frowned and said, "And then, of course, the whisper is that they never came to London because they knew they looked like Gibby and not their father."

"Which could very well be true, but, back to the story," Blake continued. "So it seems to us and everyone else in London that Gibby may have had an affair with the viscount's mother, somewhere around thirty years ago, and fathered her twins."

"Do you realize what you are accusing?" Morgan growled, doing his best to keep from limping. "You are telling me that Gibby cuckolded the former viscount and had a rendezvous with his wife."

"Yes, but not just us, Morgan." Blake rubbed his palm across his hair. "That is exactly what all of London is saying as well."

That was enough to chill Morgan.

"Things had just started to settle down for Gibby from the boxing match," Race added.

Still searching his mind to understand, Morgan said, "I've seen Brentwood. He doesn't look anything like Gibby."

"True," Blake agreed. "He doesn't, but that's not the case concerning the twins."

"What does Gibby have to say about this?" Morgan asked.

Race threw Morgan a sideways glance and said, "What do you think?"

"I would think the crafty old codger is saying nothing about this."

"And you would be right," Blake added as the three ambled down the grassy slope.

"What about these twins? What are they saying?" Morgan asked.

"Nothing that we know of," Race offered and fell in step beside Morgan once again. "One of them wears such a scowl all the time that I don't think anyone would dare speak to him about the matter."

"But someone did," Blake added. "I heard that at his brother's urging, Lord Waldo Rockcliffe said something to the man about how much he looked like Sir Randolph Gibson, and Lord Waldo has been walking around with a mysterious black eye and cut lip ever since."

Morgan grunted as much from what Blake had said as from the nagging pain in his hip.

Race leaned forward and said, "I'm sure that is the reason no one else has had the courage to say anything else to either of them."

Blake added, "And I hear the other one is as closemouthed as Gibby. They are both, of course, welcomed by the ton."

"Welcomed?" Race exclaimed. "They are encouraged, even eagerly sought out by everyone who hasn't fled London for their summer homes."

Blake huffed and said, "You know there's nothing Londoners love better than scandal."

"That is if it's not about them," Race injected, "and if it's not, they love to get close to it. In just the past week, we've received a flurry of invitations to late summer parties."

Race picked up the conversation by adding, "I've never seen anything like it. The goings on at Parliament have taken a back seat with this rash of invitations. It seems all the pushy mamas who are left in London are holding parties just so they can invite the viscount and the twins, and get acquainted with them. They figure it will give them a jump on the Season next year."

"Yes," Blake said. "Everyone wants to be able to say that they've had the twins in their homes, so they can gossip about them. You know how polite *Polite* Society can be."

"Right, which means they can make a circus out of anything."

The three cousins laughed.

"And then there is the viscount, who has his own troubles to deal with, but we won't go into that."

Morgan deliberately slowed the pace, not wanting to limp in front of his cousins. "What a nightmare. I can't even imagine what it must be like to arrive in London and find that you look just like another man, a man who is not your father."

"Needless to say, that is the reason why you need to come back to London while we are away," Blake said.

"And on this, we won't take no for an answer," Race added with a grin. "Just handle the gossips the best you can, and be there should Gib need you for anything."

"Wait? Me?" Morgan stopped again, glad for the respite. "What's this? Just a bloody minute, you two, it won't be possible for me to go to London. You both know I've made my plans to winter at Valleydale."

"You have to," Blake said. "We just told you we are going away with our wives."

Ah, the wives.

"And while they are understanding ladies most of the time, they will be disappointed if they don't get to take this holiday we promised them."

"Your wives?" Morgan said disgruntled.

"Yes," Race said. "And I might add that it is your turn to handle Gibby."

"My turn? No, you're mistaken. It was not more than a few weeks ago that I handled that time machine debacle. Remember?"

"Sorry, Morgan, that was several months ago, not weeks," Blake said. "And after that, I took care of his association with Mrs. Simpleton and her bloody balloon venture."

Race held up his hand. "And I'm still not over trying to talk him out of that travesty of a boxing match with Mr. Prattle a couple of months ago. So you see, my dear cousin, it is your turn."

"You both have known for almost three months now that I've had no intentions of going back to London in the foreseeable future."

But as Morgan said that, another thought flashed through his mind. Arianna would be going to London soon.

Perhaps he should think about going to London and keeping an eye on Gibby—just until his cousins returned. It would give him an opportunity to check in with Arianna, too, to make sure she found a place to lease and settled into London properly.

"What are you thinking?" Blake asked. "Suddenly, it was as if you were miles away from us again."

"Nothing," Morgan said and started walking again.

"Yes, you were thinking about something. I could see that faraway look in your eyes for the third time since we've been here."

"'Fess up, you blackguard, and tell us why you are so pensive."

"Damnation, Blake, don't be ridiculous. I can see that marriage hasn't changed a thing about either of you. I was just wondering what I would do if I found out I looked like someone other than my father. That is one hell of a situation to be in."

"You are lying through your teeth," Blake said good-naturedly.

Morgan grinned, hoping to throw them off guard. "If you are going to force a man to answer a question he doesn't want to answer, you can't be upset if he lies to you."

"Did you just quote Lord Chesterfield?" Race asked, grinning.

"Bloody hell, I hope not," Morgan mumbled. "And I hate to admit it, but you two might be right for a change. If it is my turn to take care of the old dandy, I will. I hadn't planned to return to London, but as you said, perhaps I should go and do what I can to stop the flow of the gossip, and to be there for Gib should he need anything."

"Something's definitely wrong. That was too easy," Race said.

"Yes, I agree," Blake said, nodding. "There is a reason he wants to come back to London, and he's not telling us."

Morgan laughed. "I'm going to hate myself for admitting this, but I've missed you two jackanapes."

Blake and Race laughed, too.

"But, we are not going to let you change the subject that easily," Blake added. "You are suddenly too eager to return to London."

"I'm not eager to do anything but enjoy the carefree life I have here."

All of a sudden, Blake stopped dead in his tracks, a stunned look on his face.

"What is it?" Morgan asked and threw a glance toward Race as they stopped walking, too.

"I'm seeing the most amazing apparition," Blake said in a husky voice.

"That is no vision," Race said, looking in the same direction as Blake.

"Who is she?" Blake asked.

Morgan froze.

"And what is she wearing?" Race asked.

"How does she move her hips, her body like that?" Blake added on a whispery breath.

"And what is she doing in your house?" Race whispered hoarsely.

Morgan felt as if he were moving in slow motion as he turned and looked toward the side of his house where Blake and Race stood staring. From where the three of them were on the slope, they were at a perfect angle to stare straight into Arianna's bedroom window on the first floor of the house.

Morgan's heart jumped into his throat, and the air swooshed from his lungs. Arianna was dancing. She looked like an exotic goddess, dressed in a scandalously small, buttercup-colored tunic similar to the one she had worn to the stables, only this one glittered invitingly from the soft lamplight in her room. The skirt of the same color looked as if it had been sprinkled with gold. It swung low on her hips and appeared to be made of a sheer, gossamer-thin material that looked as if he could see right through it.

Her hips moved from side to side, and her stomach undulated in a way that instantly aroused him. She swayed gently, smoothly, as if she were intently listening to music only she could hear. Her outstretched arms moved sensuously, and her shoulders rolled suggestively, simultaneously with the rest of her body. She brought her hands together high over her head and clasped them as she continued her slow, sumptuous dance.

Since Morgan's body was reacting to her intense movements, he knew Blake's and Race's were, too.

"Morgan?" Race and Blake somehow managed to say at the same time.

"Cousins," Morgan said in a gravelly voice, "you picked a most inopportune time to visit."

Ten

My Dearest Grandson Lucas,

While reading through his letters, I came across these wise words from Lord Chesterfield. "Should you be unfortunate enough to have vices, you may, to a certain degree even dignify them by a strict observance of decorum; at least they will lose something of their natural turpitude."

Your loving Grandmother,
Lady Elder

GRAY SKIES HAD DARKNESS FALLING QUICKLY, SO ARIANNA lit the lamp in her bedroom after she had changed into her Indian dance costume. She knew Beabe would be below stairs for quite a while, helping Mrs. Post in the kitchen, so it was the perfect time for Arianna to see if she was now strong enough to move her stomach and hips the way she could before she had the fever. She had tried a couple of times before, but she had been too sore and too weak to do very much. But every day now, she felt stronger. And, as much as she hated to leave the earl and the contentment she had found in his home, she intended to tell Morgan tomorrow that she was well enough to travel on to London so that she could meet with Mr. Warburton and begin her work for her father. She didn't want to wait any longer for Mrs. Pepperfield to arrive.

Arianna had discovered early on that it was always best to dance when Beabe wasn't around. Her British maid had never approved of her learning any of the Indian *nritya*, but through the years, Beabe had remained loyal and never told her father that her *naukrani* was teaching her the beautiful dances of India.

The Indian maid had told her dancers always wore bells on their wrists and ankles when they danced, and sometimes bells were stitched to their costumes. Beabe hadn't unpacked Arianna's bracelets or anklets at the earl's house, but when she had her dancing costume made, the seamstress had attached three rows of tiny bells to the hem of the skirt, and they jingled lightly every time she moved.

Arianna closed her eyes, and in her mind she played the music she'd often heard at the market in Bombay. As she swayed, she stepped and twirled in time with the music she heard in her head. At first, her movements felt awkward and stiff, but the more she moved, the easier it became to follow the steps and maneuvers of the dance she'd learned from the *naukrani*.

Lord Morgandale came to her mind. She imagined him watching her with his intense blue eyes. She moved as if she were dancing for him. As she moved her stomach muscles and arms the way she'd been taught, she remembered the taste of his kisses, the caress of his hands on her body, the sounds of his whispered sighs. She remembered the feel of the light rain falling on her passion-heated skin.

A loud knock sounded on the door, interrupting her dance and her wonderful thoughts.

"Bapre," she exclaimed to herself. She had thought it would take Beabe longer in the kitchen to get her evening tray.

Reluctantly, Arianna padded barefoot over to answer the door and opened it without inquiring as to who might be on the other side. She gasped when she saw a scowling earl standing before her, devouring her with his hot, angry gaze.

In that first horrifying second, she thought of slamming the door in his face or making a mad dash for a wrap to cover herself, but in the end, all she did was quickly fold her arms across her chest, trying unsuccessfully to hide as much of her bare skin as possible.

Looking at the very upset man, she said as calmly as if she were talking about the weather, "My lord, I didn't expect you. I'm afraid you caught me at a very unfortunate time. I'm not properly dressed."

"I'm quite aware of that," he said tightly. "That is exactly why I am here."

Arianna took in a deep breath and quickly assessed the situation. She was caught, and there was no use in trying to hide what she was wearing now that he had already seen her. There was nothing to do but explain and inquire as to why he was standing at her bedchamber door.

She lifted her shoulders, dropped her arms to her sides, swallowed the lump in her throat, and began, "Contrary to what you might be thinking, I heeded your words of yesterday, and I have not worn this costume outside of my bedchamber."

"That is good to know," he said too quietly.

His admission of that surprised her, but she continued. "And besides that, my lord, I have been here several days now, and you have never once come to my door. I had no reason to suspect you would be standing there this evening."

"That is true."

It struck her that he was being a bit too amiable, considering what she was wearing.

"And I had no cause to think that you might come to my door today and see me dressed like this."

"I agree," he said, pushing the door open wider and stepping inside. He closed the door, reached behind him, and turned the key in the lock.

Arianna's breaths shortened, and she took a wary step back. "What are you doing?"

"Making sure that neither your maid nor anyone else comes in while I'm in here. So you are certain no one has seen you, dressed like this?"

"Absolutely. Like I said, I have not left this room today. No one could have possibly seen me dressed like this."

"Really? Then how do you suppose I knew what you had on?"

Confusion clouded her mind. "I didn't know that you did."

Morgan walked over to her window on the right

side of her dresser and then motioned for her to come to him.

She hesitated only a moment and then did as he beckoned and walked over to him, the bells on her skirt gently jingling as she went.

"What do you see when you look out of this window, Arianna?"

She stepped closer. Darkness lay on the air, but in the distance she saw lights at the stables, indicating workers were still there.

"I see the stables and the paddock, my lord, but they are so far away, I swear to you that no one there could see me here in my room."

His intense blue eyes searched her face. "Do you know where I was late this afternoon?"

Her throat tightened, but not from fear, from his being so close that she wanted to reach out and touch him.

"No," she said, her voice sounding softer than she would have liked.

"I was at the stables, trying to ride Master Brute."

Surprise lit her face. "Did you?"

He shrugged. "Not yet." He turned and looked out the window again. "What do you think I saw a few minutes ago when I was walking down the slope that leads from the stables to the house?"

Arianna's gaze followed his, and she cringed. Why hadn't it dawned on her to close the draperies? On impulse, she had quickly donned the costume and started dancing without much thought. Certainly she had not considered that anyone might be able to see her through the window.

"There's a point on the slope where you can look directly into this room. And the lamplight from your dresser makes everything in here very easy to see."

She glanced down at her short buttercup-colored tunic, decorated with faux jewels sewn around the low neckline and the banded, low waist of the skirt. The sheer material was more revealing than the fabric of the sari she had on the day before.

She squeezed her eyes shut for a moment and then opened them and stared directly at him and whispered, "You saw me dancing."

He nodded, reached over, freed the drapery panels from the brass holders, and let them come together.

"I don't think I'll ever get that image of you out of my mind, and neither will my cousins."

Arianna gasped. "Your cousins? Lady Elder's other two grandsons were with you?"

"Yes. Unfortunately, Race and Blake decided to pay me a surprise visit and were walking with me."

Heat flamed in her cheeks. "I don't know what to say, my lord. If there is any way I can apologize, I'm willing to try. They must have been horrified."

"Take my word for it, Arianna, they were not horrified. Quite the contrary, they were mesmerized, as was I, to see so much of you doing that very provocative dance."

"I am seldom at a loss for words, but I have no answer for this."

"I can only assume you learned to do this when you were in India. Did your father approve of this?"

She wrinkled her brow. "Of course my father had no idea I learned the *nritya* of India or had a costume such as this made. He would never have permitted either. I caught one of our Indian *nauker* dancing one day and asked her about it."

"Your what?"

"*Nauker.* Servant. I insisted she teach me and had her arrange to have the costume made for me. I have always danced only for my own pleasure. I swear to you, Morgan, my father never knew, and you and Beabe are the only people ever to see me dressed like this."

"Make that four people, since my cousins saw you, too, but who is counting?"

"Well, as the old saying goes: there is nothing I can do now but face the music."

"Arianna, if you knew how badly I hated the man, you would know this is not the time to start quoting Lord Chesterfield to me."

She lifted her shoulders. "Did he say that? I believe I mentioned that I don't know of Lord Chesterfield, but I feel sure if he said it, he had good reason, and that he bravely faced the consequences of whatever his actions were at the time. I intend to do the same."

"From the moment you arrived, your bravery has never been in question, Arianna."

It pained her to say it, but she swallowed and added, "I'm quite prepared to leave your home at once if that is what you desire."

His blue eyes stared down into hers. "You know that is not what I desire. I think you know that you are what I desire right now." He stepped in closer to her. "I love seeing your hair down like this, spilling over your shoulders and down your back. The lamplight makes it shimmer like the gold thread embroidered on your costume."

Arianna's heartbeat raced, but she remained still. He picked up a length of her hair and gently rubbed it between his fingers. He lifted it to his nose and inhaled deeply.

"I love the spicy scent of the perfumed water you wear," he said, his gaze tracing down her face and lingering on her lips. "I find myself waking in the night and believing I smell you lying next to me."

Arianna stared at him, not wanting to move as his hands caressed her hair and his words filled her senses with longing.

He bent his head until his lips brushed lightly, invitingly, across hers. It wasn't nearly enough to fill her deep craving for his kiss. His touch was much too brief to savor as much of the sweet taste of him as she wanted. He smelled of leather, wet earth, and shaving soap. She yearned to be caught up in his arms and crushed against his broad chest.

Keeping his lips very close to hers, he whispered huskily, "You know, some say that Bathsheba knew King David went to his rooftop each evening, and that is why she chose that time of night to wash herself. She knew he would see her. Desire her. Defy heaven and move the earth to possess her."

Arianna had imagined Morgan watched her. Had she somehow known he was where he could see her dancing in front of the window? She lifted her lashes and looked directly into his very blue eyes. They were filled with humor. He wasn't judging. He was teasing.

She smiled. "You think I dressed like this and danced because I knew you and your cousins would be walking down the slope?"

"Not my cousins. Just me."

"If so, it was planned for me by destiny, and destiny is very hard to change."

"I'm beginning to believe that."

Morgan chuckled softly as his tongue swept the outline of her lips before his mouth settled confidently over hers. Instinctively, she parted her lips, and his tongue darted inside and played, plundered, and teased hers. Tightness squeezed her chest, and warmth settled low in her abdomen.

His arms slipped around her, and he pulled her against his chest. This was what she had been waiting for since he entered her room. She melted into his embrace; her arms went over his strong shoulders, and her hands met at the back of his neck.

Short, choppy breaths merged with long, whispered sighs as his lips roamed hungrily over hers. He kissed across her cheek to softly nuzzle the area behind her ear. Arianna kissed his cheek and felt the light stubble of beard. He pulled the lobe of her ear into his mouth and gently nibbled at it. Her skin pebbled deliciously at the touch of his moist breath and warm lips.

Shivers of desire and excitement shuddered through her. She wore little clothing, but she had never felt hotter. It amazed her that just his touch could make her feel as if she were on fire. His lower body strained to get closer to hers. She felt his hardness beneath his riding breeches. She longed to lift his shirt and feel his firm skin beneath her hands.

As they kissed passionately, his hands ran up her back, over her shoulders, and down the front of her tunic. His palms lay against her breasts. He lifted their weight into his hands and gently, firmly, caressed them. Arianna moaned softly and allowed herself to enjoy the heady sensations he stirred inside her.

"I know poets have written about hearing bells, but I swear this is the first time I've ever kissed anyone and heard bells."

Arianna laughed and then kissed him deep, long, and hard. "You are really hearing bells, my lord."

"I am?" he asked with a grin, his hands slowly caressing their way to her bare waist. His thumb found her navel and played with the tiny indentation.

"It's the custom for bells to be sewn onto the hem of the skirt."

"What?"

"See? Look." She turned him loose and lifted the hem of her skirt and shook it.

He looked at her and grinned. "Arianna, I fear you are a wicked angel sent to torment me."

She placed her lips on his and kissed him passionately with all the love she was feeling.

Love?

Is that what she was feeling for the earl?

No, it couldn't be.

It must be.

But he was a handsome, arrogant rogue. Nothing like her father.

But what else could be as glorious as her feelings for Morgan but love?

Morgan's lips left hers, and he kissed his way over her chin, down the slender column of her neck, past the hollow of her throat, to the swell of her breasts. He kissed down the center of her tunic to her midriff and suddenly dropped to his knees in front of her.

His hands circled her bare waist, his fingers splayed down her hips, and he thrust his tongue in the center of her stomach and teased her navel. Arianna gasped from pleasure, and her knees went weak with desire. She wound her arms around his head and pressed him closer. His hands slipped around to her back and lower to cup her buttocks and press her body into his face.

Arianna held her breath for fear if she breathed, the magic of the moment would break and disappear. His every touch thrilled her to new heights, and her fear was that he would stop.

She knew what she was allowing him to do was beyond the pale in Polite Society, but with Morgan, she simply had no inclination to stop him and no inhibitions where he was concerned. She had already flagrantly disobeyed so many rules, and simply disregarded others, that there seemed to be little reason to worry now.

Slowly, his hands, his tongue, and his mouth stilled. He raised his head and looked up at her. She saw in his eyes that his desire for her was great, and she would not deny him.

"Tell me you have been with a man like this before, Arianna. Please tell me so that I can take you to that bed and give us both what we want."

Arianna was conflicted. "Should I lie to you?" she asked.

He scowled. "No. Never."

"Then I can't tell you that, Morgan. It's not true. I've never known a man in that way. I have never wanted to before you."

Morgan shook his head, took a deep breath, and laid his forehead on her stomach. "That is not what I wanted to hear, Arianna, but I knew it to be true before I even asked. As much as it pains me, I must stop."

He rose quickly and groaned as if he was hurt.

Worried, she grabbed his shoulders. "Morgan, what's wrong? You are in agony."

"No, I'm all right," he said, adjusting his stance and wincing again.

"I did not lie to you just now, so please don't lie to me."

"All right." He winced. "If you must know, I have a pain in my hip from a fall, but I'm sure I will be fine in the morning."

She reached out and laid an open palm on his hip to offer comfort. "When did you fall?"

"When Master Brute decided he didn't want me on his back," he said and gently took hold of her wrist and removed her hand from his side.

"You should have told me sooner. I can help you. I have an herbal mixture that will make you feel better by morning."

"I have taken many falls in my time, Arianna. I do not require anything but rest."

"Nonsense."

Arianna went over to the bed and reached down and pulled out a small satchel from underneath it. She lifted it onto the coverlet, opened it, and began pulling out little bottles and reading the labels.

"What is all that?" Morgan asked.

"These bottles contain rare and useful plants, herbs, and spices that are used by apothecaries, herbalists, and physicians all over the world to help people with aches and illnesses."

"And you just happened to have these with you?"

When she found the one she wanted, she looked up at him and smiled. "They were my father's, and they have been very useful in helping me heal from the fever."

Arianna walked over to her dresser and poured a portion of the mixture into a glass and then added water from a pitcher. As she walked back to Morgan, she swirled it in the glass.

Handing him the potion, she said, "Take this and drink all of it."

He smelled it. A wrinkle formed in his brow. "What is it?"

"It's a potion that my father made from herbs and plants. As he got older, he often had pain in his joints, and he said it helped him." She paused and let her gaze sweep down his face. "Trust me, Morgan, and take it, please. I promise it will take away the pain, and you will feel better by morning."

He extended it back toward her. "If this has laudanum in it, no thank you. That puts me to sleep and leaves me with a headache the next day."

"It doesn't and it won't. Please try it."

He took the glass from her and drank it all. He winced and coughed as he brought the glass down from his lips.

"Was that supposed to taste like ground leaves in dirty rainwater?"

"Yes." She smiled and dropped the little bottle into his coat pocket. "It's made from several different plants. Take another spoonful the same way, in water, before you go to bed, and one tomorrow morning. Your hip will be feeling much better."

He nodded and handed her the empty glass. "I will take your word for it, but I fear my other pain will still be with me."

He turned and walked out the door without looking back.

Eleven

My Dear Grandson Lucas,

When I read things like this from my dear friend Lord Chesterfield, I do wish that I had met him before the winter of his life. "A wise man, without being a Stoic, considers, in all misfortunes that befall him, their best as well as their worst side; and everything has a better and a worse side."

Your loving Grandmother,
Lady Elder

MORGAN LEANED HEAVILY AGAINST ARIANNA'S DOOR AND composed himself, forcing his rigid body to relax, trying to swallow the foul taste of the tonic she had him drink. It amazed him how quickly he was completely focused on Arianna and all the wonderful things he wanted to do to her that he forgot all about his cousins below stairs, waiting for him. He chuckled mirthlessly, took a deep breath, and sighed softly. He had wanted to take Arianna so badly his body trembled and ached all over.

But he had to stop thinking about that. He had to stop thinking about her. She confirmed what he suspected. She was an innocent. An innocent who had a very healthy and eager yearning to taste desire, but he could not oblige her.

Making love to her would bind her to him in a way he wasn't ready for. He would stay with women like Miss Goodbody. He chuckled softly to himself as once again he questioned his sanity in sending the courtesan away before he thought things through. That was so unlike him. But everything he'd done since Arianna had arrived was so unlike him.

He rubbed his forehead and shook his head. What had happened to the quiet country life he had had just a few days ago? Ah, but then he remembered thinking not too long ago that coming to Valleydale had not been one of his brighter ideas, and that hadn't changed. Morgan always took the time to develop a thorough plan, and he didn't like anyone or anything upsetting his plan.

Recently, nothing was going according to the way he wanted it, from designing every detail of Miss Goodbody's visit to wanting to invite Arianna to have dinner with him tonight. His cousins' surprising him with a visit had spoiled that. Now he had to go to the drawing room, face his cousins, and somehow explain Arianna to them.

As Morgan hobbled down the stairs, he straightened his shirt, pulled on the tail of his coat, and combed through his hair. He didn't know what Arianna had made him drink, but his hip wasn't feeling better yet.

There was only one way to handle his cousins, and that was with all the confidence he could muster. When he made it to the bottom of the stairs, he started whistling and continued all the way down the corridor and into his drawing room, limping as little as possible. His cousins were sitting in the two upholstered wingback chairs, each drinking a glass of wine. They were chatting but fell silent as soon as he rounded the doorway.

"Ah, I see you two made yourselves at home, as I suggested," he said in a convincingly jovial tone, considering the weight he still carried between his legs. "Good."

Morgan walked over to where the decanter sat on the marble-topped table and looked down at the claret in the crystal decanter. His thoughts went immediately to Arianna. He kept seeing her fair skin, the slight indention of her waist, the gentle flare of her hips. He remembered the soft yet firm feel of her body. He remembered the taste of her lips, her skin, and the hauntingly exotic scent of her that still filled him night and day and drove him to distraction.

There was no doubt that if he had ever needed the false courage that Lord Chesterfield said came from a bottle, he needed it now. He had to force himself to get his desire for Arianna under control and off his mind. If he didn't, his cousins would know, and they would make mincemeat out of him in no time.

With his glass full, he walked over and sat down on the settee that stood opposite the two chairs where his cousins were seated.

They looked at him curiously, but neither man had said a word since he entered the room. That made Morgan more uncomfortable than if both had been badgering him with questions at once.

"Now, where were we?" he said and took a much-needed drink of his wine.

His cousins remained silent, looking at him as if he might actually have taken leave of his senses.

So Morgan added, "Tell me exactly what day you will be leaving London, and I'll plan to arrive the day before so that there will be no chance Gibby will be left with none of us in Town."

Blake guffawed. "Do you think we are going to let you get by with not telling us who that woman is that we saw dancing in your window?"

Suddenly feeling devilish, Morgan said calmly, "What woman?"

"What woman indeed?" Race asked incredulously, moving to the edge of his seat. "The woman you ran upstairs to see the second we walked in the door! The woman you just spent a quarter of an hour with."

"Who is she?" Blake demanded, taking up the argument. "And what the bloody hell is she doing in your home dressed that way?"

Morgan smiled. "Curious, are you?"

"Yes," they both chimed in.

Race leaned back in his chair again and crossed one leg over the other. "You're damned right we are, and by the way, where the devil are all your servants? We asked Post to have someone retrieve our satchels from our horses, and he said he would have to do it, as you've given everyone except him and his wife a holiday."

"Forget the absent servants, Race," Blake said.

"How can I?"

"Because that's the least of our concerns. What the devil is going on here, Morgan?"

"I think it's already quite apparent why the woman is here," Race interjected.

As Race and Blake argued among themselves, Morgan chuckled. It felt damn good to know something the two of them didn't, and he would absolutely love to leave them in the dark about her, but he couldn't. As Arianna would be going to London and establishing a life there, so he had to advise them about her. The trick would be to do it with as little fanfare as possible. Though how he could do that after her dance he had no idea.

"Calm down, both of you," Morgan finally said. "It's not what either of you are thinking."

Morgan once had hopes of Arianna's arriving in London without anyone, other than Constance, knowing she'd been to Valleydale, but Arianna had obliterated that possibility. Now he had to try to make them see she wasn't what she appeared to be from what they had seen in the window.

"It's a long story," Morgan began.

"We're staying the night, and dinner hasn't been served, so I think we have time to hear everything you have to say."

"And if we haven't heard a sensible story by sunrise, we're not leaving," Race grumbled.

Morgan took another sip of his wine to keep from smiling. "All right. I suppose I have made you wait long enough for answers. The story is not as risqué or even as interesting as it seems from appearances."

"And we are to believe that?" Race snapped irritably.

"It's true. Her name is Miss Arianna Sweet. She came from India, and she was very ill when she arrived here a few nights ago."

"That does not pass the sensible test, Morgan," Blake said with a huff.

"Perhaps you should try telling us the truth," Race grumbled.

"I am," Morgan interjected.

"Really? She didn't look Indian."

"And she certainly didn't look ill to me," Race added combatively.

"She's not. Indian, that is. She's as British as we are, but believe me, she was quite ill when she arrived here what must have been about a week ago."

"All right, I'm not saying I believe you or that I don't, but why did she come to Valleydale?" Blake asked, finishing off the wine in his glass and then getting up and walking over to the decanter.

"Yes, this estate isn't exactly on the way from India to London," Race complained as Blake held up the wine to see if either Race or Morgan wanted a refill, and both shook their heads.

Morgan waited for Blake to sit down and then proceeded to tell them about the night Arianna arrived, minus the part about Miss Goodbody. They listened with few interruptions, and he ended the story with: "I've seen her less than a handful of times since she arrived, and not at all for the first couple of days, as she was too ill to leave her room."

"If she arrived at your door dressed in any way similarly to the way we saw her just a few minutes ago, I can certainly well understand why you felt the need to insist she recuperate here."

Suddenly the tables had turned, and now Morgan was the exasperated one and they the ones having the fun. "I can assure you she was not dressed like that, nor did she look anything like she looked in that window tonight."

"We believe you," Race said and tried to hide his smile behind the rim of his glass as he took a drink.

"Yes, I'm quite certain I would have demanded she recuperate here, too."

Suddenly, the wine tasted foul in Morgan's mouth, and he scowled. He didn't want them thinking the worst about Arianna.

"She was wearing a very proper dress and cape," he defended irritably. "But she's been in India for ten years; her clothing is bound to be a little different from what we're used to."

"A little?" Blake said with a grin. "How far can you stretch credulity, Morgan?"

"You blasted devils. She was in the privacy of her room and had no reason to believe anyone would be in a position to look into her window. Now, I have no idea what her clothing looks like, but if needed, Constance can help her in that area when she gets to London."

"Constance?" Blake asked, his tone changing from humorous to inquisitive.

"Yes, since Grandmother is no longer with us, I wrote to Constance and asked if she would come to Valleydale and escort Miss Sweet to London. She needs help finding a place to live and a suitable companion. The things her father expected our grandmother to help her with. And things I know nothing about."

Morgan drained his glass. "What are you two scoundrels laughing about?"

"You," they said in unison.

"Why?" he said, feeling more defensive than he wanted to. "I had to allow her to stay here. She was very ill when she arrived. You both know our grandmother would have turned over in her grave if I had not taken her in and helped her. You bloody blackguards. Have some respect."

"We do," Race said.

"You're not acting like it. She's Sir Walter's niece, you drunken devils."

"We aren't drunk. And I agree, you had to help her," Blake said.

"Me too."

Morgan hated the feeling that he had to defend Arianna and his choice to help her. "Damnation, she came here hoping our grandmother could assist her. I did the next best thing and asked someone who could."

"You don't have to convince us, Morgan," Blake said, trying his best to hide a smile but not succeeding. "You did the right thing."

"I agree," Race added.

"And so you sent the servants away so they wouldn't know she was in the house with you and start gossip that would be difficult to stop?" Blake asked.

"Yes," Race answered for Morgan. "Can you imagine the gossip there would be if a servant had seen her dancing as we did? It's all very believable, Morgan. Everything you did was completely appropriate, and we would have done the very same thing."

"Hell yes, we would have," Blake added.

Race laughed again and said, "Morgan, it's a damn

good thing you left London to avoid being snared by a beautiful young lady."

"You know what," Morgan said, rising and walking over to pour himself another glass of wine, "you two can go to hell."

"We probably will," Race said, "but not tonight."

"Right," Blake added with a grin, "tonight we go only as far as India."

Race and Blake howled with laughter.

Twelve

IT WAS BLOODY AWFUL.

It had been two days since his cousins left, and Morgan was waiting to feel better about their visit, but that hadn't happened yet. He would have given anything if his cousins hadn't seen Arianna dancing. What a hell of a thing to have happened. Sometimes his cousins could be such bastards. For once, he thought as he walked into the drawing room to wait for Constance, he was glad they hadn't stayed longer than overnight.

Post had told him that Mrs. Pepperfield had arrived and was resting from the exhausting trip from London. She would be in the drawing room at six o'clock to meet with him. He walked over to the marble-topped table to make sure a fresh bottle of wine had been opened, but should have known he didn't need to do that now that all of Valleydale's servants had returned. Post and his wife no longer had to do everything.

He stood at the table and stared out the front window that showed a magnificent view of the front lawn with its lush greenery and tree-lined drive. But it took only seconds for his mind to drift back to Arianna. He hadn't seen her since the night his cousins arrived and proceeded to have one hell of a wonderful time at his expense. Knowing those two, they were probably still laughing. But he found some consolation in thinking they were probably also wondering how much he hadn't told them and never would.

The only way he'd been able to stay away from Arianna was sheer willpower. He'd had to search long and hard for it but finally found it when she had told him she was an innocent. He hadn't lost interest in her, far from it. And keeping his distance from her hadn't been easy.

It had been sheer torment, but Morgan didn't want the strings that came with deflowering a maiden. He would feel duty bound to marry her, and that was what finally gave him the willpower to resist her allure.

Being leg-shackled at age thirty wasn't in his plans—no matter how desirable Miss Arianna Sweet was.

So whenever his body yearned for her, whenever he couldn't get the taste of her, the feel of her, the smell of her out of his mind, whenever he thought he would go mad with wanting her, he would simply remember her innocence and the price he would have to pay if he took that from her. That alone allowed him to stay away from her. It was hard, though, damned near impossible, but so far, in the end, his willpower had come through for him in the nick of time.

"Thank God, Constance has finally arrived and can see her safely to London."

"Are you talking to me, my lord?"

Morgan turned around and saw Constance standing just inside the doorway to the drawing room. He smiled. "Yes, as a matter of fact, I was."

She wore a pale lavender dress trimmed in dark purple velvet that made her look absolutely fetching. Her vibrant auburn hair had been shaped into tight curls on the top of her head. Her wide green eyes sparkled, and she walked toward him with the confidence of a woman who knew where she stood with a man.

He couldn't help but notice that although she and Arianna were both beautiful women, they looked nothing alike. Constance's hair and eyes were lighter than Arianna's. And Constance looked strictly British through and through, while there was something teasingly exotic about Arianna, and for him, that set her apart from all other women.

Morgan remembered Blake telling him that several men had offered for Constance's hand this past Season, but she had declined them all. Looking at her now, he could easily understand why so many men had sought her favor. It wasn't that her face was absolutely lovely or that her pockets were deep. It was her control, her self-confidence that made her beautiful.

And if what Blake said was true—and Morgan had no reason to doubt that—she would continue to rebuff any gentleman's attentions if he was looking for matrimony. Obviously Constance was enjoying the life of a wealthy widow and all the freedoms it afforded her. Only one thing would make a woman like Constance want to give up her freedom: true love, and it didn't appear Constance was in the market for that any more than he was.

Morgan met her in the center of the room, where she curtseyed. He bowed and then took her hand in his and lightly kissed it.

"You look absolutely lovely, Constance. I'm honored you came."

She smiled sweetly at him. "Nonsense, my lord. You knew I would as soon as I could make the necessary arrangements."

He didn't, but there was no reason to tell her that.

"How could I not heed your plea? I have never read such enticing puffery from a man as what you wrote to me in your letter."

Morgan gave her a cautious grin. "You make puffery sound like a vulgar word."

She arched an eyebrow and asked, "Is it not?"

"No, nothing could be further from the truth. I meant every word I wrote."

"Ha!" she laughed. "If that be the case, Lord Snellingly could certainly take a lesson or two from you on how to write words that actually flatter and entertain a lady."

Morgan laughed, too. "Now you are the one full of praise and sweet talk, but I'll gladly accept it. However, I have been unfortunate enough to have heard some of Lord Snellingly's poetry, and it doesn't take much to write better than that tight-shoed poet."

"Too true."

"Make yourself comfortable, and I'll pour us a glass of wine."

"Tell me," she said, stopping by the floral-printed settee. "Is that a painting of Lady Elder when she was younger? And are those the famous Talbot pearls that I've heard so much about?"

"Yes to both. Shortly after Sir Walter gave the pearls to her, my grandmother had at least four or five, maybe more, portraits painted of herself wearing them, but only that one made it to the place of honor here in the drawing room."

"Where are the others?" she asked and seated herself on one end of the settee.

He handed Constance a glass of claret and said, "In the attic."

As he sat a respectable distance from her on the other end of the settee, she gave him a disapproving look.

"Shame on you, my lord. Paintings of your grandmother should not be hidden away in the attic to collect dust and lord knows what else. Surely in a house this large you can find a place to hang them."

"Probably, but I didn't put them there. She did. I remember that she wasn't satisfied with the first one, the second, or the third, so she kept commissioning different painters from all over the world until she finally had one she was satisfied with."

"I can see why she stopped at that one. She looks regal and commanding."

Morgan looked up at the portrait. "Yes, the artist captured her perfectly. As for the previous paintings, I see it this way. If my grandmother didn't want them to see the light of day, I'll respect her wishes and leave them in the attic where she decided to put them."

"I don't suppose I can argue with her wishes either," Constance said and then sipped her wine.

Morgan's gaze caught Constance's over the rim of his glass, and they stared at each other for a moment, each giving the other a second look to ponder attraction and possibilities. Constance was beautiful, unattached, and available if he so desired. From his cousin Blake, Morgan knew she was a widow who enjoyed taking a man to her bed. With her there would be no recriminations, no misgivings, and no strings attached. No doubt she would be an excellent bedmate for him, for any man, so why were his thoughts on Arianna?

Why were his thoughts always on Arianna?

"You look pensive, Morgan," she said, obviously letting him know that the moment of awareness between them had passed without either of them acting on it.

"Do I?" he questioned, giving himself a mental shake.

"I think so. Why don't you tell me why you needed my help so desperately that you swallowed your pride and wrote to me?"

He smiled ruefully and then chuckled. She was such

a clever and charming woman. How could a man not appreciate her directness? It was no wonder she and Blake had remained such good friends after their affair had ended last year.

"You do know how to make a man feel good about himself, Constance."

She smiled, sipped her wine again, and then said, "I try—from time to time."

"All right, the short of it is that there is a young lady staying here at Valleydale, and she needs help in a couple of different ways."

"Oh dear," she said dryly and blew out an exasperated breath. "Morgan, please don't tell me a young lady arrived at your door and she has insisted that you are her guardian and all of her previous five guardians have died."

Morgan laughed, remembering how his cousin Blake and his wife, Henrietta, had met. Though the feelings he had for Arianna could never be considered what a guardian has for his ward.

"I can assure you I am not this lady's guardian, nor is she in need of one. That said, however, I feel a certain amount of responsibility for her welfare because she came here in hopes that my grandmother might help her."

"Your grandmother? That's odd. Didn't she know your grandmother died over a year ago? If not, she must be the only person in all of England who didn't."

"That is part of the problem. She hasn't been in England. She came from India, where she had lived with her father up until his death. When she arrived in England a few days ago, she came straight here, hoping Lady Elder could assist her in finding a suitable place to live in London as well as aid her in suggesting a respectable companion for her."

"Why come to Lady Elder? Has she no family she can turn to?"

"None that she has mentioned to me, so I assume not."

Constance seemed to study over that. "And how did she know your grandmother?"

"She didn't. Her father was cousin to my grandmother's second husband Sir Walter Hennessey. Before his death, her father suggested she come to Valleydale and seek help from Lady Elder."

Constance gave him a knowing smile. "I'm sure there is more to her story than that."

"There always is," he said.

Morgan didn't feel it necessary to mention anything about Arianna's father's research, so he remained quiet about all of that. He had felt there was more to Arianna's story than she was telling, too, but he didn't see the need to confide in Constance.

"Anyway, her relationship to my grandmother, however distant, is why I feel I must help her get settled in London. Naturally, she would be more comfortable having another lady help her with that sort of thing, which is why I wrote to you."

"What is she like?"

"She's ill," he said.

"Oh, wait a minute, Morgan." Constance held up her hand and moved restlessly. "I am not a nursemaid."

"Perhaps I should have said she has been ill."

"I don't care. I faint at the sight of blood, and I

don't have the patience or the desire to talk soothing words while wiping a fevered brow."

Morgan couldn't help but laugh. He enjoyed Constance's confidence to be so completely honest with him.

"I understand, and I wouldn't ask that of you. But you don't need to be her nursemaid, I assure you. Mrs. Post has been taking care of her, and of course, she has her maid. I saw Miss Sweet a couple of days ago, and she said she is feeling much better, and she looks stronger…" He paused. *And more beautiful and more enticing.* "…than when she first arrived."

"Hmm. So it's been two days since you've seen her, and she lives in your house?"

He shrugged. "It's a big house. Besides, because she's been resting, she takes all her meals in her room."

"What is her age?" Constance asked.

"Twenty-seven, I believe she said."

"Most consider that old enough to be put on a shelf and declared a spinster, but maybe not, if she is pretty."

"She is," he said without hesitation.

"Perhaps I should start by asking you what I failed to ask Blake concerning Henrietta. Do you have designs on her, Morgan?"

Without faltering, he said, "I am not in the market for a wife, and she doesn't qualify for anything else."

Constance nodded. "I understand."

Morgan was sure she did. He suddenly felt restless, so he rose, took Constance's glass, and walked back over to the decanter to refill their glasses.

"With Miss Sweet's beauty and appeal, I'm sure she would have no trouble finding a husband of considerable means, if she wanted to. I, of course, have no idea if marriage might be in her immediate future. She has indicated to me only that when she gets to London, she has to do some work her father left unfinished for the Royal Academy of Apothecary Herbs and Spices, or some ridiculous name like that."

"That sounds extremely boring."

"I'm sure it is," he answered and splashed more wine into their glasses.

"What are her means?"

"She says that her father left her well set, and I have no reason to doubt her. I haven't talked extensively with her about this, you understand, but you should feel free to question her as to her resources and let me know if you think she needs assistance in that area."

"I will. And if she has the means, I agree that she needs to employ a companion to keep the gossips at bay, especially if she plans to enter Society. She certainly doesn't need to live alone with her maid."

He handed the glass back to Constance and then retook his seat. "My thoughts were that you might put her in touch with the right person to find her a suitable place to live."

Constance's eyes suddenly widened. "Oh, Morgan, I think I might have the perfect place for her."

"Really?"

"Of course, I can't say for sure, but there's a possibility she can assume the lease on Susannah's house. Her mother has been living there but is returning to Chapel Gate in Blooming as we speak. I'm quite certain Susannah doesn't want to keep the place now that she's married to Race. I believe Susannah would agree to

Miss Sweet taking over her lease, since you say the lady is somewhat distantly related to Lady Elder by marriage. Should I mention this possibility to Susannah?"

"Of course. Her house would be perfect for Miss Sweet."

Morgan couldn't help but note that Susannah's place was only a five-minute carriage ride from his house.

"Good. I'll send a letter to her first thing tomorrow morning, asking her to hold it for Miss Sweet until we can get to London."

"And perhaps you can help guide her with seeking a suitable companion?"

"That is personal taste, Morgan, but I do know of a couple of older ladies who might be available. The Countess of Leesberth has a cousin who is looking for employment as a companion. I've never met the relative, but I do like the Countess."

"Yes, the Countess seems a sensible woman, so one would hope the cousin would be as well."

"And there's the Dowager Duchess of Elliston. She constantly grumbles and complains. Companions don't seem to stay with her for very long at the time. There is a Miss Gilberta, who recently left her and is not yet employed, and there might be others. I'm sure any lady would readily accept a position with Miss Sweet if there were a recommendation from you."

"That goes without saying, Constance." Morgan sipped his wine and then continued. "There is one other thing I would like to discuss with you."

"What's that?"

"I think Miss Sweet might need help with her clothing."

"You said she's twenty-seven, Morgan. Surely she knows the proper way to dress."

"One would think, but remember, she's been in India for ten years. And while I'm certain, or maybe I should say, from what little I know, her father tried to keep the influence of her British heritage, as her maid is British. But keep in mind her clothing has been made with the fabrics and trimmings of India, and the styles may…" He suddenly searched for the right word.

"Never mind. You needn't say more. I understand. I will suggest she see my modiste as soon as she gets settled in London. You might not know it, Morgan, but there are many ladies in the ton who meet every ship that comes from India so they can have first choice of the fabrics, spices, and herbs."

"Really?"

Constance nodded and then relaxed against the back of the settee and sipped her wine. "While India has some of the most beautiful and finest fabrics in the world, I agree that some of them, and certain styles of the country, are not suitable for our climate or culture."

He cleared his throat and said, "I'll leave fashion to those who know more than I do."

"That's probably best."

"On another subject," he said, "tell me, have you seen Viscount Brentwoood's twin brothers?"

Her eyebrows shot up. "Yes, several times. They are at all the parties."

"What did you think about them?"

"You mean other than the fact that they look exactly like a much younger Sir Randolph Gibson?"

Morgan sighed thoughtfully. "So you think they resemble him, too?"

"I believe everyone in London does."

That's not what Morgan wanted to hear. He had subconsciously been holding out hope that his cousins had been wrong.

"How did you hear about the twins?"

"Blake and Race were here a couple of days ago."

She smiled. "I should have guessed. I learned a long time ago that what one of you knows, you all three know."

"Well, maybe not everything," he answered.

"Did they meet Miss Sweet?"

Morgan cleared his throat. "Not exactly. They saw her from a distance. In fact, I should have—" Morgan stopped when he heard footfalls in the corridor and humming. It was Arianna. His chest tightened. He rose and turned in time to see her walking past the doorway with several books in her arms.

"Miss Sweet," he called, and she turned toward the drawing room. She stopped and smiled at him.

His heart tripped like a schoolboy getting his first glimpse of a woman's bosom. He hoped to God Constance couldn't tell what he was loathe to admit to himself. He was besotted with Arianna.

Constance rose and stood beside him.

Arianna's glance swept over to Constance, and she took a tentative step forward. "My lord," she said.

"I'm glad you happened by. Put the books down and come meet Mrs. Pepperfield. She's finally arrived."

Arianna placed the books on a blue velvet bench near the doorway and walked closer. She looked the perfect English lady, with a prim-cut, high-waisted dress of pale robin's egg blue. Morgan didn't know how he managed to make the introductions, because all he wanted to do was pull Arianna to him and greet her with a warm kiss on her beautiful lips. He was beginning to believe he would never get the taste of her off his tongue or the scent of her out of his mind.

Constance walked closer to Arianna. "Lord Morgandale told me you have been ill, and I do see some lingering effects of the sickness around your eyes. How are you feeling now?"

She smiled confidently. "Much better, thanks to Lord Morgandale. I've had more than a week of rest, and I'm feeling quite strong now. Thank you for asking."

"Good. The earl was just telling me of your needs for a place to live and a companion. I believe I can help you easily achieve both."

Arianna's eyes brightened with surprise and appreciation. "Thank you, it's very kind of you to travel all this way to assist me."

"And as we journey back to London, perhaps you can repay the favor and tell me about India."

"I would be happy to."

"I'm quite fascinated by the country, the culture, and its people, but I doubt I shall ever travel that far from England."

"It's a long and exhausting voyage that should take only forty to fifty days, but sometimes unexpected things happen to make the journey much longer." Her gaze darted from Constance to Morgan and then back to Constance, and she asked, "When will we leave for London? Will it be tomorrow?"

Morgan didn't like hearing that Arianna was eager to get to London, even though he'd known since the night she arrived that was her destination.

Constance smiled and then laughed lightly. "Good heavens, no. Not that soon, Miss Sweet. I need at least a day of respite from traveling, myself, but we'll plan to leave bright and early the day after tomorrow, if that suits you and Lord Morgandale just as well?"

"Yes, of course, whenever you and the earl say will be perfect for me."

"Good."

Morgan forced his gaze away from Arianna and turned his attention to Constance. "As for tomorrow, why don't I arrange for a picnic at the cottage by the coast?"

"A day by the coast? I think that would be lovely," Constance said.

"Good. I told Miss Sweet that it was very possible her father stayed in the house when he visited here with Sir Walter, and she had mentioned she would like to see it before she leaves."

"That's a lovely idea. I haven't seen the coast in a couple of years," Constance said. "I think I would enjoy that very much, my lord."

He glanced at Arianna, who gave him a grateful smile and said, "As would I."

"It's settled then."

Morgan stared at Arianna and returned the smile. A light pink tint had returned to her cheeks and lips. Her green eyes were sparkling. All he could think was, thank God Gibby needed him and he had a reason to go back to London.

Thirteen

My Dear Grandson Lucas,

*Think upon these words from my devoted friend Lord
Chesterfield: "Your moral character must be not only pure, but,
like Caesar's wife, unsuspected. The least speck or blemish upon
it is fatal. There is nothing so delicate as your moral character,
and nothing which it is your interest so much to preserve pure."*

Your loving Grandmother,
Lady Elder

ARIANNA'S EYES POPPED OPEN. SOMEONE LOOMED OVER
her. Her heart pounded in her chest. She opened
her mouth to scream, but as her gaze focused, hastily
swallowed it to a whimper. In the shadowy light of her
room, she realized it was Morgan, not the man who
had killed her father, who was sitting on the edge of
the bed beside her.

Her chest heaved.

Her fear dissolved.

He gently placed two fingers on her lips, bent closer, and said, "Shhh."

She nodded, still shaking from the fright he'd given her.

"I didn't mean to scare you," he whispered, the pads of his fingers outlining her lips as he talked. "Are you all right?"

She nodded again. His light touch sent shivers of awareness shooting through her.

He smiled. "Good."

She couldn't imagine why he was in her room. He had done a fine job of avoiding her for the past few days, even opting out of the afternoon picnic up at the cottage with her and Constance yesterday. He had sent Post with them instead.

"What's wrong?" she asked quietly, her words whistling through his fingertips.

"Nothing, except that you'll be leaving in a few hours, and there's something I want you to see before you go. Are you willing to come with me?"

Willing? Absolutely!

Anticipation rippled through her.

"Yes," she whispered, knowing she would follow him to the moon if he asked.

"Then there's no time to talk or to dress. We must hurry. Throw on a cloak and shoes, slip quietly from your room, and meet me by the back door."

"Are we—?"

"Shh." He rose from the bed. "Don't say anything, just quietly follow me."

Arianna pushed the covers aside, and he walked soundlessly from her room, leaving the door ajar for her easy exit. She looked down at the thin, short-sleeved shift she wore for her night garment and contemplated throwing a dress on over it but, instead, she took Morgan at his word that time was of the essence.

She rushed barefoot to her wardrobe and quietly opened it. With hasty movements, she hunted through her clothing until she found her black velvet cape and a pair of low-heeled slippers. She would wait until she was below to put them on.

Excitement built inside her as she hurried out of her room, carefully closing the door behind her. She rushed down the stairs.

What could he want to show her?

She picked her way through the spacious, dark front hall to avoid stumbling over furniture, and down the wide, dim corridor that lead to the back door of the house. Morgan was there waiting for her. He helped settle the cape on her shoulders as she stepped into her shoes, and as easily as if they'd done it a thousand times, they slipped quietly out the door and into the night.

Morgan took her hand in his, and they made their way down the steps. She had no idea where they were going, and she didn't care. She was eager to see whatever he wanted to show her.

They continued to walk fast, and Morgan led her away from the house to where he had tethered Redmond, far enough so that no one would hear the horse if he whinnied. Morgan let go of her hand and pulled on gloves he took from his coat pocket.

The leather creaked, and as Morgan climbed on the saddle, Redmond snorted and shifted. Just as Arianna had the last time she'd ridden with him, she turned her back to Morgan, and he placed his hands under her arms, only this time she knew how to hold her cape so that it wouldn't get twisted under her. On his count of three, she jumped, and he hoisted her sideways onto the saddle in front of him. She felt his powerful warmth at once and sighed contentedly, immediately slipping one arm around the back of his waist and leaning into him.

Morgan kicked Redmond in the flanks, and he took off at a canter. Muggy air blew in her face and whipped her hair around her shoulders. The night was clear, tepid, and a bright hunter's moon lit the way as the horse kept up a steady pace. After having been to the coast twice, Arianna knew that the smooth gait of the horse beneath them was taking them there.

Anticipation rippled and curled inside her. It thrilled her that Morgan was willing to steal her away in the middle of the night because there was something he wanted her to see before she left Valleydale.

But what could it be?

He had avoided her like the plague since the evening of that debacle with his cousins seeing her dance, and then later when he came to her room. Arianna had not given up hope of seeing the earl glance her way with longing in his eyes or a special smile just for her. But she hadn't seen a glimmer of the man who had held her and kissed her so thoroughly that she knew she would never be the same. And she would always yearn to once again feel the way he had made her feel when he'd held her so close their bodies seemed to melt into each other.

Arianna tightened her hold on Morgan. It was mere hours before she would have to leave Valleydale with Mrs. Pepperfield and travel to London. But until then, she had this time alone with him, and she intended to enjoy it.

Their journey remained silent. Redmond slowed his pace. As the horse climbed the rise that led to the craggy coast, he had to pick his way around stone and rocks. Within minutes, Morgan pulled the bay to a stop at the edge of a peak.

When Arianna looked out over the calm sea, she gasped. A round, luminous Dorset summer moon shone down from a black, starry night to illuminate the channel with a wide, shimmery streak. The peaceful sound of water rushing to shore cut through the silence of the night. A noiseless, salty breeze shuddered the stillness of the mild air. Lights from a lone ship twinkled in the distance as it made its way across the channel.

"It's seldom this clear on the coast at night, Arianna," Morgan said. "And it's even rarer for it to be this way when the moon is full and there's not a hint of fog, mist, or chill in the air."

Arianna was filled with wonder. "It's the most beautiful night I have ever seen. And I know I have never seen the moon glisten on water like that."

"Not even when you were on the ship?"

"Beabe and I seldom left my room, and never at night."

"That was probably best," he answered.

"It's so clear and still; it makes me think that I can see forever."

Morgan chuckled softly. "I've thought the same thing at times myself."

For a moment Arianna found herself wishing she would never have to leave this place. But she knew she must. She had to convince Mr. Warburton to help her recover her father's formula and get it to the Academy. Besides, Lord Morgandale certainly hadn't said or done anything to make her think he wanted her to stay with him.

She leaned against his chest and sighed. "This view is something I will never forget, my lord. It will stay with me always. Thank you for showing it to me."

"I thought you would appreciate its beauty."

"I do."

"When we were much younger, my cousins and I would watch and wait for nights such as this."

"I can understand why. Beauty like this should never be missed."

Morgan laughed again, and Redmond shifted underneath them. "We didn't watch and wait for the beauty of the night, Arianna. When it was this warm, clear, and bright, which wasn't often, we would climb down the cliff to the beach and swim if the water was calm enough. If it was too rough, we would walk along the shore to see what urchins might have been left on the shore. Even with the path we made, it's much too treacherous to make it down unless it's a night like this."

"Can we do that, Morgan?"

"What?"

She turned and looked up at him. "Climb down the cliff right now and walk the shore."

He stared down into her eyes and smiled. "No, it is much too dangerous for you."

She moistened her lips and thought for a moment. "Did you and your cousins ever have an accident?"

"No, but remember, we were agile youths and, at the time, we had no fear of anything. You are not capable of such a climb."

Arianna tried to hide her disappointment by turning her face away from his and looking out over the water again. "Nonsense, Morgan, I am more than capable. I am very agile and light on my feet." She turned back to him and scrutinized his face. "You can hold my hand. I promise I will be careful going down the cliff."

"It's perilous even under such favorable conditions," he argued. "The rocks can be slippery or shift under your weight. And besides that, you are not properly dressed or shod for climbing down or up a ten-meter cliff."

Arianna folded her arms across her chest and said, "Perhaps you are the one who is old and not able to make the climb anymore."

His gaze swept across her face. "Do you really believe that?"

"No, but you do have that injury to your hip. Perhaps that is what is making you reluctant."

"The bottle you gave me is empty, and there's no pain in my hip."

"I'm glad the remedy worked." Arianna placed her hand on his chest over his heart. "You awakened me in the middle of the night and brought me here. It would be unforgivable of you to make me leave until I have walked on the shore."

He sighed in agreement before saying, "All right, but you must do exactly as I say."

Excitement soared inside her. Her lips widened into a heartfelt smile. "I promise."

Morgan helped her slide down the horse, and then he dismounted. Arianna took off her shoes while Morgan tethered Redmond to a low-lying bush. The ground was cool and scratchy to her feet.

"You must stay right behind me," Morgan said and sat down on the mossy ground and took off his riding boots and gloves.

"Of course I will. You need not fear, Morgan. I do not want to fall. I will do everything you say."

He took the time to roll his riding breeches farther up his legs to just below his knees. He then he stood up and shrugged out of his coat and threw it over Redmond's saddle.

"I'm not sure I believe you about that," he grumbled good-naturedly. "And something tells me I will probably regret doing this."

She reached out for his hand. "I will make sure you don't."

"Going down can sometimes be harder than coming up. Watch where you put your feet."

"I will follow you, my lord."

"The night is dry, so the rocks shouldn't be slippery, but there's one other thing. You'd best take off your cape. It drags on the ground and could very easily trip you on the slope. The night is warm enough you shouldn't get chilled."

She instantly wondered if he remembered she had on nothing but her nightshift. But she wasn't going to say anything and let a little thing like modesty keep her from climbing down to the shore and wading in the cool water.

"Oh, yes, I suppose you are right." She took off the cape without hesitation and handed it to him.

He seemed to take no notice of what she was wearing, and took the cape and threw it over the saddle, too. She supposed most women would be mortified to have a man see them in their plain white night rail, but Morgan had already seen her in far less clothing than what the shift covered.

"Follow me. The path is not too far from here."

They quietly made their way along the edge of the cliff to the clearing Morgan had mentioned. When he started down, he looked back over his shoulder to Arianna and said, "Stay behind me, and don't let go of my hand. Step exactly where I have stepped."

"You are worrying far too much about me, Morgan. I will be fine."

The narrow path down the rocky hillside was steeper than it looked in the moonlight. She watched Morgan carefully and did as he'd said, putting her foot on the exact spot his vacated. They remained quiet and concentrated until they reached the bottom, and her feet hit the wet, rocky shore. She immediately glanced up to where she'd come from. The craggy cliff stood like a huge chunk of rock jutting out over the shore. She turned around and looked at the dark, crashing water, not far from her, and suddenly shivered, memories of her weeks onboard the pitching ship washing over her. She knew how violent the water could be, but she was no longer threatened by its power.

The longer she stared at the rushing blue, the stronger she felt. She had a lot to be thankful for. She had finally made it to England, where all she had to do was see to it that her father's formula was found and delivered to the Royal Apothecary Scientific Academy before Mr. Rajaratnum sold it to the highest bidder. And she had faith that Mr. Warburton would help her get that done.

Morgan stepped close to her and touched her arm. "Are you cold?"

"No, it's the water." She turned and settled her gaze on his face. "I was just thinking that it is so different from this level than it is looking from the bow of the ship. It even sounds different. I know that it's powerful, destructive, and menacing at times, especially to a small ship, but here from the shore it almost looks peaceful."

He smiled, and his eyes questioned her. "Menacing? I've never thought of it like that, but I supposed it can be at times. If not treated with respect, the water can be dangerous. We can't stay down here long or walk very far, but come, let your feet get wet."

Arianna followed Morgan to the edge of the water. It washed over her feet, lapped at her ankles, and the sand shifted beneath her toes. As they started down the shore, a breezy wind tossed her hair away from her face and fluttered her clothing against her skin.

In her wildest dreams she never could have believed she was walking barefoot on a wet, sandy shore with a handsome earl beside her, the moonlight shining down on them. If only she could stay a little longer. If only she didn't have responsibilities that must be attended to.

A rogue wave splashed up to her knees, wetting the hem of her night rail and cascading down her legs, but Arianna didn't mind the cold water. She found it invigorating and kept walking. She looked over at Morgan. The wave hadn't bothered him either.

Morgan broke the silence by asking, "Are you smiling at me?"

She'd been caught. "Me? What? Was I smiling?" she answered playfully.

He seemed amused. "Yes. What were you thinking about that made you smile?"

You.

"Oh, several different things."

"Hmm. Like what?"

Like what am I going to do now that you have awakened feelings and desires inside me that have never been brought to life before? Like how wonderful and safe it is here. Like how right it feels to be here with you on the shore at Valleydale.

But she couldn't say any of that. Instead she offered, "One of the things I was thinking is that this will probably be the last time I see you alone. Thank you for allowing me to stay here. In a lot of ways it has reminded me of my early years in the Cotswolds. Not the landscape, of course. It's the feeling of safety and contentment that I feel here that is the same."

"Safety? Why do I still, at times, get the feeling there are things about your life that you haven't told me."

She averted her eyes from his gaze. "There are always things about our lives that we don't share with others, are there not?"

"Perhaps. Probably. Yes."

She laughed. "There's one other thing I want to say. I'm sorry if I caused you embarrassment when your cousins were here. I fear I must have, yet you denied it."

Morgan stopped and stared at her. The moonlight was so bright she had no trouble seeing his eyes sparkling with a teasing light.

"Embarrassment?" He chuckled lightly. "Never. What makes you say that?"

"They saw me dancing in my costume. I'm sure you didn't wish that."

"No, I didn't wish it, but embarrassment is not what I felt, Arianna, and I can assure you, neither did my cousins."

"We haven't had the opportunity to talk since they left. What did they say about me?"

"They asked, who is that beautiful lady with her light auburn hair shimmering around her shoulders? What does she have on, and how does she move her body like that?"

Her eyes widened. "Truly?"

He chuckled again and started walking. "Maybe not in those exact words, but close. It doesn't matter what they said, Arianna; believe me, they will never forget they saw you, and neither will I."

"And you swear I didn't embarrass you."

He glanced over at her and grinned. "I swear."

"Good. Do you mind if I ask you a personal question, my lord?"

"Of course not."

"Is Mrs. Pepperfield your mistress?"

He frowned. "What? That's rather a bold and awkward question for you to ask."

"You gave me permission to ask you," she said innocently.

"I didn't know what you were going to ask," he argued in a tone that let her know he wasn't miffed by what she asked, just stunned.

"I said I wanted to ask you something personal," she reminded.

"Arianna, have I ever told you that it is times like this that I want to change your name from Miss Sweet to Miss Tart?"

She tried not to smile. "Maybe more than once."

"Oh, well, to answer your question, no, Constance is not my mistress. She has been a good friend to my family for a long time."

"She is very beautiful, commanding, and she is a widow."

"Yes, I agree. She is all those things and more, but she is not and never has been my mistress."

"And what about Miss Goodbody?"

He continued to look straight ahead and never missed a step. "What about her?" he returned.

"She is the lady you were expecting the night I arrived."

He nodded, but said nothing.

"Is she your lover?"

He laughed low in his throat, and he shook his head. "No, I can truthfully say that she has never been my lover, either." He looked toward Arianna again and said, "You know I take back what I said."

"What? You know you can't take anything back once it has been said."

"That sounds like more wise words from Lord Chesterfield, but this time I can. You can no longer ask me personal questions. I've said all I'm going to say about personal matters."

They walked on quietly for a few moments, Arianna feeling very pleased to know that neither lady had been his lover.

Morgan stopped and bent down. "Look, here is a crab."

He picked up a crab about the size of his hand and extended it toward her. The crustacean's legs and pinchers moved frantically.

Arianna squealed with surprise and backed away from him.

"Throw it down!"

Humor glinted in his eyes, and he continued to advance on her. "I thought you wanted to come down to the beach so you could walk on the shore and look at what the sea has brought in."

"Yes, I want to look but not touch!"

"So you are afraid of crabs, are you?" He stepped closer, still holding the excited crab toward her.

"Yes," she shrieked again, started laughing, and bolted away from him.

Her feet kicked water up on her legs and on the tail of her nightshift, but she kept running and laughing. She heard Morgan splashing in the water behind her saying, "Where's your courage? It's only a little crab."

Morgan caught up to her a few steps later and spun her around. Forced to face him, Arianna laughed and squealed again.

She closed her eyes tightly and said, "Don't put him on me! Throw him down."

"You are safe," Morgan said, laughing. "I've already let him go."

Arianna opened one eye and looked at him, not knowing if she should believe him. He held out his empty hands, palms up, for her to see.

Arianna opened the other eye. She liked the way his eyes glistened with pleasure. She loved it that he felt comfortable enough to tease her with the crab.

"Thank goodness." She shivered. "Why do crabs look so frightening?"

And then, without prompting from Morgan, and not knowing why, she stepped up to him and circled his waist with her arms, laid her head on his chest, and melted against his warm body. His arms immediately went around her and hugged her close. He laid his nose on the side of her head. She heard him breathe in deeply and then let out a contented sigh.

"I don't know why crabs are scary-looking," he whispered. "I didn't really frighten you, did I?"

She shook her head and then raised her face to him. "But it was enjoyable running from you. I haven't felt that carefree in a long time."

"Neither have I, and since you enjoyed it so much, may find another crab and chase you with it?"

She hugged him tighter and placed her head on his strong, firm chest again. "Don't you dare!"

He chuckled lightly and buried his nose in her hair again and kissed her head. His hand ran up and down her back. "Hmm, I shouldn't have touched you," he whispered. "I promised myself I wouldn't touch you tonight."

Arianna felt her heart pounding in her chest. She leaned back so she could see his eyes. "Why not?"

His gaze was busy on her face, as if he were searching for a sign from her. And she wondered if he could sense the desire for him that filled her.

He brushed her hair away from her shoulders to her back, and then his hands skimmed down the length of her arms. "Because you feel too good to me, and when I start, I don't want to stop with just touching. I am a greedy man, Arianna, and I always want more, more than touches, more than kisses. I brought you here because I wanted you to see how beautiful the coast is in the moonlight when there is no mist or fog to hide its splendor."

Awareness that hadn't been there mere moments before simmered between them. They stood ankle deep in the water; the gentle breeze fluttered their clothing and hair. The sand shifted beneath her feet, but that's not what made Arianna suddenly unsteady. It was the cold reality that she desperately wanted Morgan to kiss her, to touch her, to take her beyond both their boundaries and ease the longing and hunger deep within her. But he was desperately trying not to oblige her.

When she looked at him, she thought about brief glances, seductive touches, and urgent kisses. She thought about being with him today, tomorrow, and always. And she also thought about what an impossible dream that was. What made her think she could capture the heart of an honorable man like Morgan? She couldn't.

If Arianna knew nothing else about herself, she knew she didn't want to leave for London in a few hours and never see Morgan again, never touch him again, and never kiss him again. But that wasn't her decision to make. It was Morgan's, and as usual, when it came to intimacy, he was making the proper choice.

Morgan let go of her and stepped away. "Come on, we need to get back. It will be dawn soon, and I don't want your maid finding your bed empty. I'm sure she would wake the entire household with her screaming."

Swallowing his rejection, Arianna mumbled, "Yes, I'm sure she would."

They turned around and started back toward the path they had taken down to the shore, at a hastier step than when they started.

"So remind me," Morgan said, "what exactly is it that you have to do for your father when you get to London?"

Arianna felt constriction in her chest. If she was ever going to tell Morgan the whole truth about her father's death and the stolen formula, this was the time to do it. But she didn't want to spoil this time alone with him by talking about that horrible afternoon. There would be plenty of time to dwell on that when she left Morgan's house a few hours from now.

She chose her words carefully and said, "He had some research findings and formulas he wanted presented to the Royal Apothecary Scientific Academy for their approval. As my father expected, I will talk to Mr. Warburton, and hopefully he will help me to sort everything and get it ready for presentation to the members of the Academy."

"I remembered you said he was working on formulas for various illnesses, right?"

"Yes, among other things, including the perfumed water he made for me."

He inhaled deeply. "I could never forget the perfumed water, Arianna. The scent lingers with me."

"I'm almost out of it. I'll have to take the jar to an apothecary when I get to London to have more made."

"With all you have to do, it sounds as if you will keep busy."

As they started the climb up the cliff, he reached back and took her hand. His hold was firm and steady. It was silly, she knew, but she didn't want to reach the top, because when they did, he would let go of her again.

"For a time, yes."

They fell silent as they worked their way up the path. She followed Morgan's footsteps all the way to the top of the cliff, where she stopped and stared out over the water. She was filled with longing she didn't completely understand. When she got to London, she would miss the coast, the stables, the gardens, and watching Master Brute, but nothing would compare to the way she would miss the earl. She swallowed hard and took a deep breath. He didn't want to want her, or to touch her. She had to accept that no matter how difficult it was.

"I know you are glad we made it without any falls or accidents," she said in a happier tone than she was feeling, making her way over to where she had left her shoes.

She started to slip her wet, gritty foot into her slipper, but Morgan stopped her by saying, "Wait."

He pulled his coat off the saddle and laid it on the ground. "Sit down on my coat. I'll dry your feet before you put your shoes on."

She gave him a grateful smile and said, "That is not necessary, my lord."

His gaze wafted up and down her face. "I know, but I want to do this. Sit down."

Arianna acquiesced and sat down on his coat. She placed her hands on the ground behind her and leaned back, extending one foot to him.

Morgan dropped to his knees before her. She watched as, much to her surprise, he tugged his collarless shirt out of the waistband of his breeches and pulled it over his head. Arianna's heart jumped up to her throat and stalled her breathing. He looked like Adonis. His wide, lean-muscled chest and arms rippled with his movements. She had never seen a man's chest before, and she was amazed at how beautiful Morgan was.

He laughed. "You looked stunned. What's the matter? Never seen a man without his shirt before?"

His laughter was contagious. She relaxed and returned his smile. "No, I haven't. I had no idea you would be so beautiful beneath your clothing."

He gave her a smile that let her know he appreciated her compliment.

Arianna wasn't prepared for the shock of pleasure that shot through her when he caught her heel in the palm of his hand and cupped it gently, solidly. She was instantly engulfed by eager desire when he raked his other hand up and down the lower part of her leg, slowly wiping away the sand and traces of salt water with his shirt. As he rubbed up and down the lower part of her leg, the soft fabric sluiced away the sand.

He dropped the shirt to the ground and tenderly massaged the back of her calf all the way up to the back of her knee and down again to her ankle. Arianna gasped with pleasure at his boldness. Luxuriant sensations stirred and mounted warmly inside her. The sensual touch of his hands started a heat low in her stomach. The warmth curled and wove its way up to her breasts and teased them before skittering down to the center of her womanhood and making a nest of hunger.

She was mesmerized by his kneeling in front of her, his bare chest gleaming in the bright moonlight. His hands skimmed her skin. The motion of his palm sliding up and down her leg was decidedly erotic. She watched the bulge of his taut muscles in his chest and arms. Her breaths grew short and choppy. At times, she wasn't sure she was breathing at all.

Arianna had never even thought about the possibility of a man touching her so intimately, holding her foot, wiping her legs, and it was titillating. His hand slid down to her ankle and across her foot to the end of her toes. His palm quickly slid up the back of her calf once again and gently kneaded her firm muscle.

Morgan didn't bother to glance at her but kept his attention on what he was doing. He gently lowered her foot to the ground and grasped the other. He followed the same sensuous routine, first wiping the sand and saltwater from her skin with his shirt and then making sure every grain of sand was brushed away with the smoothness of his hand before leaving in its wake her body shaking with pent-up desire.

His hand caressed, massaged, and teased her leg and her foot. The slow spreading of sensuality was delicious, languorous, seeping into her, warming her until she thought she would reach down and grab him up to her breast and kiss him madly. She felt weak with a wanting she was frantic to explore and understand. A hot dizziness whirled in her head.

While still caressing her leg, Morgan finally glanced at her and looked into her eyes. She knew he saw exactly how he was making her feel—like a woman who wanted him to take her. She didn't have to tell him. Words weren't necessary to communicate that she wanted him to give her what his hands were promising.

He swallowed hard.

The moon glow flickered off his dark hair and sparkled in his bright blue eyes. The sensual touch of his fingers stopped, and the warmth of his hands lay still on her bare skin.

A few days ago, Arianna had wondered if she loved Morgan. She no longer had to wonder. She now knew she loved him with all her heart, but she didn't know how to let him know. She didn't know how to ask him to show her how a man made love to a woman. And she was out of time. She couldn't stay longer than a few more hours. She must go to London.

Still, with all her heart, she yearned to be with Morgan before she left. How could she let him know that?

Suddenly, over his shoulder she saw the distant streak of a shooting star light up the black sky. She quickly closed her eyes and wished that Morgan would deny his honor and finish what he had started inside her. If only once, so that she would have something to dream about in the coming weeks, months, and years.

She had to let him know.

Arianna rose up very close to him, and in a voice far huskier than she intended for it to be, she said, "You are seducing me."

His hand ran up her leg, and his gaze fell on hers with his penetrating blue eyes. "No."

"Yes, my lord, you are."

Morgan sat back on his heels. "That is not what I intended."

"No, my lord, it is what you have been offering me all night, and I accept. I want to be your lover."

Fourteen

My Dearest Grandson Lucas,

Some considered Lord Chesterfield pompous, but that was never the case with him. He was simply a Master at life's little lessons. Read this one and remember it when life becomes difficult as I can attest to the fact that it certainly will: "I always made the best of the best, and never made bad worse by fretting."

Your loving Grandmother,
Lady Elder

MORGAN WAS DOOMED.

Arianna was right. He was seducing her. But why in the hell he was doing it, he had no idea. But did she know what she was asking him? He didn't think she did, but he certainly knew the ramifications of seducing an innocent, and he wasn't prepared to accept any of them.

Arianna's gaze raked like hot coals over his body. And what the devil was he thinking to take off his shirt and offer to dry her feet?

Because she enchanted him.

There was no mystery, no doubt of his attraction to her. It was the simple truth.

His hands lay innocently on her leg. He made no attempt to move them. Bright moonlight shone down from the twinkling black sky, making it very easy for Morgan to read Arianna's face. Her eyes were glazed with passion. She was as aroused as he was. The first time he had kissed her, he'd recognized her untapped sensuality, and ever since, he had longed to explore it with her. And right now, he was dying to bring it to life and release it, and drown himself in it.

She was eager for his touch, and that made his wanting her all the more difficult. He didn't know why, but unlike all the other proper young ladies he had kissed, she put no boundaries on him. Perhaps it was that she had lived in another country and felt freer; maybe it was her advanced age, but then, it didn't really matter why. The undeniable truth was that instead of pushing him away, as any sensible young lady should do, she always eagerly accepted his touch.

And while he was thrilled she was so willing, he couldn't oblige her. He was determined not to take away her innocence, no matter how alluring she was. It was a long-standing vow he made to himself years ago. There were enough women, who had already known a man, willing to share their beds with him; Morgan had never wanted to trifle with an innocent.

But here he was, tempted, really tempted for the first time in his life to break his vow and give in to Arianna Sweet's charms.

Suddenly, Arianna smiled at him. Why the devil was

she smiling? This was no smiling matter. Damnation, she had to know that taking her innocence was a hell of a thing to ask of him.

She placed her hands on the ground behind her again and leaned back. "Has the cat got your tongue?" she asked when he remained silent for so long after her provocative statement.

Couldn't she see how weak he was where she was concerned? He had to stop the tension building between them. She was too appealing. It was dangerous for both of them.

"Arianna, you find the most inconvenient times to quote Lord Chesterfield."

"Who is this man Lord Chesterfield? You've mentioned him several times before. Would it be possible for me to meet him some time?"

This might be his salvation. If they talked about Chesterfield, it would surely take his mind off giving her what she wanted and quite possibly ease the heaviness in his breeches, too. Maybe for once in Morgan's life, the pompous Earl of Chesterfield could actually do something to help him.

"You would have to go beyond the grave to do it," Morgan said, "because he died more than thirty years ago. He wasn't so famous during his life, but shortly after his death, more than one hundred letters that he'd written over several years to his son, his godson, and others were published and have now been read by most anyone who can read. That is when and how he acquired his fame."

"He must have been a very intelligent man to have had his letters published."

"Perhaps to some like my grandmother, but to me and my cousins, he was an egotistical braggart who felt it was his duty to bend, shape, and control the life of his adult son."

"Then why do you quote him so often?"

He gave her a quizzical glance and started rubbing the bottom of her foot. "I don't, you do."

She laughed, gently shaking her shoulders. Just looking at her so relaxed made him feel good and warm inside.

"You are a puzzle. I couldn't possibly quote him. I had never heard of him until you mentioned him. You are the one who always mentions him to me."

"I guess that is because he was a good friend to my grandmother," Morgan said, his hand leaving her foot to caress its way up her leg once again and then back to the arch of her foot.

"Tell me about her."

"Lady Elder was an exceptional person in many ways, but there were numerous times in my life when I wished she had never met Lord Chesterfield. If he had not been almost deaf and infirm when she met him, I believe she would have married him."

"I think I would like to read his letters and make up my own mind about him. From what you have told me, he seems such a clever fellow."

Morgan let out a half laugh, half grunt. "Most people considered him a very wise and humorous man who had an artful way of writing words, but my cousins and I never felt that way."

"Simply because you didn't like what he wrote to his son?"

"Not exactly. From the time we were seventeen until my grandmother's death, she sent us a letter at the beginning of each month without fail, and they always contained quotes from Chesterfield."

"She penned a letter to all three of you every month? That's quite amazing."

"Yes. She always started her letters to me with 'My dearest grandson Lucas,' knowing that no one had called me by my given name since I was twelve. And she always ended her letters with 'Your loving Grandmother, Lady Elder.'"

"I think that makes her sound very protective of you, and very kind."

"I'm sure she considered it one of her great missions in life. The only thing her letters ever said was something along the lines of: 'Here are more wise words from Lord Chesterfield,' and then she would quote something from the exasperatingly pretentious old man."

"Give me an example."

"I tried my best never to remember anything the man said and usually don't until you say something that sounds like one of his quotes."

"All right," she said, "I think it's time we return to our original conversation anyway. Will you show me what happens between a man and a woman when they are all alone on the coast and sitting half dressed under the moonlight?"

She's not going to give up.

Arianna sat on her buttocks and leaned back, supporting herself with her hands open on the ground. The simple white shift she wore lay invitingly against her breasts, her stomach, and the upper part of her legs. He should have insisted she put her cape back on the minute they made it back to Redmond.

The narrow ribbon that held her gown together at her throat had come untied, revealing the hollow of her throat, the gentle slope of her shoulder, and the beautiful rounded swell of her breasts. He glanced down at her foot. Her ankle was cupped in his hands, the sole of her foot resting snugly against his abdomen.

Her gorgeous hair spilled invitingly around her shoulders. He remembered that it smelled like a day that had been kissed with sunshine, and it felt like the finest of silk from the Orient.

"You don't intend to answer me, do you?" she said.

His gaze held steady on hers, and he said, "Don't tempt me, Arianna. I'm not as strong as you obviously think I am."

Her gaze whipped down his chest to where he held her foot firmly in his hands, pressed between his legs, and then quickly back up to his eyes. "You look enormously strong to me."

"As Lord Chesterfield was so fond of saying: 'Looks can be deceiving.'"

"I won't let you divert the conversation back to him again, Morgan. I'm asking you to show me what comes after kisses and caresses between a man and a woman. Do you not want to?"

Morgan was hurting. He wanted her so badly. He was a fool to think he could bring her out here, look at her, touch her, and not take her. He wanted her too much. Why did she have to be so eager and so damned responsive to his every touch? Why did she have to encourage him instead of rebuff him?

He told himself to push her away, leave her alone, get on Redmond, and ride like hounds from hell were nipping at his ankles, but he stayed put, caressing her foot. He had lost his willpower to move away from her.

He swallowed hard and managed to say, "Hell, yes, I want to, Arianna. I am not made of stone."

She moved as if to rise up and meet him, but he lifted his hand and said, "No, stay where you are. I want to show you, but I will not."

A gust of wind blew a strand of hair across her face, and she delicately moved it behind her ear, exposing her beautiful slender neck.

"I know what I'm asking is unconventional."

"Immensely so, Arianna."

"I don't think you are giving me enough credit, Morgan. I am old enough to know what I want and to understand what I'm asking of you."

He sighed heavily. "No, I don't think you do. There are always consequences to what you are asking, and I'm not prepared to accept them."

A warm breeze drifted across his face, and he closed his eyes and took a deep, solid breath, wishing the wind had been chilling so it could cool the heat in his loins. He opened his eyes and saw her watching him with wonder, with hunger in her eyes, and he knew what he must do.

He moved her foot so he could run his palm under her arch. He let his fingers slide in between her toes, and his gaze slid up her ankle, to her long and shapely leg, to her knee.

Right now, the way she was looking at him, the way he was feeling about her, he didn't care if he ever got her back to the house. He was thinking, propriety be damned, and innocence could go to the devil. Would it really be so bad to be leg-shackled if it was to this tempting lady before him, who was so eager for his touch and all that he could show her and all he could make her feel?

"You think I would make demands on you, don't you?" she questioned him in a soft voice.

"It has crossed my mind," he admitted honestly, his open palm moving to her thigh with light caresses.

Every time he rubbed up, he went a little farther up her leg. With as little distraction as possible, he rose up from the back of his legs to rest his weight on his knees so he could continue on his present course. He caressed past her knee and let his hand disappear beneath the hem of her nightshift.

"I know you have no reason to trust in what I say, but I assure you I would not cry foul should anything unfortunate befall me from actions you took at my request."

His hand inched farther up until he found her soft inner thigh, letting his fingers stop and hover just short of the center of her legs.

Her breathing quickened. Her eyes rounded with surprise. As he very lightly touched her warm skin, making it pebble with anticipation of what was to come, she gasped and trembled. It felt damn good to see how he was making her feel.

"I do believe it is easy enough to say that now, Arianna, while you want the education I could give you."

Education? Had he really said that?

He stroked down with the pads of his fingers and up with the backs of his nails, loving the feel of her bare, heated skin. Her lips were slightly parted. Her shallow breaths were short and choppy, making her chest heave. He watched and savored the tremors of expectancy that shook her body.

"I suppose," she said in a breathy voice, "that it is easier for me to say than it is for you to believe."

"Most definitely."

Morgan smiled. He was having the desired effect on her. She was having trouble focusing on their conversation, and Morgan loved the way he was making her feel. He moved his fingers to her innermost warmth, and she gasped again.

Her body tensed and then tightened. Her thighs caught his arm like a clamp. A trace of fear outlined her eyes, but he knew it would soon disappear and be replaced with a sensation so glorious that it couldn't be adequately described by mere words.

It was almost killing him to do it, but somehow, from somewhere, he had found his willpower. He remembered when Gibby had talked about how a pugilist had to find his bottom to know the depth of his strength, and Morgan was determined to find his inner strength, too.

He took his time, keeping his gaze riveted on her eyes, teasing her, barely touching her center, but treasuring every moment.

"Open for me, Arianna," he whispered huskily.

She hesitated, but that didn't surprise him. She knew what she wanted, but she was still unsure about what exactly would happen. Her thighs parted only a little.

"Open for me," he whispered again.

When her thighs slowly relaxed against his arm, he parted the folds of her womanhood and found her soft, moist center with his thumb. He was careful not to enter her. It would give her more pleasure, but that was more than he was willing to take from her future husband. He only rubbed, circled, and explored her riches.

He took his time and was careful how, when, and where he touched her. He didn't want this experience to go too fast for her or for him. Even though it was exquisite pain for him, he wanted her to enjoy and savor the spreading, languorous warmth of being awakened to hot, indescribable desire, and then feasting on the climax of it.

And she was getting close.

Her raspy intake of breath thrilled him. His body protested its absence of participation in what was obviously giving her so much pleasure, but he savored every minuscule touch of her. The center of her desire was where he wanted to be with the heavy thickness between his legs, but he would settle for the gentle touch of his fingers and give her what she desired.

"I'm not sure what you are doing to me, Morgan, but is it supposed to make me feel like my heart might stop beating?"

He chuckled softly. "That is exactly how you are supposed to feel."

"I might stop breathing, too," she whispered breathlessly.

"If your heart stops beating, you will definitely stop breathing, but I don't think either of those things will actually happen."

She had wanted to know how a man could make a woman feel, and he was showing her the shortcut way. By doing this, they would both be somewhat satisfied. After it was over, she would still be a virgin, and while she wouldn't exactly be untouched, he wouldn't feel duty bound to marry her.

Her dampness gave him the indication that she was ready, so he slipped his thumb over to the small nub of her core, and within seconds her thighs slammed against his hand and arm. She closed her eyes, threw her head back, and moaned softly, her body pumping against his hand and arm. And then slowly, slowly, she stopped, relaxed, and fell back onto the ground, gasping for breath.

Morgan looked at her and smiled even as his body protested that it too needed release. Her face was serene, beautiful. He had never pleasured a woman without taking his own pleasure, too. But tonight, it seemed the right thing for him to do, and somehow he'd managed. He felt quite good about that.

He had enjoyed giving her pleasure, and now she wanted to lie still and bask in the glow of fulfillment, but he couldn't allow that. Dawn was fast approaching, and they would have to ride like the wind to get her back inside her room before the servants started stirring.

One thing was for sure; he now knew that he would have to see her while he was in London. There was no way he could not call on her and see that all was well with her. He didn't know why he hadn't told Arianna or Constance that he would be traveling to London as well in a few days. He rather liked the idea of surprising them both. He would give Arianna time to get settled, and then he would pay her a visit.

"Arianna, I hate to disturb your peacefulness, but we must go."

She opened her eyes, pulled her nightshift over her legs, and sat up. "I've never felt that way before. It was as if one moment I was soaring through the air without wings, and then suddenly I exploded. What did you do to me?"

Morgan smiled, chuckled low in his throat, and started pulling on his stockings. "There are a number of different ways to explain it, but I think the best way for me to say it to you is simply to say that I satisfied you, did I not?"

"Without question. Completely."

Hearing her say that made him feel damned good. "That is what I set out to do."

"But what about you?"

"What do you mean?" he asked, rolling down the legs of his riding breeches.

"I have not satisfied you, and while I don't know everything about the intimate life between a man and a woman, I do know I was supposed to do the same for you."

He grabbed a boot and shoved his foot inside. "That is not always the case, Arianna. In some cases, such as this, it is perfectly acceptable for one person to be satisfied and not the other."

Concern shadowed her face, and he thought he saw a touch of sadness in her eyes. She grabbed one of her shoes and slipped it on her foot.

"Why the long face?" he asked.

"Your explanation seems unfair," she argued, putting on her other shoe.

He rose and settled his feet into his boots. "Nonsense, Arianna."

"It's not nonsense. I'm disappointed you didn't want me to satisfy you. Is it that you didn't think me capable?"

"Of course not. That's not true." He then bent down and took her hands in his and helped her rise. He looked directly into her eyes and said, "Hear my words: my desire for you is great, but my desire to keep you an innocent miss is far greater. Do you understand what I am saying?"

The concern on her face deepened. "Of course, I understand. I am not a simpleton. I do not agree with you."

He frowned. "You don't agree with what?"

"I do not agree with keeping me a maiden."

Morgan took a deep breath, reached down and picked up his coat, and shook it. He shoved his arms into the sleeves and fitted it over his shoulders while thinking about how to respond to her.

He looked at Arianna and with blunt honesty said, "Then the only option you have is to find someone else willing to relieve you of that, Arianna. I will not."

Fifteen

My Dearest Grandson Lucas,

What do you have to say about these wise words from Lord Chesterfield? "When evils are incurable, it may be the part of one friend to conceal them from another."

Your loving Grandmother,
Lady Elder

"YOU SHOULDN'T BE HELPING ME WITH THE WORK, MISS Ari, it isn't right."

"I believe I told you I didn't want to hear such nonsense as that again, Beabe," Arianna said, reaching into another barrel and gently pulling out a large piece of bright red cloth. She carefully laid it on the kitchen table of her new home and opened the bundle.

"But you have more important things to do than maid's work."

"At the moment it is important to me that I preserve as many of my father's vials, potions, and

tonics as possible. It's more than an hour before I have
to leave to meet with Mr. Warburton. Besides, I am
letting you and the other servants take care of most of
the unpacking. Which leads me to ask, how are you
getting along with the new staff?"

"Me?" Beabe said as she opened a small box and
looked inside. "I'm getting along fine with them, but
I think they are wary of me."

"You? Why would they? You are one of the most
pleasant people I know."

"I think it's because I've been with you for over ten
years, and they think I will get special treatment."

"And you will."

Beabe's hands went still, her eyes widened, and her
mouth formed an oh. Arianna laughed at her maid's
shocked expression.

"Don't look so surprised. Remember, you saved
my life when we were put off that ship in Egypt. You
found us a safe place to stay, and you took care of me.
You will always be special to me."

"It was mostly your father's medicines that saved
your life, Miss Ari."

"But you were there to give them to me. But don't
worry, I will make sure that Lady Raceworth's former
employees know that I'm very pleased they stayed on
and will now work for me. And in time they will see
that I'm fair with them."

"They should have known that when you didn't
turn off any of them after you took possession of
the house."

"I do believe they were all pleased about that. And
I don't mind earning their respect and their trust," she

answered and looked at the label on the bottle she was holding. "And you shouldn't either."

"I don't. They won't have cause to find fault with me."

"Good, because I am so pleased to be settled, Beabe. I never dreamed we could lease a house so quickly. And that it was already staffed and had enough furniture for us to get by until I can purchase more was a godsend. And it's the perfect size for me. I had fears of it taking weeks to get settled."

"Mrs. Pepperfield knows how to get things done; that's for sure."

Arianna unwrapped another bottle from the red cloth and looked at it. Her stomach did a flip. It was the same mixture that she had given to Morgan when he hurt his hip. Suddenly, vivid memories flashed through her mind of when she was nestled with Morgan on his horse, to their passionate kisses in her room, to when she was sitting on the coast with his hands divinely working their magic on her body. She squeezed her eyes shut and lightly shook her head. Taking a deep breath, she placed the dried concoction in line with all the other small bottles with cork tops. She hoped the day would come when she could think of Lord Morgandale and not feel such overwhelming longing.

It had been a week since she'd seen him, but already it felt like years. He had been most circumspect on the morning she left Valleydale. He didn't come below stairs until it was time for her and Constance to board the large, comfortable coach that had brought them to London. He had been the perfect gentleman when he walked them outside, chatting easily about how the remarkably good weather would make their journey shorter.

She would have loved to have seen a possessive smile from him or feel a brief squeeze of her fingers as he helped her board the coach, but he had been the perfect, distant gentleman, leaving her no doubt that he felt none of the things for her that she had felt for him. There was nothing about his manner or his words that would have suggested that only a few hours earlier, he'd awakened her womanly desires and showed them how to flourish.

Arianna took in a deep, cleansing breath, trying to clear her thoughts. She missed the earl desperately and wanted to see him again so badly that there was a constant ache in her chest. She had decided that after she finished her work for her father, she would make a visit to Valleydale to thank him for all his help.

She reached into the bottom of the barrel and pulled out a piece of dark blue fabric. In India, she had lined all the barrels with straw and then used fabrics as an extra cushion for the contents on the long voyage, knowing she could make the material into dresses when she settled in London. She ran her hand over the very fine cloth, feeling its slightly rough texture. She immediately knew the fabric would be a stunning color for Morgan. It would highlight his beautiful blue eyes.

As Arianna stared at the fabric, an idea popped into her mind. She would have a banyan made out of the fabric for Morgan. She had read somewhere that the long coat with a banded collar, that had long been fashionable in India, had become quite popular in England, too. Though the article stated that most of the gentlemen who had them wore them only in their homes and not out in Society. Presenting the coat to him for his kindness toward her would be the perfect reason to visit Valleydale and see him again.

Arianna hugged the fabric to her chest and smiled.

"What's made you so happy?" Beabe asked.

"Oh," Arianna said, having forgotten for a moment that her maid was in the room, "I was just thinking how delighted I am that all of these bottles and jars seem to have made the trip across the seas in perfect condition."

"Excuse me, Miss Sweet."

Arianna turned to see her new housekeeper, Mrs. Hartford, standing in the doorway.

"Yes?" she said with a smile for the tall, slender woman with small eyes and thin lips.

"Mrs. Pepperfield is here to see you. I hope it's all right that I asked her to wait in the drawing room for you."

"Yes, of course. I wasn't expecting her, but I have time to see her before I must leave. Beabe, I'll let you add these bottles I've lined up on the table to that shelf in the cupboard that I designated for healing aids."

"Yes, Miss Ari."

Arianna left the kitchen and headed toward the small drawing room of the house. She was indebted to Constance, too, for all the help she'd given her. Arianna knew she had packed some exquisite fabrics in the storage barrels, and after all of them had been unpacked, she would pick out a trio of the finest and present them to Constance as a gift.

Constance rose from the settee when Arianna walked in.

"How lovely to see you so soon," Arianna said.

"I would never have called on you this early if I didn't have good news."

Arianna's breaths shortened. Did she have word from Morgan?

"Nonsense. You can call on me at any time. Sit down and tell me," Arianna said. "May I get you a cup of tea or other refreshment?"

"No, no, I can't stay. I'm not even going to sit down again. I only wanted you to know that I've set up two appointments for you next week to meet prospective companions."

"So soon. How wonderful," Arianna said, hoping disappointment that the news wasn't about Morgan didn't show as much on her face as it felt in her heart.

What was she thinking?

Constance would have no reason to come rushing over to tell her anything about Morgan, even if she had heard from him. And Arianna would have loved to ask her if she had, but she didn't.

"I wrote down the dates and times. I hope they work for you." She handed the folded paper to Arianna.

"Thank you. I'll make sure they do. I'm at a loss for how to deeply thank you for all you've done."

Constance smiled. "I was happy to aid you for Morgan. He and his two cousins have been my friends for a long time."

"Yes, of course," Arianna said.

"But had I not liked you the moment I saw you, I would not have done as much as I have. There's something about you that I find intriguing and deserving of help."

Arianna stared into Constance's sympathetic eyes.

For a moment, she had the desire to drop to her knees and pour out to Constance what had happened to her father and the fear she had that Rajaratnum would sell the formula to someone who would make it known to the world before she could find it and present it in her father's name. But Arianna swallowed hard and let the moment pass.

She simply said, "Finding this house for me, helping me get to the freight company, all the things you've done. You have been my salvation, Constance."

"What poppycock." Constance's green eyes sparkled, and she laughed. "But I do like for people to lavish praise on me. It was destiny that you should have this house. I had nothing to do with it. Now I have one other thing to ask, and I won't take no for an answer."

Arianna smiled. "What?"

"Lord Windham and her ladyship are having a party on Saturday night, and I want you to go with me. We will be companions for each other."

"A party? I'm not sure. I'm certain I don't have proper clothing for a party, and I—"

"Of course, you do," Constance said, interrupting her. "You just don't know it yet. Why do you think I wanted to borrow your green dress with the gold threads circling the hem of the skirt?"

"I don't know."

"To give it to my modiste, of course, so she would have your measurements and could start making your gown." Constance started walking toward the doorway, and Arianna followed her. "I'll pick you up at half past eleven tomorrow to take you to your first fitting."

"Ah—I… but you don't understand. I have other things to do. I… my father's papers. That is, I won't feel right about going to parties until I have certain things completed."

Constance stopped walking. "You seem flustered."

"Maybe a little. I, you've been so kind to me. I hate to tell you no."

"I hope I wasn't too forward in having the gown made. I meant it as a good surprise, not a bad one."

Arianna hesitated when she saw concern on Constance's face. "Of course you did. All right, I will go with you to this one party. But I must get my father's work finished before I start spending my days with a modiste and my evenings at parties. I hope you understand."

Constance smiled kindly. "I understand. In fact, I think I rather like the idea that you attend only one party, and then you won't be seen again for a time. That will certainly add a bit of mystery to you. Everyone will be asking about you and wondering when you'll reappear."

"They will?"

"Absolutely. If there is anything Londoners love, it's a mystery. Look how the entire Town is in a dither over the twins."

"The twins?"

"I don't have time to explain about them or their older brother Viscount Brentwood right now, as I'm late for an appointment." Constance headed down the corridor toward the front door. "See you tomorrow."

Arianna slumped against the door after she shut it behind Constance. Attending a party was the last thing she wanted to do, but how could she decline after all Constance had done to help her? Arianna looked at the tall clock in the vestibule. Thankfully, it was time for her to go see Mr. Warburton.

∽

An hour later, Arianna sat in the drawing room of Mr. Robert Warburton's house, waiting impatiently for him to see her. Beabe had perched herself on the farthest window seat and was quietly working on her knitting. Arianna had already finished two cups of tea and had nibbled on an apple tart.

She wouldn't have minded so much the man being so terribly late had she not had an appointment with him. The first day she arrived in London she had written to Mr. Warburton, asking for a scheduled time to see him. She explained that she was most anxious to meet with him but would be available for whatever time and arrangement best suited his schedule. He had given this date and time.

"Miss Sweet, pardon my tardiness," Mr. Warburton said, walking into the drawing room. "I was rushing to get here, but the traffic in London has become ridiculously heavy. Sorry for the delay."

Mr. Warburton was a tall, robust man with a thick gray beard. The crown of his head was completely bald, but the sides and back of his head were covered with bushy gray hair. She had first met the man before she and her father left for India. While there, her father allowed her to read Mr. Warburton's letters, and by the time he first visited them in India three years ago, Arianna felt as though she knew him. Mr. Warburton and her father had worked on many research projects together over the years.

"Please sit back down. I trust your journey from India was uneventful."

She hesitated and then without compunction said, "Yes. It's a long and tiring journey, of course, as you know, but not too many eventful things happened." She had nothing to gain by telling the man she had almost died more than once.

Mr. Warburton seated himself in an upholstered side chair near the settee. "I was devastated to get your letter with the news of your father's passing. Albert Sweet was one of the most intelligent men I've ever had the pleasure of knowing, and he'll be missed by me and the Royal Apothecary Scientific Academy members."

"Thank you for the kind words about my father." Arianna moved to the edge of the settee. "Mr. Warburton, I must tell you that my father didn't just pass away."

He frowned. "What do you mean?"

"He was—my father was murdered."

The man jerked back and blinked rapidly. "My goodness, Miss Sweet, surely you don't mean that."

"I do. My maid and I came home one afternoon to find his *bhagidar,* Rajaratnum, standing over his body. The man stole my father's private journal before he fled."

Mr. Warburton shook his head and made a clucking noise low in his throat before saying, "I find that difficult to believe. As you know, I met Rajaratnum when I visited your father in India a year ago. He was very respectful and, perhaps, even in awe of your father."

"Nonetheless, it's true. My maid and I saw him standing over my father's body."

"Good heavens! But why? Why would he do it?"

"I can only assume it was because my father was working on a formula that he had kept very secret. I think Mr. Rajaratnum killed my father and stole his journal with the formula in it because he wanted to sell the formula to someone else."

"I knew your father was working on something he considered extraordinary, but then Albert worked on many different experiments, so I'm not sure which one you are referring to."

Arianna felt a moment's hesitation now that it had actually come to the point of her telling Mr. Warburton about her father's discovery. But she had to put jumpy feelings aside and remember that her father had trusted this man, and she must trust him, too.

"My father had discovered what he thought could be a cure for consumption."

Mr. Warburton moved to the edge of his seat. "My dear girl, that would be a very important find."

"My father knew that, which is why when he was killed, we were already making plans to return to England for him to present his findings to the Academy. I believe Mr. Rajaratnum stole the formula either to sell to someone else or to present the findings in his own name in a country other than India."

"That seems farfetched to me, child."

Arianna bristled. "I am not a child, Mr. Warburton. And I can come up with no other reason why my father's partner would betray him, kill him, and steal his private journal of formulas."

Mr. Warburton sat back in his chair and pulled lightly on his beard. "You are right. You are not a child. I do keep up with the latest discoveries in remedies, medicines, and the like, and I can assure you no one has come forward with anything to do with consumption. That kind of news would travel very fast."

"Good, that means Mr. Rajaratnum hasn't managed to sell the formula, or if he has, whoever has it isn't ready to make the formula known."

"If anyone does, of course I'll be the first one to go to the Royal Apothecary Scientific Academy and object to the claim on your father's behalf."

Arianna smiled and relaxed a little. "Thank you, I appreciate that. I hope there is something else you can do to help me, that is, for my father."

He held up his hands. "If I can help, I will, but I have no desire to get embroiled with intrigue," he said and shook his head, letting Arianna know he had little patience.

"Mr. Warburton, I have all my father's research papers, books, and journals, except, of course, the one Mr. Rajaratnum stole. I was hoping you would go through them and help me either find or reconstruct the formula, and then present it to the Academy for him before someone takes the credit my father deserves."

"Do you have all his notes from this particular experiment in one journal?"

"No. All I know is that the formula is somewhere in his papers, and they are quite extensive."

The old man chuckled. "I would think so. He was in India a long time."

"I was my father's assistant long before Mr. Rajaratnum came along, and even after he joined my father, Father still allowed me to rewrite some of his papers and notes for him in a neater hand during the evenings. I can read everything, but much of it I don't understand. I need your help to find the right formula among all his written experiments."

"That seems as though it would be a huge undertaking, Miss Sweet, and I have my own research going on that takes so much of my time. I've gotten old, and I'm not as fast as I used to be."

Arianna leaned forward in desperation, feeling her best chance of finding the formula slipping through her fingers. "But you must, Mr. Warburton. If you won't, I will have to struggle through his papers on my own or go to someone I don't know. I shudder to even think about my father's life's work being handled by a stranger."

His eyes softened, and he pulled on the end of his gray beard again. "I understand your reluctance in doing that. Let me think on it, and maybe I can come up with the name of someone trustworthy who might be able to help you."

"No," she said firmly, resignation setting in. "I really can't trust anyone but you not to take my father's discovery and make it their own."

He sighed heavily. "I'm afraid that's the best I can do for now."

"Thank you, but I think I should like to try finding it on my own first." She rose. "I'm sorry to have troubled you."

He stood up. "You are no trouble, dear girl. I wish

I could be of more help. I'm more than willing to make inquiries for you."

❧

Overton, Gibby's stiff butler, stood to the side and allowed Morgan to walk into the house.

"Would you like me to make you a cup of tea, Lord Morgandale, or perhaps you'd prefer something stronger?"

"No, thank you, Overton. I'll just sit in the drawing room and wait for Gib."

Morgan had sent Gibby a note yesterday, saying that he would be around to see him late in the afternoon today. But sometimes Sir Randolph Gibson lived by his own rules. He was just as likely not to be home, even if he knew to expect you. But thankfully he hadn't played the disappearing act today.

Morgan rounded the doorway into Gibby's drawing room and was immediately struck by all the bright colors he saw in the room. The bold, cheerful fabrics immediately brought Arianna to his mind. Not that she wasn't already constantly in his thoughts and had been since the evening she arrived at his door, looking like a weary waif.

He didn't know why, but he'd never really noticed the décor of Gibby's drawing room until today. It was spacious and filled with dark wood furniture that was covered in embroidered silk fabrics of astoundingly vibrant colors and patterns in shades so rich and striking that he decided they must have come from the Orient.

The only window in the room was framed with a strikingly bright shade of red draperies. Each velvet panel was tied back with large gold velvet tassels, exposing fancy lace panels covering the panes.

Morgan sat on the chair he had always used, but this was the first time he'd ever noticed that the bright green fabric had a red and black embroidered dragon on the seat and back. He tried to remember the last time he'd been in Gibby's home; it had been several months at least.

Looking around, he wondered if he'd been inattentive of his surroundings through the years or whether the old man had recently redecorated. And if he had, why had he gone to the brilliant colors of the Orient? Morgan remembered the life-size statuaries of Venus and Athena that held up the marble mantle that graced the ornate fireplace. The gold-framed mirror over it was shaped like a large pagoda, so if he had refurbished the house, he hadn't changed those. Morgan couldn't remember ever having seen such vivid reds, yellows, and greens in upholstery before. But with a closer inspection, he could see the fabrics showed signs of aging. Most were frayed and worn.

Suddenly, Morgan knew Gibby hadn't changed anything. He had the same furniture, the same paintings and sconces on the walls, and the same figurines and lamps on the tables that he'd always had.

Morgan had changed. He never noticed color until Arianna. Because of her, Morgan was looking at everything in a new light.

He reached into his pocket and withdrew the empty bottle of perfumed water that he carried with him. He pulled out the stopper, closed his eyes, and inhaled the scent of Arianna. He chuckled to himself and recapped it. Every time he opened the small jar and breathed in, he swore it would be the last time.

Had she left the container on purpose to remind him? To tempt him? It was almost empty. Maybe Arianna left it because she had another, or several, and didn't need it. Maybe she expected the maids would simply throw it away. Or had Arianna known the servants would give the remnants of the perfumed water to Mrs. Post and that she would bring the bottle to him for direction? Had she wanted to leave a memento of her time with him? She needn't have bothered. There was no way he could forget her scent or the taste of her.

He looked closely at the bottle for the hundredth time. It had strange writing on it. He could only assume it was the contents of the bottle written in one of the languages of India. When he left Gibby's house, he planned to take it to his apothecary and have the man find someone who could read it, and then have more made for her.

Whenever Morgan thought about the last thing he said to Arianna when they were on the coast, his gut wrenched. Had he really told her to find someone else to take her maidenhead? What kind of fool was he? What madness had possessed him that night? That kind of folly was taking honor too far. She had been in London over a week now. What if she had taken his words to heart and had already found someone to oblige her? His stomach tightened with anger.

What if she…

"Morgan, what's wrong?" Sir Randolph Gibson said, striding into the room with a curious expression on his face and looking as fit as a man half his age.

"What? With me? Nothing!" Morgan said, rising from the side chair.

"There must be. Last I heard you were going to winter at Valleydale, and now here you are back in London."

"I was, but now I'm not," Morgan said, giving Gibby a brief hug and a clap on the back as he tried to push Arianna from his mind.

"So the tranquility of the countryside got to be too much for you, and the debauchery the city offers lured you back into its clutches."

Morgan grinned. "Not exactly."

The old man's eyes brightened and sparkled. "Then what's her name?"

Morgan laughed but didn't say anything. Gibby had always been too damned clever.

"All right," Gibby said, "You don't have to tell me her name. I'll find out soon enough."

And he probably would.

"You are what brought me to London."

"Me?" He raised his thick gray eyebrows. "Don't tell me; let me guess. You were sent here to mind my affairs."

"Someone probably needs to, but I prefer to say I'm here to monitor your affairs."

Gibby smiled, showing unusually straight and healthy teeth for a man in his sixties. "When Blake and Race went missing for a few days last week, they went to see you, didn't they?"

Morgan nodded. "They came to see me."

"And what did the guardian fools tell you that made you want to hightail it back to London before the first frost?"

"That there are adult twins in town who look just like you did when you were a much younger man."

The old man's eyes widened, and he leaned back in the settee as if startled. "There are?"

Morgan laughed. The man was an unbelievably crafty old dandy. "Yes, and you damned well know it, so don't play dumb with me. So what do you have to say about them?"

"Me?" He held out his hands as if showing he had nothing to hide. "I don't have anything to say about them, except that they are fairly handsome fellows."

Morgan shook his head and chuckled again.

"You're not going to talk about them, are you?"

"I'll talk about anything you want to talk about; you know that."

"All right, let's take this one question at a time," Morgan said. "Did you know there were two men in London who look just like you?"

"Do you think they look like me?"

"I don't know. I haven't seen them. I just arrived in Town yesterday. I'm going by what Blake and Race said."

Gibby rose. "You can't believe anything those two tell you."

"Except they are not the only ones who have told me about the twins."

"Somebody else rode all the way to Valleydale just to tell you about gossip? Hmm. Wonder who it was?"

"If you must know, it was Constance Pepperfield who also mentioned this to me."

Gibby's eyes narrowed. "So she's the one who brought you back to Town early."

"No, she isn't. You brought me back to Town early. I want to know about these twins."

"So would I. Let me know what you find out. Now tell me, what are you drinking? Is it too early in the afternoon for a nip of brandy? Blake brought a bottle of his favorite over to me that night after my boxing match. I guess he thought I might need it, but I didn't."

"Sure, brandy would go down nicely about now," Morgan said and watched the dapper man walk over to his side table to pour a little splash into two glasses.

Morgan settled back in the chair and made himself comfortable. He knew he'd gotten all he was going to get out of Gibby.

For now.

Sixteen

My Grandson Lucas,

You should never be without a book of Lord Chesterfield's letters. If by some chance you have misplaced yours, let me know and I'll send you another. These words from him should be set to memory. "In the evenings, I recommend to you the company of women of fashion, who have a right to attention, and will be paid it. Their company will smooth your manners, and give you a habit of attention and respect, of which you will find the advantage among men."

Your loving Grandmother,
Lady Elder

ARIANNA SAT IN THE MUSIC ROOM OF HER NEW HOUSE and looked at the vast quantity of books, journals, and papers in front of her. This room had the least amount of furniture in the house, so she had chosen it for her work room.

After her disappointing meeting with Mr. Warburton

a couple of days ago, she'd had the servants move everything out except the pianoforte, which was pushed against the far wall, when she learned that Mrs. Hartford had learned to play the instrument. Arianna enjoyed hearing her play late in the evenings when the house became quiet and before she and the servants retired for the night.

Arianna had a long rectangular table—which was now littered with her father's life's work—and a comfortable chair brought in and set up for her. She knew that somewhere among his writings he had listed the basic ingredients that formulated the medicine he'd created, which he said would cure consumption. He had tested it on several people, and all of them had overcome the illness and were completely well after having several days of treatment with the mixture.

Her father had told her it was written in the journal that he always kept with him, the one that Rajaratnum had stolen, but her father had also told her that if for some reason his journal was lost or destroyed at sea by water damage, or some other mishap, he had it written down elsewhere. He didn't tell her where. At the time, she had no reason to believe she would ever need to know.

She had worked with him enough to know that a lot of medicines and remedies used many of the same compounds and ingredients. It was her hope that if she couldn't find the complete formula, she could find the correct notes, and given time, reconstruct the formula. If Mr. Warburton had agreed to help her, it would have been far faster and easier to distinguish formulas for consumption as opposed to ones that might be for gout or some other ailment.

Arianna looked up at the clock. It was three in the afternoon. She had been in the room since early morning, sorting her father's notes and making her own notes. She didn't know why she had ever agreed to go to a party with Constance tonight. Maybe it was because she already had her modiste making a gown for her. The French dressmaker had wanted Arianna to come back for two more fittings, but thankfully, Arianna had insisted she couldn't possibly do that. Mrs. Hartford had told her the dress had been delivered earlier in the day, and it had been laid out on her bed.

"Why didn't I simply say, 'I can't go'?" Arianna mumbled to herself.

Because Constance had been extremely kind and very helpful, Arianna owed it to her to go and to do her best to have an enjoyable time. The good thing was that Constance easily agreed that she should not go to another party in the near future. She said something about it adding an air of mystery to her.

What nonsense!

Arianna smiled and rested her elbow on the table, placing her chin in the palm of her hand. She was tired. Her eyes were tired, but she must keep reading, every page of every journal, every loose sheet of vellum and foolscap that she had found in every barrel. She pushed thoughts of the party from her mind and returned to reading the long laborious notes and jotting down anything that looked like it might be part of a formula.

Arianna was so deep in thought, when Mrs. Hartford spoke to her from the doorway, she jumped.

"I'm terribly sorry, Miss Sweet. I didn't mean to startle you."

"It's all right, Mrs. Hartford. It wasn't your fault. What can I do for you?"

"The Earl of Morgandale is here to see you."

Arianna gasped. Her throat immediately went dry, and her heart started hammering. "Here in my home?"

The woman gave her a nod. "I showed him into the drawing room."

He had come.

"Good. Thank you, Mrs. Hartford. Tell him I'll be right in to see him."

As soon as I catch my breath! As soon as I straighten my hair!

Had he come all the way from Valleydale just to see her, or had something else brought him to London? It hardly mattered. He had come to see her now. She felt like shouting with joy, but instead she pinched her cheeks and bit her lips to give them color. She pushed stray strands of hair behind her ear and looked down at her dress. She had ink stains on her apron, so she quickly took it off, showing her soft pink morning dress that was banded with light green ribbon around the sleeves, neckline, and waist.

She lowered her arms to her side and sucked in three long, deep breaths. She wouldn't allow herself to speculate about why he had come. She would simply go in and find out, as soon as she managed to settle the rapid beat of her heart, catch her gasping breath, and steady her shaking legs.

After what happened between them on the coast the last night she was at Valleydale, she didn't know if he'd ever want to see her again. He'd made his point about their relationship very clear to her.

A couple of minutes later, as calmly as she could, Arianna walked to the doorway of the drawing room and saw Morgan standing by the window. As if sensing she was there, he turned and stared at her so intently it made her heart rate jump right back up to a maddening level. He filled out his clothes better than any man she had ever seen. His black coat, white shirt, and camel-colored waistcoat fit him the way well-made gloves fit a man's hand. His neckcloth was perfectly yet casually tied, and his hair fell long at his nape, giving him that roguishly handsome appeal.

As Arianna stared at him, she felt weightless and exhilarated and knew more than ever before that she had fallen victim to his charm. No, more than that, it was as she had suspected before—she had fallen in love with him.

"Lord Morgandale," she said, her voice sounding more composed and more confident than she felt as she stepped inside the room and curtseyed. "This is a surprise."

"A pleasant one, I hope," he said, sauntering toward her with a self-assured expression that let her know he knew exactly how pleased she was to see him.

She gave him a tentative smile and walked farther into the room. "Do you even have to ask that?"

"I would never take how you feel about seeing me for granted. I had to come to London to check on an old friend, and while I was out and about today, I thought I should stop by and visit you, too."

So much for thinking she might be the reason for his presence in Town.

"I trust it's nothing serious with your old friend."

A wrinkle of concern formed between his eyes. "Unfortunately, that remains to be seen." He extended something toward her that looked like a book that had been banded with a wide blue ribbon tied in a bow. "Since I was coming by, I thought you might like this."

She noticed his hand as he gave her the book. He had strong, manly, and attractive hands.

Arianna cleared her throat. "Thank you," she said, taking the book. She untied the bow and read aloud the bold black lettering. "Lord Chesterfield's Letters to His Son and to Other Notables." A glow of unexpected pleasure covered her. She looked up at him and smiled. "The man you often spoke about. So he actually wrote letters that were published?"

Morgan's gaze locked on hers curiously, and he asked, "Did you doubt me about the man's existence?"

She moistened her lips and looked down at the book. Heat flooded her cheeks. "Yes, I believe I did."

Morgan chuckled, obviously amused by her honesty. "Then I'm doubly glad I took the time to pick up the book for you to prove Lord Chesterfield was not made up from my imagination. He was a living, breathing man who was quite vain and so full of himself that many now herald his letters as required reading."

"I shall never doubt you again."

His eyes narrowed with humor. "And I doubt that, Arianna. You said you would like to read the letters for yourself and form your own opinion of the man. I'll look forward to hearing what you have to say about him after you've read his letters."

Was he telling her he wanted to see her again, or was

he merely indicating that she should send him a post? "I will get started on it tonight," she said softly, placing the book and ribbon on the small rosewood table behind her. "Thank you. It was kind of you to remember me."

"I will always remember you, Arianna."

A gentle expression softened his gaze and his smile. Arianna had an overwhelming urge to rush into his arms and bury her nose in the warmth of his neck and tell him how much she had missed him. Somehow, she managed to hold herself in check.

"It looks like you are settled into your new home. How do you like it?"

"It's perfect for me," she said softly.

"Good. You look tired."

"No," she said defensively, her hands automatically going to smooth her hair. "I feel in very good health. I've just been very busy since I arrived."

"I can see that. You have ink on your fingers and on your cheek."

"Oh!" She looked down at her hands and quickly raised one hand to rub first on one cheek and then the other with the back of her palm.

Morgan chuckled softly. He took hold of her wrist and slowly lowered her hand down to her side. Her skin prickled with anticipation at his comforting touch.

He stepped closer to her and said, "Allow me." He stuck the pad of his thumb to his tongue, moistened it, and then lightly rubbed her cheek near the corner of her mouth.

The dampness of his thumb, the gentleness of his strokes, and pressure of movements caused a tightening in Arianna's chest that skittered along her breasts. She wanted to grab hold of his hand, place it over her face, and inhale the scent of his palm. She wanted to drown in his warmth and drink in the heavenly smell of shaving soap that lingered on his skin.

"There, that looks better," he said, letting his arm drop to his side.

She lowered her lashes and looked down at her ink-stained fingers. "I'm sorry, my lord. It seems as if you are always catching me when I am not properly attired and ready for guests."

He lifted her chin with the tips of his fingers. She raised her lashes and looked directly into his cool blue eyes. "I don't see that as anything to apologize for. I rather like the fact that I never know if you will be wearing a sari, a dancing costume, or ink."

They chuckled lightly together for a moment. His gaze swept down her face, and her gaze lingered on his eyes. As their laughter died down, Arianna once again had such a great desire to hug him and tell him that she had missed him terribly, but she held that inside and said, "How long will you be in London?"

The merriment faded from his face, and a wrinkle formed between his eyes. "I'm not sure, but I suspect it will keep me here at least until my cousins return."

"And how long will that be?"

"Probably a month or two."

"I see. Tell me, how is Master Brute?"

"Mastered," Morgan said, the smile returning to his face. "He was a difficult horse to break."

Like his master.

"I took a scraping of sugar to him the day before I

left Valleydale with Constance, and I found him quite docile even then."

"You definitely had an influence on him."

"Well," she said shyly and then suddenly said, "Forgive me for not asking you to sit down or offering you refreshment. I don't know what happened to my manners."

He grinned. "Yes, you do. You were so thrilled to see me that you forgot them."

At first she tensed, thinking he had read her thoughts, but quickly realized he was teasing her. And she loved it.

She gave him a knowing smile. "You are exactly right. So now why don't you tell me the real reason you came to see me today."

"So, you know the book on Chesterfield was a ruse. I came for this," he said. His hand cupped her neck, his fingers sliding around to grasp her nape. His thumb caressed the soft lobe of her ear, and his face moved closer and closer to hers. Her heart fluttered; her stomach quickened. She had longed to be this close to him once again. She had dreamed he would come to her again.

Desire for her shone in his eyes, and it elated her. He hadn't been able to forget her either. She felt the tremble of wanting in his touch. His longing for her had not been sated any more than hers had been for him. What he had done for her when they were up on the coast that night only made her ache for more.

As he lowered his head and closed his eyes, Arianna heard his intake of breath. His breath fanned her face, and his lips touched hers with a kiss that was possessive yet cherishing. Soothing warmth flooded her. She had wanted this, too.

She relaxed and leaned into him. His lips pressed hers harder and became more demanding. With natural ease, her mouth opened, and his tongue slipped inside, tasting her briefly before kissing his way down her neck.

"Mmm, I've missed you," he murmured and breathed in deeply, kissing the crook of her neck and then over to the hollow of her throat. "I've missed you, Arianna," he whispered a second time. "I haven't been able to get thoughts of you, the taste of you, or the smell of you out of my mind."

Morgan's words sent a shimmering thrill spiraling through her.

He had missed her!

"I consider that a good thing, my lord," she whispered and rained kisses on his cheek, over his jawline, and down his firm neck.

A hunger she couldn't control clawed inside her, and she wrapped her arms around his neck and pulled him closer. His arms circled her back and caught her up tight against his chest. His tongue probed her mouth, and his lips searched wantonly over hers. His hand slid up past her waist to cover, cup, and caress her breast.

Arianna sighed. Immense pleasure coated her like a warm blanket, and she gave herself up to the wonderful sensations exploding inside her.

But as she tried to get closer to him, suddenly Morgan stepped away from her.

Arianna blinked rapidly, feeling rebuffed and confused.

"Damnation," he whispered under his raspy breath. "I don't know why I can't control my passions when I'm with you, Arianna. I think to take one little kiss, and before I know it, I'm ravishing you."

She swallowed hard and said, "I don't feel ravished. I don't feel violated, Morgan. And I don't know why I continue to let you trample on my affection for you."

"Arianna, the only thing I can offer you is desire. You are a lady and deserving of more from a man than his passion."

"I haven't asked for anything more than passion from you."

He advanced on her. "You really want me to make you my lover?"

No, I want you to love me!

"*Bapre*, Morgan!"

He frowned. "What does *bapre* mean?"

A hesitant laugh blew past her lips, and she shook her head. "It's a curse. Not a bad one, but swearing nonetheless."

"I thought so."

"I am almost twenty-eight years old with no prospect of marriage any time soon. What does it matter whether or not I remain a maiden at my age?"

"You know it matters to me."

She didn't know exactly why, but anger suddenly welled up inside her. "Yes, I do know. You have made me aware of that time and time again. Now, let me make you aware of this, Morgan: do not ever kiss me again unless you intend to follow through with your kisses and make me your lover. I don't want any more of your kisses that lead nowhere. Now excuse me. I have work to do. I'll send Mrs. Hartford to show you out."

❧

Her words stung.

Hours later, Morgan was still feeling the effects of her parting words. Feeling out of sorts with himself and not knowing what to do about it. Late in the evening, Morgan decided to dress and go to Lady Windham's party. He handed off his coat, hat, and gloves to the servant at the countess's door and went in search of a pretty miss he could ask for a dance. The best way to get Arianna off his mind was to replace thoughts of her with an equally beautiful and charming lady. And at Lady Windham's party, that shouldn't be too difficult to do. She was known for always having the cream of Society at her affairs.

When he had first arrived in London a few days ago, he'd thought about calling on Miss Goodbody, but for reasons he didn't even try to comprehend, he had no desire to reacquaint himself with her or any other paid woman. For reasons that only his body knew, he couldn't seem to think about touching, tasting, or even kissing anyone but Arianna. He hoped to put a stop to that kind of thinking tonight.

Perhaps some new lady had arrived in Town while he'd been away, he thought and looked at the crush of people filling the house. If not, surely there would be a charming lady he could talk to and dance with to put him in a better frame of mind than his present one. He refused to believe that only Arianna could enchant him.

And there was also the chance that he might meet

the twins his cousins had told him about. He'd really like the opportunity to see them and decide for himself if he thought they looked just like Gibby. Perhaps Constance and his cousins had simply fallen victim to the gossip gadding about Town.

Morgan saw Constance standing on the far side of the crowded room and started toward her. Now there was a woman whose company he could certainly enjoy. As he waded through elegantly dressed ladies and fashionably suited gentlemen, his gaze strayed to the dance floor. Suddenly he stopped. Was that Arianna on the dance floor, dressed in that flowing alabaster-colored gown with an indecently low neckline? And who the devil was she dancing with? He'd never seen that lad before. He couldn't be more than twenty if he was a day. What was she doing dancing with someone so young at her age? What the devil was she doing dancing anyway? She'd been ill with a fever for weeks. If she became overly tired, she could have a relapse. He remembered she had looked a little peaked when he saw her at her house earlier in the day. It was well after one o'clock in the morning. She should be in bed, reading the book he had given her, not twirling under some young blade's arm and laughing at his inane jokes.

He'd have a word with Constance. What was that woman thinking to drag Arianna to balls and keep her out to all hours of the night? Constance knew how ill she'd been.

Morgan swiped a glass of wine from the tray of a server passing him. He picked his way through the noisy, bustling crowd, ignoring friendly smiles, bumping shoulders, and sidestepping groups that had gathered to chat, until he finally made it to where Constance stood. She was trying her best to get away from Lord Snellingly. Any other time, Morgan would never approach anyone if that man was nearby. He was a fop of the highest order and could irritate the wool off a lamb with his incessant talk of poetry.

"Good evening, Constance, Snellingly," Morgan said, walking up to them and trying his best to hide his growing irritation.

Constance greeted him with a grateful smile and hello, as did Snellingly, who immediately sniffed into his lace handkerchief after speaking. The man had so many ruffles on the cuffs of his sleeves, his hands were completely hidden by the frills.

"You look lovely tonight, Constance," Morgan said, though he had hardly even looked at her. He had eyes for no one but Arianna.

"Thank you, my lord. I'm surprised to see you here. When last we spoke, you planned to stay all winter in Dorset."

"Yes, that was my plan, but a business matter brought me back to Town."

"Morgandale," Lord Snellingly said, "you are just the person I wanted to see."

Bloody hell!

Morgan grimaced and mumbled, "That can't be good."

Snellingly lifted his chin a little higher, which must have been difficult to do, considering his collar and neckcloth were already so ridiculously high on his neck he looked like a baby bird trying to see over his nest.

"I beg your pardon; I didn't understand you."

Morgan cleared his throat. "I said then it's good that I walked up."

Snellingly smiled. "Oh, right. I was hoping I might be able to persuade you to join me and a small group of other friends tomorrow evening at my home for some poetry readings. I was just trying to talk Mrs. Pepperfield into joining us, too."

Morgan scowled at Constance and then turned to the earl and said, "I'm certain I can't, Snellingly, I'm otherwise committed. Perhaps another time. Would you excuse us? I need a private word with Mrs. Pepperfield about Miss Sweet."

"So you've met her, too," Snellingly said. He let his eyes flutter between open and closed and sniffed into his handkerchief again. "She has the face of an angel and the voice of a lark." He smiled at Morgan. "I met her earlier, and she's promised me a dance."

Over my dead body.

Morgan threw a questioning glance toward Constance, took hold of her elbow, and started propelling her away from the astonished earl.

"What do you mean by having Miss Sweet out this late and letting her dance with every fop, fribble, and popinjay who asks?"

Surprise lit in Constance's eyes, and she stepped away from Morgan. She set her gaze firmly on his and said, "I will forgive you for your tone and your implication this once. If you want to know anything from me, you had best use the puffery you were so famous for when you asked me to travel to Valleydale."

Morgan relaxed. "You're right. I was out of line. Forgive me."

"That's better."

"I wasn't expecting to see her here, dancing."

Looking so beautiful, so enticing, so womanly!

"Why shouldn't she?"

"She's just getting over her sickness. You don't know how ill she was when she came to Valleydale. I wouldn't like to see her sick again."

Constance studied him, clearly not moved to believe him. "We've been in London almost two weeks. She's in fine shape now, Morgan, and quite frankly, I think dancing is good for her. I believe one of the things she has needed is entertainment. With her father's death, the long journey, and her recent illness, I believe she deserves a little enjoyment in her life."

Morgan looked back to the dance floor. She did look as if she were having a marvelous time.

"I bow to your knowing what is best for her."

"I think what is best for her is marriage."

Morgan's gaze darted back to Constance. "What?"

"You heard me. She's a beautiful lady of quality with means. She's not married at twenty-seven because she hasn't been in London to have a Season or to be a part of the marriage mart. No doubt, if she let it be known at this party that she was available, she'd have offers before sunrise."

Constance's words stunned Morgan, but he believed them to be true. He looked back at the dance floor and saw the young man walking Arianna toward them. They were talking and smiling at each other. Morgan's stomach constricted. She was the most gorgeous woman he'd ever seen. Her light auburn hair was swept up on her head with small golden leaves woven through it. She wore long earrings that looked like hundreds of golden threads tied together. The waistline of her dress fit tightly underneath her breasts and was banded by golden-colored cord, and the skirt fell to the floor in what looked like shimmering layers of gossamer-thin alabaster.

The blade handed Arianna over to Constance, excused himself, bowed to Arianna, and walked away. Suddenly, Morgan knew what he didn't want to believe. He was jealous. He was filled with it, enraged by it, and he didn't know what to do about it. He had never cared enough about a woman to be jealous if another man showed interest in her, but Arianna was different. With her, he didn't want anyone else touching her. When had this happened, and what was he going to do about it?

"Good evening, Lord Morgandale."

She curtseyed and said his name so properly he wanted to tell her to cut the poppycock and call him Morgan, but he dared not be so bold in front of Constance.

"Good evening, Miss Sweet. May I say that gown is quite fetching on you."

And you are so seductive you couldn't keep me from ravishing you if we were alone right now!

"No doubt you like the very proper color," she said.

"Yes," he said tightly, wondering why the devil Constance had the damned gown cut so low Arianna couldn't help but have every man in the house drooling over her beautifully rounded breasts. "It's the perfect color for you," he answered, remembering that she loved bright, vivid color, not neutrals.

"Hello, Morgan, fancy seeing you here. Mrs. Pepperfield, how are you this evening? And who is this lovely young lady standing between the two of you? I know I haven't met her because, even at my age, I would have remembered her."

Morgan turned and faced Gibby, taking a moment to collect himself as he made perfunctory introductions. He was so smitten with Arianna that he'd forgotten about Gibby and the twins who were rumored to look just like him.

"Miss Sweet, I hear a hint of an eastern accent. Have you been in the Orient?"

She smiled at Gibby and said, "Until very recently, Sir Randolph, I was in Bombay."

Gibby's eyes brightened. "I was there once many years ago. Fascinating city and culture. And how are you this evening, Morgan? I trust you have seen everyone you came to see?"

Morgan glanced at Arianna and then back to Gibby and said, "Yes and no."

Gibby smiled and said, "I think I understand that."

Morgan was certain he did.

"Excuse me, Miss Sweet, but I believe this is the dance you promised to me."

Morgan turned to see who had spoken to Arianna, and he felt like a big, meaty fist landed in his stomach, taking his breath away. The man smiling at Arianna was the spitting image of Gibby—tall, broad-shouldered, handsome. They had the same eyes, the same smile, and the same nose. Morgan watched the man walk away with Arianna and was absolutely speechless.

Realizing he had a glass of wine in his hand,

Morgan took a long drink before looking at Gibby and saying, "Did you see him?"

Gibby looked at Morgan as if he'd lost his mind. "The man who left with Miss Sweet?"

Morgan wiped the corner of his mouth with his thumb and nodded.

"I saw him," Gibby said.

"He looked just like you."

"You think so?"

Gibby looked as serious as a clergyman on Easter Sunday. Morgan glanced at Constance, who promptly excused herself and walked away.

"I know so," Morgan said, turning back to the old man. "Gib, what the hell happened thirty years ago?"

"Surely after all your grandmother's teachings, you remember Lord Chesterfield's words about that."

"No, Gib, I'm happy to say that I don't."

"A gentleman never gossips about a lady." He patted Morgan a couple of times on his shoulder and walked off.

Seventeen

My Dearest Grandson Lucas,

Read the following from Lord Chesterfield. It's one of the things that made him such a master of decorum. "Wit is so shining a quality, that everybody admires it, most people aim at it, all people fear it, and few love it unless in themselves. A man must have a good share of wit himself to endure it in others. The more wit you have the more good nature and politeness you must show, to induce people to pardon your superiority, for that is no easy matter."

Your loving Grandmother,
Lady Elder

ARIANNA SAT AT HER MAKESHIFT DESK, DILIGENTLY reading through her father's writings. Occasionally she would find a formula and copy it into her notebook, but more often than not, she would have to, at times, stop and allow sadness to consume her. Reading his writings proved more difficult than she had imagined.

Her father had a habit of writing personal comments to himself in the middle of his documentation. Sometimes his words seemed angry, and he would lash out at himself if he expected a formula to work and it hadn't. There were times his words sounded poignant, and at other times hopeful. Every once in a while she would read something that was humorous. And then there were times she would laugh out loud at his wit, and that was when she missed him most of all.

She realized that having these days alone to go over his private papers and journals was a way for her to enjoy being with him once again. It was a way to tell him good-bye and bring closure to his death in a way she hadn't been able to in India.

But other thoughts had occasionally invaded her mind as well through the long days she'd worked in the music room. Despite her best efforts at denial, every once in a while she would stop reading, lay her head on the makeshift desk, and allow Morgan to fill her mind. She remembered their laughter when he held the crab and chased her on the beach. She remembered the warmth of his body and the strength of his chest when they rode Redmond together. But most of all, she remembered his showing her how, by the gentlest of touching in just the right places, to open up a whole new world of passion she had never dreamed existed. Thoughts of Morgan always revived her, lifted her, and gave her the energy to keep going on her father's work until late at night.

She hadn't seen Morgan since Lady Windham's party a few nights ago. He had been so handsome in his cutaway evening coat that fit perfectly over his broad shoulders. He'd seemed angry at her, and she supposed it was because of her parting words to him when he'd come to her house that afternoon and given her Lord Chesterfield's book. She had spoken in haste, and those words were borne out of frustration.

They hadn't said more than a dozen words to each other at the party, but often throughout the evening she had caught him staring at her from across a crowded room. And there were times he had caught her watching him.

He had danced with lovely young ladies, and she had danced with handsome gentlemen, but they hadn't danced with each other. That had been several days ago now, and she hadn't heard from him. But she had thought of him often.

Arianna felt close to Morgan late at night when she finally stopped poring over her father's notes and went up to bed. It was then that she picked up the book on Lord Chesterfield's letters. She was thoroughly enjoying the man's writings. He had great insight to the inner workings of a titled man's mind. But she could easily understand why Morgan hated the fact that his grandmother always sent him quotes from Lord Chesterfield each month. Arianna had never read anything from so arrogant a man as Lord Chesterfield.

"Miss Sweet?"

Arianna laid down her quill and turned to see Mrs. Hartford standing in the doorway of the music room. "Yes?"

"I'm sorry to disturb you, but a Mr. Warburton is here to see you."

Arianna's stomach lurched, and she rose from her chair. Why had he come? It had been almost two weeks since she had gone to see him. "Show him into the drawing room, and tell him I'll be right there."

"Yes, miss."

"No, wait," she said impulsively, untying her apron. "I don't know why he is here, but it probably has something to do with my father's work, so maybe it's best you show him in here. And would you please see to tea and maybe some of those fig tarts we had earlier today?"

"Yes, miss," the housekeeper said but continued to stand in the doorway.

"What is it, Mrs. Hartford?" Arianna said, laying her apron on the back of her chair.

"Begging your pardon, Miss Sweet, but where will the gentleman sit, and where will I place the tea tray?"

Arianna glanced around the room and smiled. She had forgotten for a moment that she'd had all the furniture in the room removed except for her chair and makeshift desk.

"Thank you, Mrs. Hartford. You are right, of course. There is no place to entertain in here. I'm not usually so flustered. Show him to the drawing room, and tell him I will be right there."

Mrs. Hartford smiled, nodded, and left.

Arianna picked up her apron and tried to wipe the ink stains from her hands. She didn't want to wonder why Mr. Warburton had come to see her. It could be as simple as he wanted to check on her and see how she was doing. She wouldn't allow herself the luxury of thinking that he came to offer help. She had been disappointed by him once, and that was enough.

After removing the dried ink as best she could, she walked into the drawing room with a cheerful countenance and said, "Mr. Warburton, how good of you to stop by."

"Miss Sweet," he said, rising from the settee. "You're looking lovely today."

"Thank you. Please, sit back down," she said, taking a side chair to the left of the settee. "I've asked Mrs. Hartford to bring us some tea."

"That's so kind of you, dear girl, but I can't stay long enough for tea today."

"Oh," she said, feeling a stab of regret. "I understand. I know you are very busy with your work."

"I am. But I haven't been able to get your request off my mind, though often I've tried these past few days since you've been to see me. I've studied over what you asked of me, and I've reconsidered."

Her heartbeat started racing, and she felt as if she could hear Redmond's hooves pounding in her ears. "In what way, exactly?"

"I've come to the conclusion that I must help you with your father's work."

Arianna scooted to the edge of her chair. "Do you mean that, Mr. Warburton?"

"Of course, I mean it. I didn't come here just to tease you with the possibility of my input." He chuckled, and his eyes glistened.

"I would be so grateful to have your expertise. I'm carefully going over every note, every journal, and every scrap of paper that my father had ever written on, but it's difficult to know what might be important. I've found lists and notes of various formulas, but so far nothing that I've thought might be the stolen formula."

"That is what I suspected. It would be difficult for you to identify a particular formula, even though you helped him on occasion with his writings. I'm certain many of his research formulas have much of the same basis of ingredients."

"Yes, I've noticed that."

"Why don't you tell me exactly what it was that your father told you about the formula?"

A bittersweet calm settled over Arianna. That afternoon was one of her favorite memories of her father. It was the happiest she had ever seen him, and she welcomed the opportunity to share it.

"I remember he came home late in the day, extremely excited, laughing. He picked me up and hugged me, swinging me around and saying, 'I've found a cure for consumption. I've found a cure, Arianna. Start packing. At last, we're going home to England.'"

"So he was very confident that his latest formula worked."

"Yes," she said, brushing a loose strand of hair behind her ear. "After he settled down, he told me he had tried the mixture he'd created on five different people, and all of them had had miraculous recoveries."

"That's extraordinary," he said.

"I know. He knew. He said he wanted to get his discovery to the Academy so that they could begin their own testing of his formula and see what they had to say about the accuracy of his experiments."

"So what happened after that?"

"Within a few days, we started packing our things and getting ready for our journey. Most of the papers I'm looking at now were shipped to London well before our departure date. I brought some of his journals with me on the journey from India, and I've read through all of them now and made notes."

"I see," he said and rubbed his chin. "Tell me about the journal that was stolen and where you think the formula is now."

"Papa told me he had the formula written in the journal he always carried with him. He said he would keep it with him on the ship, but he realized accidents happened on long voyages, and that the book might get wet or torn or destroyed in some way, so he had also written it down elsewhere."

"And you didn't ask him to tell you specifically where?"

Arianna shook her head. "No, at the time I had no reason to think someone might want to kill him for the formula. He simply said that if I needed to find it, with a little searching, I could."

"Hmm. You know, by even telling you there was another copy, he might have had some forewarning of danger. Finding something as extraordinary as a cure for consumption would be quite a breakthrough for our world. Your father's name would live forever in the Apothecary Society."

"I know," she said, leaning toward him with eagerness. "That is why I must find it and present it to the Academy. Naturally, when I saw Mr. Rajaratnum quickly shove the journal in his coat before he fled, I knew that he had killed Papa to get the formula to sell to someone. But it's been so long now since Papa died, I'm surprised no one has come forward to present the cure."

"Well, that intrigue is probably best left to the authorities, and until the man is caught, you can't know what he had in mind. Perhaps he's not found anyone willing to pay his price. Even if Mr. Rajaratnum had a buyer when he stole it from your father, whomever he sold it to would want to test the formula to make sure it was legitimate before making any claims. That sort of thing takes time."

"I do realize that, and I know time is running out for me to find the formula."

Mr. Warburton clapped his hands against his thighs. "That, my dear girl, is why I've decided I must help you. If the formula proves true, no one deserves the notoriety but your father, and the world deserves the cure; so let's find it."

Sudden tears welled in her eyes. She had needed this man's help. "Thank you, Mr. Warburton."

"Now, now, child, don't cry."

"No, I promise I won't," she said, wiping at the corners of her eyes with the back of her hands. "Please excuse me, but I'm suddenly overcome with joy. For days, I've been reading every word my father has ever written, and sometimes I feel I've made very little progress."

"Why don't you get everything together, as you said, every scrap of paper, even what you have already been over? You never know when you might have missed something. Have it delivered to my residence this afternoon, and I'll get started on it right away."

Arianna smiled gratefully. "I'll see that you get it before night falls."

❦

Beabe rushed Arianna through the front door and slammed it shut. She dropped her packages to the floor and threw the latch.

"*Bapre,* Beabe!" Arianna said, almost stumbling over her skirts. "You don't have reason to be so frightened."

"Yes, I do, Miss Ari," her maid said, leaning against the door, her eyes wild with panic. "It was him. I tell you it was him."

"All right, Beabe, settle down."

"I know you didn't see him, but I'm certain it was that man who killed your father."

"But we are now safely locked in our house with several servants to help protect us if need be. Now, why don't we go into the drawing room?"

Beabe started to pick up the packages. "No, leave them," Arianna said. "We'll get them later. Come sit down with me, and let's talk sensibly about this."

They walked into the drawing room. Beabe rushed over to the nearest window and untied the tassels, letting the velvet panels fall together, covering the window.

"Beabe, leave the other draperies open so it won't be so dark in here. That window overlooks the herb garden, and I don't think anyone is out there. Cook probably just left the garden, as she should be preparing dinner by now. Come sit down with me on the settee."

Beabe's shoulders sagged, but she did as instructed and seated herself on the settee beside Arianna.

Not really knowing whether to believe her, Arianna picked up both Beabe's hands and held them in hers, wanting to give her faithful servant comfort. "Now without the hysterics you showed in the carriage, tell me exactly what you saw when we came out of Mr. Warburton's house.

Unshed tears glistened in the woman's eyes, and Arianna's heart ached for her. "I saw him standing in front of a carriage, not far from Mr. Warburton's house. We looked at each other. I know he recognized me. He turned and climbed into the carriage, and it took off."

"All right. What did he have on? Was he dressed in Indian garb, the banyan coats that are so popular there?"

"No. He was dressed like a fine gentleman."

"Did you ever see Mr. Rajaratnum in a gentleman's clothing the entire time he worked for my father?"

"No, Miss Ari."

"Beabe, you have always been frightened that the man would come after us and try to kill us, haven't you?"

Beabe nodded.

"But you know he has no reason to harm us. We have already told the authorities all we know. We have already identified him as my father's killer. Harming us would not keep the authorities from finding him and bringing him to justice. In fact, it would make them more determined to find him, isn't that right?"

Beabe nodded again.

"Now, is it possible that the man was another Indian who happened to look like Mr. Rajaratnum?"

"It's possible, but I won't ever believe it."

Her words were said with such conviction that Arianna's blood chilled in her veins, but she didn't want Beabe to know that.

"All right, since you are so certain, we'll take extra precautions whenever we leave the house. We will not walk anywhere. We'll always have Benson take us in the carriage. He's quite a sturdy fellow. And I'm certain that should I ever be fortunate enough to see Mr. Rajaratnum, I would not run from him, I would chase him down and beat him about the head and shoulders with my parasol until he was unrecognizable as a person."

Beabe smiled and then laughed.

Arianna smiled, too. "What's this? You don't think I would do it? You laugh, but I am serious."

"I just can't imagine you chasing anyone with your parasol."

Arianna let go of her maid's hands. "But I would. Now, you know what I think?"

"What?"

"I think this is a good time for you to take the time you deserve and go visit your family."

Beabe rose, clutching her skirts in her nervous hands. "No, Miss Ari, this is not a good time for me to leave you."

"You said it wasn't a good time when we first arrived in London, because you wanted to help me get settled in the house. Well, I am settled. You have been away from your family for a long time, Beabe. I know your sister and your aunt want to see you. The journey was difficult for you, too. You deserve the rest. You deserve a month off. Longer, if you want it."

A quiver started in Beabe's bottom lip. "But I don't want to leave you."

"And you never will want to, because you have looked after me for so long."

"And who would be your maid while I'm gone?"

"I'm sure Mrs. Hartford can help me find someone. This time I am insisting you will go to your sister's. Now, no argument. Tomorrow we will have Benson take us to the Station House and check on the schedule for the mail coach, and we'll see about getting you a seat."

Beabe's eyes welled with tears once again. "You won't really force me to leave you, will you?"

Arianna took in a deep breath and rose. "Yes, I will, Beabe. But don't worry, it won't be tomorrow, so don't look so sad. It will take us a few days to make all the arrangements for you. I remember once during our journey a violent storm came up suddenly. The ship was rocking, creaking, banging. The wind was howling viciously. It was cold and damp, and I was so sick, so weak I couldn't lift my hand or my head. Do you remember that time?"

Beabe nodded and seemed calmer.

"I was so exhausted I was ready to give up on life. I asked you to give me enough laudanum so that I would go to sleep and not wake up. Do you remember what you told me?"

Beabe shook her head.

"Yes, you do."

Arianna watched Beabe grow stronger before her eyes. Her clutch on her dress relaxed, her shoulders lifted, her chin jutted out.

"I told you that if it was your destiny for your life to end on that ship, it would happen without any interference from either of us."

"That's right. The same still holds. If it is our destiny for our lives to end at the hands of Mr. Rajaratnum, as my father's did, we cannot stop destiny. We cannot live in fear."

Beabe sniffled and wiped her eyes with the back of her hands. "If I go, will you promise never to leave the house without your parasol?"

Arianna smiled. "Yes, I promise I will always have it with me."

"Perhaps I'll have the tip of it sharpened for you before I go."

Laughing, Arianna said, "I don't think that will be necessary. Besides, I have two interviews tomorrow afternoon for a companion. If either of the ladies suit me, I will hire her. And you know, once I do that, as tiresome as it will be, I will probably never be alone again."

"Excuse me, Miss Sweet, are you all right?"

Arianna turned to see Mrs. Hartford standing in the doorway, a worried expression on her face.

A chill ran up Arianna's spine. Beabe had her jumpier than she'd been since right after her father's death. "Yes, I'm perfectly fine. Why?"

"There are packages strewn all over the floor in the vestibule."

"Oh, I forgot about that, Miss Ari," Beabe said, heading for the doorway. "I'll get them right away and take them to your room."

Arianna turned away from Beabe and Mrs. Hartford

and looked out the window that Beabe hadn't closed. A chill shook her.

What would she do if Beabe was right about Mr. Rajaratnum, and he had come to England, looking for them?

Eighteen

My Dearest Grandson Lucas,

Here are more wise words from Lord Chesterfield. Study on these and remember them. "Be convinced, that there are no persons so insignificant and inconsiderable, but may, some time or other, have it in their power to be of use to you. And remember that fear and hatred are next door neighbors."

Your loving Grandmother,
Lady Elder

"As for leisure time, well, I'm certain you can find no one finer schooled in card games than I am, and you know how we spinsters love our card games, Miss Sweet. Just ask around. Anyone in the ton can tell you all about my skills, and my even temperament, which I must say you won't find many people as composed as I am, even under the most trying of circumstances. I'm not given to fits of vapors or hysterics. And as I mentioned before, I have many other talents, though

I'm quite reluctant to mention all of them myself. However, this kind of interview necessitates it, don't you agree, Miss Sweet?"

"Yes," Arianna said, struggling not to yawn. "This is the time for all your talents to shine."

Arianna had stayed up to the wee hours of the morning, hoping to finish the book on Lord Chesterfield's letters, but still had a few pages to read. Her long days and short nights were finally catching up with her. The rather robust woman with thin gray-streaked hair and big, expressive brown eyes hadn't stopped talking since she walked into the drawing room and sat down. Arianna wanted a companion who could provide lively conversation, but she was now certain she didn't want one who provided constant conversation.

"I think so, too," Miss Gilberta continued. "And I do have many accomplishments to my credit, and talents, as well. Not that you need it of course, Miss Sweet, but I have the most superb washing cream for the face that will give the most delicate luster to your skin, and I don't share my secret with just anyone, but I, of course, would share it with you. It's much easier on the skin than the corn plaster most spinsters use to keep them looking younger long past the years of their youth." She leaned in closer to Arianna, as if she was trying to keep Constance from hearing. "And I have the perfect remedy to prevent your breath from smelling like wine or any other spirits you might be partial to, if you ever need it. Now I'm sure you're not one of them, you understand, but sometimes, we spinsters don't want anyone to know what we've been drinking, if you know what I mean."

"Well, I agree you certainly have plenty of qualifications to recommend you, Miss Gilberta." Arianna reached over and placed her tea cup on the tray and sent a quick, furtive glance to Constance that said she was ready for this interview to end.

Constance rose and clasped her hands in front of her. "We so appreciate your coming today, Miss Gilberta. Miss Sweet has just started her search for a companion, and she has several more interviews to conduct."

"Oh, of course," Miss Gilberta said, placing her dainty cup on the tray, too, and then lifting her stout frame from the settee with a loud grunt. "And I have other interviews as well, so please let me know as soon as you have made a decision."

"Rest assured, I will," Arianna said and smiled pleasantly at the woman.

"Good. I would so despair at hearing that you had your heart set on me only to learn I was no longer available. I think we would get along together delightfully, don't you?"

"Yes, I'm sure we would. Thank you for coming, Miss Gilberta. Mrs. Hartford will see you out."

When Arianna was sure she'd heard the front door close behind Miss Gilberta, she leaned back in the settee and laughed. "If she mentioned spinsters to me once, she must have mentioned them thirty times. I do believe she is obsessed."

"I'm terribly sorry about that," Constance said, looking a little concerned. "She just assumes that if you are looking for a companion instead of a match, you have resigned yourself to being a spinster."

"Hmm," Arianna said with a smile. "I guess you are right about that. The problem is that I don't know that I've resigned myself to that life. I have to admit I've been so busy since I arrived in London that I haven't given much thought to the idea that if I don't marry in the next year, I will definitely be a spinster."

"Arianna, you still have plenty of time before making that decision. You are a beautiful *young* lady. I know you declined gentlemen who were asking to call on you when you were at Lady Windham's party, and that was the right thing to do for now. But take my word for it, you will not be a spinster by the end of next year unless that is what you desire."

Morgan came easily to Arianna's mind, and her heart ached. She had enjoyed dancing with all the gentlemen at Lady Windham's party who'd sought her attention. Most of them were quite handsome and charming, too, but they were not Morgan. She couldn't imagine any of them holding her close, kissing her, and making her feel the way Morgan had… beautiful, desirable, delicious. She didn't mind talking, laughing, and dancing with them, but she didn't want any one of them to touch her in the way Morgan had.

"Thankfully it's not a decision I have to make right now when so many other things are on my mind. Once I have my father's business concluded, I will think about my own life and what I want to do."

"How is the search for your father's formula coming along?"

"Slowly, of course. I had a note from Mr. Warburton this morning, asking if I had missed sending some of my father's papers, documents, or journals to him. I was certain I hadn't, but I checked the house over again to be sure."

"I know how important that is to you. For now, you have all winter to decide if you want to enter the marriage mart next spring. And if you do, I'll be there to help you."

Arianna smiled at her new friend. "Thank you, Constance."

❧

Morgan hurried through the pelting rain and climbed into the waiting carriage. The landau took off with a jolt and a bump down the flooding street in Mayfair. He left his hat and gloves on, since it was only a short ride from his house to The Harbor Lights Gentleman's Club. Autumn was less than a month away, but there was already a nasty chill in the early evening air.

He had taken the time to dress for a party he'd planned to attend later in the evening, but unless his disposition improved, he wasn't sure he would end up going. He might just decide to spend the evening at the club, playing cards or billiards. He had spent the past two nights prowling the parties, dancing with young ladies he had no interest in, just to see if he could get a glimpse of Arianna. It was downright irritating that he hadn't seen her at any of them. It was probably Constance's blasted idea to have Arianna attend a crush like Lady Windham's party and then have her disappear and leave all the women chattering and the gentlemen wondering about the new lady in town.

He had spent most of the day in his book room,

catching up on correspondence and reading and signing documents his solicitor Mr. Saint had sent over. That man always had something urgent for Morgan to attend to. It had been slow and tedious because he couldn't keep his mind on the task at hand. His thoughts kept straying to Arianna.

She had bewitched him, enchanted him, or something. He didn't know what the hell she had done to him. He only knew he was aching to see her again. He wanted to be alone with her. He wanted to kiss her and hold her close. And damnation, he wanted to know what it was like to sit across the dinner table from her and enjoy conversation while they dined.

But the worst was that for no reason he could understand, he would suddenly see her dancing and twirling under the arm of incessantly annoying Lord Snellingly, or weak-kneed Lord Waldo Rockcliffe, or that fake Count Vigone. Knowing that Italian had even touched her hand made Morgan want to bloody the fop's nose. And then there was the gentleman who looked so much like Gibby it was eerie even to have caught a glimpse of him before he walked off with Arianna. Why the hell had anger twisted inside him every time she had a new dance partner?

But then, there were times during the day when Morgan would find himself staring out the window, remembering how angelic she looked that night they were on the coast, when she experienced her first taste of ecstasy. And despite his best efforts at forgetting, he remembered the shock and then hurt he saw in her eyes when he had rebuffed her appeal for more.

What he didn't know at the time was that it was

easier to refuse her advances when there weren't half a dozen men crowded around her, competing for her attention, looking at her with hunger in their eyes. Now suddenly, he was the one eager for more of her. He wanted to see her, talk to her, and hold her. He wanted to touch her again, taste her, and breathe in her scent.

Oh, yes, Arianna's scent. As the carriage rolled along at a leisurely pace and the rain pounded the roof of the landau, Morgan leaned his head back against the cushion and breathed in deeply. He'd taken her empty perfume bottle in to his apothecary's shop to have more of the scent made. The man had told him it might take some time to get it made, because he had to find an apothecary who could read the Hindi language to know the ingredients. Morgan made a mental note to check on that and see if the man had it ready for him.

Morgan made a tight fist and socked it into the palm of his gloved hand. "Oh, yes," he whispered aloud in the quiet carriage. "I want to see her."

The carriage rolled to a stop and, not waiting for his footman, Morgan opened the door and jumped down. Puddled rain splattered on his newly polished boots. He quickly darted inside the dimly lit club and handed off his wet coat, hat, and gloves to the attendant at the door. He then went in search of Gibby. Morgan knew the old dandy often enjoyed a light supper at the small private club before making his nightly rounds at the parties and any other clubs he might want to visit for a drink, a game, or conversation.

As Morgan rounded the doorway to the taproom,

luck was with him. Sir Randolph Gibson was sitting at his favorite table, looking out the window, a smile on his face. Morgan wondered what he could be looking at that amused him. The rain was so heavy, no one was on the walkways, and it was too dark and foggy to see even the coaches as they passed on the street.

For a man in his sixties, Gibby was still a handsome, strapping fellow with a full head of silver hair and all his teeth, which was a miracle considering his boxing match. His wealth was quite substantial, too, though Gib had never earned a dime of it by labor. He'd been damned good at managing it until a year or two ago when, suddenly, he started investing in risky business ventures. Morgan and his cousins assumed he did it just for their attention.

Gibby's father had made his fortune in the shipping business, when England was still trying to maintain control of its colonies across the sea. That war made the old sea merchant a wealthy man, and it all went to Gibby when his father died.

Over the years, Sir Randolph Gibson had been constantly sought after by young ladies wanting to better their station in life, and more recently, by aging spinsters and middle-aged widows looking to find a bit of romance or a comfortable life. But no one had ever caught his fancy enough for him to propose matrimony. He held to the fact that Morgan's grandmother, Lady Elder, was the only woman he'd ever loved.

As of late, Gibby had been getting himself into one predicament after another. Morgan or one of his cousins would always bail him out. But Morgan didn't know of any way to help him out of this latest situation.

Morgan had to admit that even though his cousins and Constance had assured him the twins looked just like Gib, he hadn't really believed it until he saw one of them for himself. The resemblance was stunning.

This latest escapade, if it could be called that, wasn't anything like the balloon venture, the time machine, or even the boxing match Gibby was involved with a couple of months ago. Those things were eventually settled. How did someone go about settling the fact that two grown men looked just like you instead of their father or older brother?

Gibby prided himself on saying that Morgan's grandmother, Lady Elder, was the only woman he ever loved, and Morgan didn't doubt that. But obviously, she wasn't the only lady he'd ever made love to. It was Gibby's and his grandmother's great friendship, that spanned thirty years, that made Morgan and his cousins feel responsible for the dapper old man.

Morgan walked over to the table where Gibby sat, put his hand on the back of an empty chair, and said, "Is this chair taken?"

"As a matter of fact, it is. I'm waiting for someone to join me."

"Really?" Morgan questioned and gave him a look that said he didn't believe him for a minute. "And who might that be?"

"Viscount Brentwood is joining me, not that it's any of your business."

That surprised Morgan. "Well, I'm impressed."

Gibby picked up his wine glass and smiled. "The hell you are."

Morgan smiled, too. "No, really, I am." Morgan

pulled out the chair and sat down. He caught the server's attention and pointed to Gibby's glass and held up two fingers. "So the two of you are going to talk?"

"We're going to have a drink, but we'll probably do a little talking, too."

"I bet you do. And let me guess. I bet it will be about the twins?"

Gibby's eyes sparkled with mischief. Morgan hadn't seen the dapper old man's eyes brim with such excitement in months.

"He's the one who asked to meet with me. I have no idea what he wants to talk about."

"I think you can easily guess that he plans to talk about his brothers."

"The twins?" the cagey whipster questioned. "I don't know. As for me, I don't have any plans. I take each day as it comes. As Lord Chesterfield used to say: 'Every morning I wake up it's a good day.'"

As the server placed a glass of wine in front of Morgan and put another in front of Gib, Morgan smiled. "I don't think Chesterfield said that. I think you made it up just now as you were talking."

Gibby smiled, too. "No, he said it. I heard him say it more than once."

Morgan nodded and sipped his wine, though he was still unconvinced. Turning serious, he wrinkled his forehead and asked, "Gib, what the devil are you going to do about the fact that everyone in the ton is talking about Brentwood's brothers looking just like you?"

Gibby held out his empty hands, palms up. "What can I do about what other people say?"

"You could say something like, yes, these men are my sons, or no, they aren't."

Gibby laughed good-naturedly. "Now why would I want to say anything like that? You should know without my having to tell you that the best way to handle gossip is not to acknowledge it."

"That sounds like more wise words from Lord Chesterfield."

"Yes, he probably said that, too."

Morgan picked up his wine, leaned back in his chair, and looked at Gibby. The dandy loved all the notoriety he was getting, and it probably ratcheted up his virility and his ego, too. That's why he wasn't trying to clear up everyone's questions.

Morgan took him to task by saying, "You don't want to say anything because you are enjoying all the attention."

"What's wrong with attention? Now, instead of trying to mind my business, why don't you tell me about Miss Arianna Sweet?"

Morgan's eyes narrowed. It made his stomach clinch just hearing her name. "So you think it's all right for you to remain as closemouthed as a turtle in its shell, but you expect me to spill everything to you?"

Gibby grinned. "Yes, I do."

Morgan grinned, too. "It's not going to happen, old man."

"You do know that your not wanting to talk about her tells me quite a bit about what your real feelings are for her, don't you?"

Morgan slowly sipped his wine. It was impossible to outsmart Gibby. "No, I didn't know that."

"Excuse me, my lord."

Morgan turned toward the server who had just walked up. "Yes?"

"There's a man at the front door, insisting that he speak to you immediately. He said it's quite urgent."

"Me? All right, I suppose I can go see what he wants." Obviously it wasn't a member of the ton, or they would have brought the gentleman to him.

"Gib, I'll come back and join you and the viscount after I see what this fellow wants."

"Hell's bells, Morgan, come back for what? We're just going to have a drink together. I can manage my own affairs quite nicely without you and your cousins' interference. Now go on, and you take care of your own urgent business. I'm doing quite well on my own."

Morgan polished off his wine and nodded to Gibby before walking to the front door where the server said the man was waiting for him.

"Where is he?"

"He's waiting outside, my lord."

"All right." Morgan opened the door and stepped outside. He saw his footman standing under the small portico, trying to stay away from the driving rain.

"My lord," he said rushing up to Morgan.

"What is it?" Morgan asked, seeing real fear in the man's eyes.

"One of your grooms just arrived from Valleydale, my lord. He says someone killed your servant Jessup, and that Post is at death's door."

Morgan's stomach lurched. "Damnation!" he swore. "What's going on? Did he say who did this and why?"

"He didn't know the man, had never seen him before, my lord, but he said he was a foreigner, maybe from India."

A chill ran up Morgan's back and made the hair on the back of his neck spike.

The footman clasped his hands together in front of him and added, "He also said the man was looking for a lady named Miss Sweet."

Nineteen

My Dearest Grandson Lucas,

You would do well to remember these words from Lord Chesterfield: "Wrongs are often forgiven, but contempt never is. Our pride remembers it forever. It implies a discovery of weaknesses, which we are much more careful to conceal than crimes."

Your loving Grandmother,
Lady Elder

As Arianna walked down the stairs, her slippers were soundless, her chest was tight, and her stomach felt jumpy. It was half past eight in the evening, and Mrs. Hartford just informed her that Morgan had called on her. It was sheer luck that Arianna was still appropriately dressed in a simple capped-sleeved high-waisted dress with a lightweight woolen shawl tied around her arms to keep away the chill.

What could have brought him to her door at this time of evening? It was well beyond the respectable time to visit anyone. And it had been storming for over an hour. Hardly the kind of weather or time of evening someone would make a hospitable call.

"Cook has already retired, Miss Sweet," her housekeeper said, following in Arianna's footsteps down the staircase. "Should I make tea?"

"That won't be necessary, Mrs. Hartford. The earl isn't given much for tea. I had Benson pick a bottle of fine brandy. I know he likes that. I will pour it myself should he care for a glass while he is here."

"What do you suppose he wants at this late hour?"

"I would have no idea, but I'm sure you know that the titled few feel quite entitled to call on whom they wish whenever they wish. He is an earl after all."

"Very true, Miss Sweet."

"You may wait in my music room until I call on you to show him out."

"But that room is at the end of the other side of the house."

When they reached the bottom of the stairs, Arianna turned back and smiled at the woman. "I'm quite aware of that, Mrs. Hartford. Should I be so fortunate that the earl wants to ravish me, I certainly wouldn't want you to hear him."

The woman gasped so loudly that for a moment, Arianna wondered if the poor woman had choked.

"I apologize, Mrs. Hartford. My attempt at humor was in poor taste. I assure you that you have no need to fear. I will be perfectly safe with Lord Morgandale. If you'll remember, he took me in when I was so ill I could hardly place one foot in front of the other, and I stayed in his care for more than a week."

"Yes, miss, I do remember that."

"Good. In fact, if you don't mind, I'd love to hear you playing some of your lovely tunes on the pianoforte for me. That will remind the earl that you are nearby. I'll call you when I need you."

Mrs. Hartford hesitated but finally nodded and turned to the left toward the music room. Arianna went in the opposite direction and headed down the darkened corridor to the drawing room. When she rounded the doorway, she saw Morgan pacing restlessly back and forth in front of the window. Only one lamp was lit in the room. She couldn't see him well, but she knew immediately something was terribly wrong. Her throat tightened, and a cold feeling of apprehension chilled her. She pulled her shawl tighter about her arms.

"Good evening, Morgan," she said, walking farther into the room.

Morgan stopped and stared at her for a moment before striding toward her. "We have to talk."

Arianna couldn't imagine what had caused the concerned expression on his face. "All right, sit down. Shall I pour you a brandy?"

"No, I won't sit down, and I don't want anything to drink. What I want from you is the truth."

That statement stunned her for a moment. She studied his face. She had never seen such strain around his eyes and mouth. Something disturbed him greatly, and that worried her.

Arianna moved closer to him and stopped by the upholstered side chair. She quietly said, "That implies I have lied to you, my lord, and I have not."

He remained in front of the settee. His arms hung stiffly

by his side. A frown twisted between his eyes. "Haven't you, if only by not telling me the whole truth?"

She didn't know exactly what he might have discovered about her but she was about to find out. "That can hardly be called a prevarication, my lord."

"What happened in India that caused you to leave?"

Although she remained calm on the outside, all of a sudden her insides were shaking, "I told you my father died, and—"

He took another step toward her. His blue eyes pierced hers. "The truth, Arianna, I need the whole truth."

Within a second or two he covered the short distance between them. He grabbed her upper arms and held her firmly. For a moment fear gripped her, but she quickly saw that he wasn't really angry at her but at something else.

She gazed into his troubled eyes. "What's wrong, Morgan?"

"I just received word that an Indian man went to Valleydale looking for you, and when he left, my groom Jessup was dead, and Post is barely clinging to life."

"No, oh, no!" Suddenly, Arianna couldn't breathe. She couldn't think. She managed to whisper, "He killed someone? Post is injured! How?"

"You tell me, Arianna."

"I can't. I don't know. Beabe told me she thought she saw him, and I didn't believe her. I should go to Post right away and check on him. I have medicines from my father that might help him."

"Arianna, slow down and take one thing at a time. Your maid saw whom?"

"Mr. Rajaratnum. He was my father's Indian *bhagidar*."

"What? Blast it, Arianna, use English. This isn't the time to use Indian words."

"Partner. He was my father's research partner in India. He killed my father and stole the formula he was working on."

"Formula? What kind of formula is worth killing someone for?"

"My father discovered a cure for consumption. That is the kind of discovery that would bring fame and fortune to any man."

"Why didn't you tell me this at Valleydale? You are the impulsive one. You should have blurted it all out to me."

She struggled to find the right words to say to make him understand her feelings at the time. "I don't know. When I first arrived, you were so brusque I hesitated to tell you anything. And later, I didn't want to burden you with my troubles. You were already doing so much for me by allowing me to stay in your home. I had no idea Mr. Rajaratnum would follow me to England or that he would harm anyone. He has the formula. Why would he come for me? Why would he kill anyone else?"

Morgan let go of her and said, "Sit down and tell me everything, from the beginning. And do not leave anything out."

They sat on the settee facing each other, and Arianna quickly told him the story, starting with when her father said they would be going back to England. Morgan sat quietly and didn't interrupt her. She finished with Beabe telling her she thought she had seen Mr. Rajaratnum a day or so ago near Mr. Warburton's house.

"And you didn't think your maid would know the man who killed your father?"

For the first time since he arrived, Arianna felt his tone was accusing, and that hurt. A breathless fluttering filled her chest. "I think I didn't want to believe it. I didn't want to believe he had followed us to England. It's not the first time she thought she saw him."

She gazed into his anxious eyes and, all of a sudden, it hit her anew that this tragedy was her fault. She shouldered the blame because one servant was dead and another was severely wounded. That grieved her.

What have I done!

She must do something. She rose from the settee. "I've put your employees and mine in danger. You are at risk, too, and Mr. Warburton. I must warn Mr. Warburton, and then I'll leave London immediately." She spun and was going for the door, but Morgan jumped up and grabbed her arms, holding her back.

"Arianna, you aren't going anywhere."

"I have to," she said, knowing she was close to losing control. "I can't put anyone else in danger. Let me go, Morgan." She struggled against his hold. "He's killed twice now. I can't let him hurt anyone else. It's me he wants. If I leave London, he will follow me, and then you will be safe. Beabe will be safe, and Mr. Warburton will be safe to continue to search for the formula."

"Where do you think to go?"

Her chest heaved, and her heartbeat raced. Inside she trembled. Her forearms rested tentatively on his chest. His face was so close to hers she heard his raspy breathing.

Her heart was so heavy with pain and guilt she could hardly speak, yet she continued to try to wrest herself free from his grasp. "I don't know where I'll go. I don't care. I can't let him hurt you or anyone else. Please, Morgan, let me go."

His hands tightened on her arms, but his eyes softened, and his features relaxed. "I'm not going to let you run away."

She couldn't bear his sympathy.

No, not that!

She didn't deserve it. She was unable to keep her eyes from filling with tears.

"Don't cry, Arianna. Do not let that monster reduce you to tears. You are too strong for that."

She bit back a sob. "No, you don't understand. I'm not."

He gave her a little shake. "Yes, you are. You are too strong for him. He will not make you cry, and he will not make you run. Do you hear me?"

Morgan was right. Her father deserved her tears, but his killer did not.

"I don't know what else to do," she said on a broken gasp and felt the first tear roll down her cheek.

He placed his warm hands on each side of her face, his thumb raking away the lone tear. He looked deeply into her eyes. "You don't have to do anything. I'm here. Trust me, Arianna."

She closed her eyes against his compassion. She loved him so much her body ached. "I do trust you," she whispered earnestly. "You know I trust you."

"Arianna."

As if with a will of their own, her lashes lifted and she met his blue, blue gaze. She knew he was going to kiss her. She didn't want to stop him but knew she must.

His head descended toward hers, and she twisted her face away from his. "Don't," she said softly. "Don't kiss me, Morgan. I've told you I don't want your kisses."

"I don't believe you," he said huskily. "You said you have never lied to me. Are you lying now?"

Why must her own words come back to haunt her? Especially at a time like this when her own heart was wounded from the pain of what Mr. Rajaratnum had done to her father and Morgan's servants.

"Yes," she said honestly. "You know I want your kisses."

"Yes, I do know."

Morgan's lips came down on hers with such hard driving passion and desperation it took her breath away. Arianna had never felt such intensity in his kisses. The depth of feeling should have frightened her, but it thrilled her, and she matched his ferocity. She shoved her hands beneath his coat, her body craving his warmth. His hands tangled in her hair. Their lips and tongues clung together. There were no words, no thoughts, just hunger, deeply rooted hunger.

With nimble fingers, Morgan quickly untied the knot in her shawl and threw it onto the settee. They fell together on top of the shawl, and Morgan rolled on top of her. With frantic movements of hands working together for a common goal, her dress was thrown up and her drawers pushed down. His trousers were unbuttoned. Their kisses were wild, fierce, and uncontrolled. The feral sounds they made were soft, whispered, but eager and passionate.

Morgan's body bore down on hers with something thick, hard, and probing. In a single motion he thrust inside her. It was sharp, burning, and painful. Her gasp of surprise was caught by his mouth and swallowed. As the pressure built inside her, she felt full. Suddenly Morgan moaned as if something exploded inside him, and then he collapsed on top of her, shuddering and quietly gasping.

Arianna winced silently when she realized it was over almost before it began. It hadn't lasted nearly long enough.

"Oh, damn," Morgan whispered on an uneven breath into the warmth of her neck. "I can't believe I did that to you. Arianna, I didn't mean to be such a violent, greedy beast."

She loved the feel of his weight resting on her body. Her hands moved languorously over his strong back. "What do you mean? You were not violent, nor were you a beast."

"Do not try to assuage my shame or my guilt. I have no excuse for my clumsy haste, for taking my own pleasure and not thinking about you. I wanted you. I wanted you with such fury that I didn't care that I was ruining you. I didn't care that your servants might come in and catch us. I cared for nothing except possessing you."

Arianna didn't understand his remorse. "I am not unhappy about what happened, Morgan. How could I be? I was able to do for you what you did for me on the coast. I've wanted this, and for the first time you wanted me. How can that upset me?"

Morgan chuckled into her neck and then raised his head and looked deeply into her eyes. "No, not for the first time, Arianna. I have wanted you a million times since the first night I saw you. It has never been my right to take you. But tonight I felt your fear and saw your tears, and the only way I can explain it is to say I could no longer control my emotions. I never intended for this to happen, and I certainly didn't intend for it to happen like this."

His words pierced her heart with such sadness that all she could say was, "I know."

There was so much uncertainty in her about where she should go from here that she suddenly wanted to weep again, but she dare not show him her weakness a second time. She swallowed hard, closed her eyes, and summoned an inner strength.

When she lifted her lashes, she pushed at Morgan's chest. "We shouldn't be doing this, not now, not knowing what happened to—"

"Shh." He silenced her by placing a finger tenderly upon her lips. "Listen to me. Nothing can be done for the man who is dead except for me to take care of his family, and I will. I have already dispatched a doctor from here in London to go to Post. The man is already on his way. All that can be done for him will be done. There's nothing more I can do right now for him. I have already talked to a man on Bow Street, and by now, there should be runners arriving to guard your house and to make sure no one gets in here. What I can do now is right the wrong I did to you."

She was puzzled by his words. "What wrong?"

He touched her cheek with his fingertips and smiled. "I'm going to show you how a man makes love to a woman, starting right now. Where are your servants?"

Suddenly Arianna felt as if a million butterflies were fighting to get out of her stomach. "All retired but Mrs. Hartford, who is in the music room playing the pianoforte."

He smiled. "So that is real music I hear?"

"I asked Mrs. Hartford to play the pianoforte while she waits to show you out."

He chuckled low in his throat before saying, "I always hear music when I'm with you, so I had no idea there was someone actually playing this time."

His words thrilled her. Arianna felt as if her heart opened up and was filled with Morgan.

"Is there any chance she'll bother us?" Morgan asked.

"I don't think she will come until I call her."

Her lips parted for a final, feeble protest, but all they found was the warmth of Morgan's mouth covering hers, softly, sweetly, briefly. He cupped her waist with one hand and with the other gently massaged her breast. He rocked his lower body against hers, and Arianna felt him filling her again. All the pent-up tension left her body, and she melted beneath his gentle touch.

"All right, you had your turn, I've had mine, and now it's time for our turn. You and me together this time."

Arianna smiled. "I would like that."

As he kissed her lips, her cheeks, and her eyes, his movements were confident, commanding. His mouth and tongue ravaged hers in a hungry kiss, and his body leaned heavily, deeply into hers, pressing his hardness into her softness. She met his ardor with a surprising fervency of her own.

He propped himself above her with one hand, and with the other, he grabbed hold of the neckline of her dress and pushed it off her shoulder and down her arm. With little work, he freed her breast and cupped it before closing his mouth over her nipple.

Arianna gasped with pleasure that was too wonderful to put into words. Her nipple stiffened beneath his gentle touch. Waves of pleasure radiated through her. He bent his head and closed his mouth over the rosy tip of her breast and suckled. Arianna moaned with exquisite delight. She slid her hands up to let her fingers tangle in his thick, luxurious hair. Her hand traced the line of his shoulder and down his muscled arm. His hand molded over the fullness of her breast, and he gently sucked, giving her immense pleasure and satisfaction.

Pulling his neckcloth and collar down with her teeth, she nuzzled the warmth of his neck with her nose and lips, letting her tongue explore his scratchy skin, tasting him. Her hands combed over the solid wall of back, hips, and buttocks.

"Lift your hips and move with me, Arianna."

And she did, matching his rhythm as he pressed against her. He kissed her lips, her eyes, the tip of her nose, and down to her breast again.

"I have dreamed of this, Arianna, so many times."

Suddenly, when that sensation she couldn't explain, couldn't control, settled in her womanly core, her heart beat so loudly in her ears it was frightening, exhilarating.

His lips left her breast and brushed up her chest and across her shoulder. He buried his nose in the crook of her neck. Arianna rose up to cup his body to her, and an explosion of sensation spiraled through her that was so heavenly she thought she might lose her breath and faint. She wanted to cry out that she loved him with all her heart, but she swallowed the words and kept them hidden in her heart, and the sensation slowly ebbed.

Moments later, Morgan's body jerked, his rough breathing slowed, and he settled himself deep within her. He moaned softly, breathlessly, and kissed that soft area between her neck and shoulders.

Morgan slipped his arms beneath her back and hugged her tightly to his chest before raising his head and looking down into her eyes. "I didn't want this to happen between us like this, Arianna, but now that it has, I can't say I'm sorry it did."

She smiled. "I'm not sorry either. I've wanted this for a long time."

He nodded. "Forgive me for being in a hurry. I will make it up to you."

To Arianna there was nothing to forgive, but if he thought there was, she wanted him at peace. "You're forgiven," she whispered.

He kissed her so tenderly Arianna wanted the kiss to last forever, but she knew that couldn't be. They lay that way only for a few moments before Morgan rose, turned his back, and quietly started adjusting his clothing. Arianna rose and quickly did the same to her clothing and hair.

When he turned to face her, he said, "I have many things to do, Arianna. You'll be safe here. I don't want you leaving this house until I get back to talk to you."

He reached down and picked up the shawl that was spotted with the evidence of her virginity and handed it to her. "You don't want your maid to see this. Now go call Mrs. Hartford and tell her I'm ready to leave."

Twenty

My Dearest Grandson Lucas,

I'm sure Lord Chesterfield had a particular person in mind when he wrote this, but he never made mention of the name. "A strange concurrence of circumstances has sometimes raised very bad men to high stations, but they have been raised like criminals to a pillory, where their persons and their crimes, by being more conspicuous, are only more known, the more detested, and the more pelted and insulted."

Your loving Grandmother,
Lady Elder

ARIANNA LOVED MORGAN WITH ALL HER HEART, BUT SHE simply couldn't obey his every command. She had to warn Mr. Warburton about Mr. Rajaratnum. She would have loved to have gone straight to bed and dreamed about every touch, every taste, and every whisper from her time with Morgan, but that would have to wait until sometime in the future. Right now, duty demanded that she think about her wants later. The first thing she had to do was go to see Mr. Warburton.

Morgan thought Mr. Warburton could take care of himself, but she wasn't so sure of that. He was a man her father's age, and her father certainly hadn't been a match for Mr. Rajaratnum's youth and strength. The old man needed to be warned. Arianna was sure of it. And just a note via a footman might not convince Mr. Warburton that he was in danger.

It was bad enough that she had the death of Morgan's groom, Jessup, on her head, and possibly Post's, too. She wouldn't be able to live with herself if any harm came to Mr. Warburton and she hadn't alerted him. Morgan said he had someone watching her house so that Mr. Rajaratnum couldn't get in, so she felt comfortable that her servants should be safe.

As soon as Mrs. Hartford showed Morgan out of the house, Arianna dismissed her for the evening. But instead of going straight to bed, Arianna went to her room and found a black, hooded cloak and her reticule. She opened her jewelry chest, took some coins from the bottom of it, and dropped them into the drawstring purse. She had a moment's hesitation, thinking maybe she was once again being too impulsive. What would she do if it was too late in the evening to find a coach to hire? Arianna pushed those thoughts away as just being jittery. What little she'd seen of London's streets the evening she went to the ball with Constance, they were very busy with traffic. She would be fine. And just in case she had to wait for Mr. Warburton, as she had the first time she visited him, she picked up her copy of Lord

Chesterfield's letters from her night stand and stuffed the small book into her reticule with the coins. She picked up her cape and turned to leave. Beabe was standing in the doorway.

"I thought you were already in bed," Arianna said.

"Not yet. I was doing some mending, getting ready for my journey next week. Right now, I'm thinking it looks like it was a good thing I was busy. What are you doing with your cloak and reticule in your hands at this time of night?"

Arianna took in a deep breath. "It's not that late, yet. I must go out, Beabe, but I don't want the rest of the staff to know, so I would appreciate it if you would speak quietly."

"If you are going out, Miss Ari, I'm going with you."

"I must do this alone."

"No, Miss Ari, I can't let you do that. I told your father I'd take care of you, and I will. I don't know where you are going, but you are not going without me."

Beabe was so fearful of Mr. Rajaratnum, Arianna didn't want Beabe to know that she had been right and the man was in London. "All right, just to keep you quiet, you can ride in the coach with me, but I must go into Mr. Warburton's house by myself. Now get your cape and meet me at the front door."

When Beabe came down with her cloak, she also had Benson with her. She had taken it upon herself to wake the driver to take them to Mr. Warburton's rather than risk the chance of not finding a coach to hire. Arianna easily agreed, seeing the logic and safety in having her own driver.

It took longer for Benson to go to the mews

and ready the carriage than it did to drive to Mr. Warburton's house. But finally, Arianna was standing on the man's front steps, waiting for someone to answer the door. A steady rain fell, and there was a chill to the foggy air, but somehow she knew she was doing the right thing in coming to see the man.

At last, an older woman opened the door just enough to peek around it and asked, "Who is it?"

"Miss Arianna Sweet. I met you about a week ago when I brought some papers to Mr. Warburton. I realize it's late, but it's important that I speak to him."

"Hold on, I'll see if he's available," the woman said and shut the door again.

Arianna looked back to the coach and waved to Benson to let him know all was fine. A couple of minutes later the door jerked open and Mr. Warburton stood in front of her.

"Miss Sweet. I—ah—come in. This is unexpected, but do come in."

"Thank you, Mr. Warburton," she said, stepping into the warmth of his home. "I needed to talk to you. It's quite urgent, and I felt it couldn't wait until morning."

"I don't know what has brought you out so late on a night like this, but I was just thinking that I must call on you tomorrow."

"About my father's work?"

"Of course. Let me have your cloak and gloves, dear girl. You didn't come alone, did you?"

"No. My maid is in the coach, waiting for me, but I wanted to talk to you about something in private, so I asked her to remain with my driver."

He took her cape off her shoulders while she

untied her bonnet and removed it. She then took off her gloves but left her drawstring reticule hanging on her wrist.

Mr. Warburton laid her gloves, cape, and bonnet on a chair and said, "We shouldn't be too long. Why don't you come with me into my laboratory? It's quiet in there. We'll have complete privacy. That's where I have your father's papers. I was going over some of them again when my housekeeper told me you were at the door."

"I suppose it's too much to hope that the reason you wanted to talk to me is because you have found the formula," she said as they walked down the corridor toward the back of the house.

"Found it, no, no," he said, glancing back at her. "But that is what I wanted to talk with you about."

He opened the door, stepped aside, and allowed her to enter ahead of him. She walked into a rather large, well-lit room, but the first thing she noticed was that there were no windows. For a moment, she was reminded of the ship, and a sudden fear gripped her. She had never wanted to be in a room without windows again.

Arianna took a deep breath and tamped down those irrational feelings. Except for the lack of windows, Mr. Warburton's laboratory looked much like her father's had and nothing like the small room she and Beabe shared on the ship.

On one wall was a series of counters and shelving lined with varying sizes of jars, bottles, and vials, all holding different amounts of substances. Some looked to be filled with plants or herbs, while others contained clear and lightly colored liquids. On the back wall stood a desk littered with papers, her father's journals, and more containers of liquids and what looked like jars of dried leaves. It surprised her to see some loose papers scattered on the floor around the desk.

"Now tell me what brought you here," Mr. Warburton said.

The papers looked like her father's work. Arianna walked over to the desk and started picking up those that were on the floor.

"I'm sorry about that," Mr. Warburton said, helping her gather the last few sheets of foolscap. "I'm afraid I'm a careless old fool at times."

"I understand." She stacked the papers neatly on the desk.

Shaking off the unsettling feelings that didn't seem to want to go away, she said, "I came here at this late hour because I heard on very good authority that Mr. Rajaratnum is in London, and I wanted to warn you that he might try to contact you. He is a dangerous man, and I feared for your safety. If he had any idea you were trying to find or even reconstruct the formula for me, I'm sure he would do anything to stop you."

Mr. Warburton waved his hand dismissively. "The problem I have is that I've been unable to find your father's formula. Not even a part of it. I can only believe that you failed to give me all of your father's writings."

"No, I kept nothing."

He shook his head. "Perhaps he wrote in a book that you didn't know about, and it's now just sitting on your bookshelf."

Arianna's hands gripped into fists at her sides. It was frustrating when he talked to her as if she were a child. "Mr. Warburton, nothing is more important to me than finding that formula and turning it in to the Royal Apothecary Scientific Academy. I can assure you I gave you everything my father had ever written on."

"But you must have it somewhere, because it's not here," he stated flatly.

His sudden, quarrelsome manner stunned her, and for some reason she couldn't shake that feeling of uneasiness.

"Tell me again exactly what he told you about how you could find the formula, because I find it difficult to believe that out of all this—" His hand swept over the desk. "—I can't find anything that even remotely resembles a formula that will cure consumption."

She gasped.

"You must have forgotten something," he said feverishly.

"But I haven't," she said, jerking her hands to her waist, her drawstring reticule dangling loosely from her wrist. "I know it has to be there. You've just missed it."

"No, Miss Sweet, I have not. You have it somewhere."

"You can't really think that," she said, suddenly confused by his insistence. "I want my father to get recognition for what he discovered. I want the medicine to be available to help people who are sick. Why would I keep it from you?"

"Then you are going to have to come up with something better than the drivel your father has written thus far, because there is no formula that could possibly cure consumption in this jumble of papers you gave to me."

Arianna's shoulders lifted at his shocking words. "Drivel? Did you call my father's writings drivel? Is that what his life's work means to you?"

"Yes. That is exactly what this is."

Waves of indignation shook her. "In that case, sir, I will not bother you further. I will collect all of his papers and journals right now and take them home with me."

"Good evening, Miss Sweet."

Arianna's blood ran cold, and chills prickled over her skin at the accented voice that came from behind her. She twirled to see Mr. Rajaratnum stepping inside the laboratory, a diabolical smile on his thin lips. He gently closed the door and turned a key in the lock.

She gasped.

He dropped the key into the pocket of his coat.

As she looked at the dark-haired man with the smirk on his face, fear rose up in her chest and throat. She couldn't move. She couldn't breathe.

She was looking straight into the eyes of the man who had killed her father. She had an overpowering impulse to rush him, hit him, choke him with her bare hands, hurt him in some way, but just before she leapt toward him, she remembered that it was a misguided impulse that brought her to this point. There was nothing but folly in trying to attack a man twice her size. She needed to stay still and think.

Her gaze flew to Mr. Warburton. He gave her a cold, calculating smile.

Something was very wrong. Another chill peppered her body.

"You see, Miss Sweet, I have been working with Rajaratnum since the first time I visited with your father in India."

"No," she whispered, knowing she hadn't misunderstood him but not wanting to believe him. "You were my father's friend!"

He shook his head.

An anguished gasp passed her lips. Her ears started ringing, and her chest tightened in disbelief. She suddenly felt as if she might faint, but that she could not allow herself to do.

She would not let these evil men win!

Taking in a large, gulping breath, she tried to think. She was locked in a room with the *bure log* who had planned and carried out her father's murder.

What could she do?

"Oh, yes, I knew your father was on to something," Mr. Warburton said. "I was certain it would take a lot of research on his part, and I was content to bide my time and allow him. I knew Rajaratnum would bring the formula to me when it was ready. But this is the problem. The journal your father always said the formula was in, the one Rajaratnum took from him the day of his demise, doesn't have the formula." Mr. Warburton walked closer to her. "You still have it, and I want it."

"I don't have it. You have it," she said, retreating until the back of her thighs hit the desk.

"He was a sly *bhagidar*, your *pitaji*," Mr. Rajaratnum said. "He wrote it down somewhere else and only pretended to write in the journal he always carried with him."

She was confused. Her glance darted from Mr. Warburton to Mr. Rajaratnum. "You mean you don't have the formula after all?"

"No, but I am not worried, Miss Sweet," the Indian said. "We will get it."

Her father had fooled them both!

Arianna suddenly felt lighter. The thought that her father had outsmarted his killers thrilled her. Her fear dissipated. Renewed strength flooded through her.

"Yes, you will give it to us," Mr. Warburton added. "Rajaratnum is well versed in how to make people talk, and it doesn't take long for him to accomplish it."

Arianna's euphoria waned, and she swallowed hard. They didn't believe that she didn't have the formula. What could she do? They were between her and the door, and it was locked. She remembered there were containers of liquids on the desk. Did they hold water, alcohol, or something else? Could she use one of them as a weapon? Whatever the liquids were, would they sting and burn if they got in the eyes?

"We were just discussing how and when to approach you about this complication, and you came to us," Mr. Rajaratnum said. He folded his arms indolently across his chest, widened his stance, and smiled lecherously at her. "I've always wanted to spend some time alone with you."

The idea of being touched by either of these vile men made her throat ache with a suppressed scream. But screams would do her no good. There were no windows for Beabe, Benson, or anyone else to hear.

"My maid and driver are outside, and my entire staff knows I'm here," she said, remembering

Morgan's warning for her not to leave her house until he returned.

Mr. Rajaratnum laughed. "But they do not know I am here, Miss Sweet."

"That's true," Mr. Warburton agreed. "Once he's finished with you, and I know where the formula is, he can bind my hands and feet to a chair before he leaves you dead. The authorities will be looking for him and never know of my involvement in your murder. I'll present the formula in my name and secure my place in history. Rajaratnum gets the rest of his money from me."

"You can't take credit for the formula," she said. "I've told others that you were helping me recreate the formula for my father."

"That is very easy to remedy. I'll simply tell them that you wanted to believe your dead father discovered it, so you told several untruths about his accomplishments. The Academy will believe me, because neither you nor your father will be around to plead your case."

Anger grew inside Arianna, and she inched closer to the containers lined up on the desk. Her father had trusted these two men, and they had betrayed him, murdered him. She was not going to let them get away with that.

"If you kill me, you will never find the formula," she said, stalling for time so she could move closer to the liquids.

"Oh, I won't kill you until after you have told me where the formula is," Mr. Rajaratnum said.

Fury rose up inside her again. "Even if I knew where it was, I would never tell you."

Mr. Rajaratnum smiled; his eyes glinted with malice that shot fear to her core. "You think not?"

"There are mixtures I can force you to swallow that will lower your inhibitions," Mr. Warburton said. "We will get the formula, Miss Sweet. It's up to you how much pain it will cost you before you succumb."

Arianna ignored the fear and anger mounting in her chest and focused on her plan. Warburton was the closest one to her. She could grab the first container and fling it on him, and try to get another to hurl on Mr. Rajaratnum before he reached her. It was her only chance.

But did the containers hold something more than water?

If she could disable one of them, she would fight the other as if she were one of the tigers that roamed India.

Without further thought, Arianna swayed, feigning dizziness. She turned toward the desk and clasped the nearest jar in her hand.

Mr. Warburton took a step toward her, and she threw the liquid into his shocked face. He screamed. Clawing and tearing at his eyes, he fell to the floor, writhing in pain.

She turned and grabbed a second jar. Mr. Rajaratnum appeared before her, snarling. He knocked the container from her grasp and slammed the back of his hand across her cheek.

Arianna's head snapped back. Pain splintered up her face, and lights flashed in her eyes. Gritting her teeth against the blinding pain, she stumbled. Finding her footing, she scrambled to get away from the Indian, but his hand snaked around her arm. He threw her against the wall. Both his hands clutched her neck, his thumbs sinking into the hollow of her throat. Terror rose up in her.

She couldn't breathe!

"The formula, Miss Sweet," the man yelled in her face. "Where is the formula?"

Her chest burned. She struggled to drag in air. She raised her hands to pry at his fingers and felt the weight of Lord Chesterfield's book in her velvet reticule. She fumbled with the purse. If she could somehow manage to strike him with the book, maybe she could… But the thought was lost.

Black spots formed in front of her eyes. She couldn't die here. Morgan would never know how much she loved him. Her father would never get his recognition.

The door slammed against the wall, and Arianna heard Morgan call her name.

Mr. Rajaratnum released her and spun, pulling a pistol from his pocket. He pointed it at Morgan.

"No!" she screamed with her first gasping breath. With every ounce of strength she had left, she swung the book. It connected with the Indian's head at the same moment she saw the spark of fire leave the barrel. The Indian howled in pain. Another shot rang out. Mr. Rajaratnum jerked. A red stain appeared on his white shirt, and his eyes widened. Moments later, he crumpled to the floor.

Morgan's arms circled her. He pressed her face to his chest, and with his body, he shielded her from the two men lying on the floor.

"Get them out of here," Morgan yelled to someone.

Arianna coughed and struggled to regain her breath.

She heard the sound of shuffling. She didn't know how long she stood there, just letting Morgan hold her, but when the room became quiet and her breathing eased, she looked up at Morgan. His eyes were heavy with concern. He touched the side of her face, under her eye, and she winced and turned away.

"You're hurt."

"I'm fine," she lied. Her throat felt raw, and her chest burned from struggling to breathe. "Where are…?"

"The runners are taking care of them. It's you I'm concerned about."

"Mr. Warburton was Mr. Rajaratnum's partner, not my father's. Together they planned my father's murder."

"I'm sorry about that, Arianna, but there is no reason for you to worry about either of them again. Rajaratnum is dead, and the runners are taking Mr. Warburton to the magistrate as we speak. I can assure you, I will see to it that he will never be a free man again."

"How did you know I was here?" she asked, pushing out of his arms.

"I told you I had runners watching your house. Their instructions were not to let anyone get in. I didn't think it was necessary to tell them not to let anyone get out of the house, but knowing you, I should have. Luckily, two of the men followed you here, and once you came inside, one of them rushed back to tell me. When the maid refused to let us in, we forced our way inside."

Morgan reached for her, but she stepped away. There was comfort in his touch, in his arms, but she didn't want to be comforted. Not now. She wanted to go home. She had to find a way to deal with the heartbreaking fact that her father's formula was lost. Mr. Rajaratnum didn't have it. She had given Mr. Warburton everything she had of her father's. If he couldn't find the cure for consumption written in the notes, there was no way she could ever find it. Her father's discovery would be lost forever, and that was almost more than she could bear.

Arianna had a sudden overwhelming feeling of loss. "I am very tired, Morgan," she said, trying to hold herself together. "Would you please let whoever is in charge know that I will come back at a later time for my father's papers?"

"I'll see they are collected and returned safely to you."

"My book." She searched the floor and saw it. "I must have my book." She bent down to pick it up, but Morgan got to it first. He looked at the cover. "Is this what you hit Rajaratnum with?"

She nodded and took the book from him and held it to her chest.

"Do you realize that because you hit that man with Chesterfield's book, you saved my life? You caused his bullet to miss me."

She nodded. "I'm thankful, and I'm thankful you saved me."

He ran the backs of his fingers down the side of her cheek that wasn't bruised and smiled. "Looks to me as though you were taking good care of yourself before I got here."

"I need to go home now."

"All right. I must speak to the magistrate about what happened here. I'll come to your house after I'm finished with what needs to be done about this."

She shook her head and turned away from him. "Please don't. I can't talk to anyone right now."

He touched her arm, trying to get her to respond to him, to look at him, but she couldn't. "Arianna, you don't need to be alone."

"But that is what I want."

"All right, if you are sure."

She saw confusion in his eyes but didn't have it in her to settle his mind.

"I am," she said and turned and walked out of the laboratory.

Twenty-One

My Dear Grandson Lucas,

One of the many things I loved about Lord Chesterfield was his enchanting wit. "Nobody can be more willing or ready to obey orders than I am: but then I must like the orders and the orderer."

Your loving Grandmother,
Lady Elder

FEELING QUITE PLEASED WITH HIMSELF, MORGAN STOOD on Arianna's doorstep, waiting for the door to open. He could hardly wait to tell her the good news he'd discovered earlier in the day and what he'd just come from doing. He wanted to tell her all that was in his heart, too. He wanted to pick her up, swing her around, and tell her he loved her.

He reached into his pocket and palmed the bottle her perfumed water had been in and smiled. He still couldn't believe he'd been so impulsive as to have made love to her in her drawing room. Not that he was unhappy they had, but not even in his youth had he been reckless enough to seduce a lady in her drawing room. But then Arianna had him doing a lot of things he would have never done before meeting her.

The door opened. He took off his hat and said, "Good afternoon, Mrs. Hartford, I'm here to see Miss Sweet."

Her eyes rounded, and she blinked rapidly for a few seconds before saying, "I'm sorry, my lord, Miss Sweet is not here."

"No matter, I'm sure she will not mind my waiting until she returns, if you will be so kind as to show me where I might wait for her."

Her eyes widened more, and Morgan got the first hint that all was not well.

"But, my lord, I don't know when she will return."

"Nonetheless, Mrs. Hartford, I have valuable information for her that I know she will want to hear. If it takes all evening, I shall wait for her." Morgan walked past the woman and into the vestibule. He handed the woman his hat and started taking off his gloves.

"But, but..."

"But what, Mrs. Hartford?"

"I don't think she's coming back today. She took her trunks with her."

Morgan's hands went still on his gloves. He felt as if he turned to stone. He couldn't move. He couldn't think. Arianna had left? She had wanted to run yesterday when she'd first heard about Jessup and Post. But he thought he'd settled that for her last night when Rajaratnum was killed and Warburton was turned over to the magistrate.

"Where did she go?" he asked.

"She didn't say."

"Do you expect me to believe she just packed her bags and left with no word to you about where she was going or when she would return?"

"Yes, my lord. It's the truth. Benson already had the carriage ready by the time I came below stairs."

"What exactly did she say?"

"For me to take care of everything until she returned."

That gave him some comfort. At least she didn't expect to be gone forever. But why would she have left without telling him?

"Who went with her?"

"Just her maid Beabe, Benson her driver, and the footman."

Thank God she wasn't alone. "What time did they leave?"

"Sunrise."

Morgan swore under his breath. It was already after five. Wherever she was going, she had a full day's head start.

"Have you checked her room? Perhaps she left a note."

"Yes, my lord. Her room has been cleaned, and there was no note."

Morgan felt as if his stomach was twisting. "Then I want you to assemble all the servants immediately. I want to talk to them, maybe the scullery maid, the gardener, or perhaps the cook overheard a conversation. I want to talk to them all."

"Yes, my lord."

"Immediately, Mrs. Hartford."

The housekeeper rushed away. Morgan felt like putting his fist through a door. After what she went through with Warburton and Rajaratnum, Morgan should have insisted he come over last night. Why had he listened to her and stayed away? Because he had to plan everything out. He had to put everything in order, and what did Arianna do, she simply left. No planning, no thought.

But he would find her. He had no doubt he would find her. He just needed to think about where she might have gone. He knew she was overwrought because she didn't have the formula. She wanted that legacy for her father. He was trying to be sensitive to her needs about that last night and give her the time she needed to collect herself.

Maybe she'd sent a note to his house. He hadn't been home since early morning. It could have arrived after he left. Yes, there was the strong possibility that she had sent him word about where she was going. As soon as he talked to the servants, he'd go home.

Morgan swallowed past a lump in his throat. Surely she wouldn't leave town without saying something to him, would she?

She would. She was impulsive, and it was one of the things he loved about her. He remembered seeing her dressed in the sari, when on impulse she had walked to the paddock. He was sure it was on that same kind of impetus that she'd donned the dance costume that afternoon in her room, and the thing that drove her to race to Warburton's after he had told her to not to leave her house.

Yes, one of the things he loved about her was also one of the things he found so frustrating about her.

Morgan paced in the small vestibule, waiting for the servants to arrive. Damnation, why hadn't he told her he loved her when he made love to her? Because he wasn't sure he had fully realized it himself at that time. He'd been so selfish when he'd first taken her and then so eager to make it up to her. Maybe that had scared her. No. He shook his head. He was certain that hadn't made her run away. She would never have responded to him the way she had after that if he had traumatized her, would she?

Why hadn't he told her he loved her?

Because he didn't want to believe it. He didn't want to love her. He didn't want to marry. Probably all those reasons. But last night when he'd seen her shoved against the wall with Rajaratnum's hand around her neck... he knew then he couldn't live without her.

Why hadn't he told her he loved her then?

Because he had to make plans first. He had to do everything right, get everything settled. He wanted everything in place before he told her the good news he had for her and before he told her he loved her.

A low, bitter chuckle passed his lips, and he shook his head. And what had all his planning gotten him? He had just come from applying for a license to marry her, and now he didn't even know where she was.

What would he do if she had gone back to India to look for that blasted formula? Could she have booked passage on a ship that quickly?

No, she wouldn't go all the way back to India, looking for the formula, would she?

Yes, Arianna would.

But she hated being on that ship, and she had been so sick.

Morgan swore softly again and combed his hand through his hair. He was making himself crazy with ideas. He had to stop letting his imagination run wild. He had to plan. If none of the servants knew where she was, he would go home and see if he had a note from her. Constance's house was on the way to his, so he'd stop there first and see if she had news from Arianna. If not, he'd pray he had a note from her. He couldn't plan past that.

Less than half an hour later, Morgan was walking through his door, throwing off his coat, hat, and gloves as he went.

"My lord," his butler said, rushing into the front hall, "Sir Randolph is in your book room, waiting to see you."

"Did I receive a letter, a note, or anything this morning?"

"Several, my lord. Most everyone knows you are back in Town, and the invitations are pouring in. They are all on your desk."

Morgan strode down the corridor toward his book room. He was in no mood for Gibby's antics. What could the old fellow want anyway? Morgan couldn't remember the last time Gibby had come to his house.

It had been raining almost steadily for two days, and the gloomy weather matched Morgan's mood. He walked into the book room and saw Gibby standing at the window, but Morgan went immediately to his desk and started looking through the mail.

"It's about time you got home. I've been waiting for you for over an hour."

"You should have told me you were coming," Morgan said without looking up from the correspondence. If he couldn't tell who the note was from by the outside, he ripped it open, letting it fall to the desk and picking up another as soon as he could see it wasn't from Arianna.

"You must be looking for something," Gibby said, walking over to stand in front of the desk.

"Yes, but damnation, it isn't here." Morgan let the last letter flutter to his desk.

"You seem full of merriment this afternoon. What has you so happy?".

Morgan plopped down in his chair. "I'm not in the mood for your humor, Gib."

"Really? I couldn't tell by the gloomy look on your face or the frantic way you tore into your mail."

Gibby walked over to Morgan's sideboard and splashed port in two glasses. He set one down in front of Morgan and said, "Thank you, I don't mind if I do have a drink with you," when Morgan remained quiet.

Morgan picked up the glass and took a long drink before bringing the glass down from his mouth, coughing as he did. Port was too strong to drink so fast, but right now, he didn't care. He didn't want to believe Arianna had left without sending him some kind of word about where she was going. His denial that she had done that was fast turning to anger that she had.

"Since you are always minding my business, I think I might better mind yours for a while."

"There's a difference," Morgan muttered. "You like for me to mind your affairs."

"The hell I do," Gibby said, taking a seat in front of the desk. "So did you ask her to marry you, and she turned you down?"

"Not exactly," Morgan said, swirling the port around in the glass.

"What does 'not exactly' mean? She wants time to think about it? Most women do. That shouldn't have you so riled."

"It means I applied for a license today to marry her, but I haven't told her about that because she's left town, and I don't know where the hell she's gone. Now are you happy that you know?"

It was Gibby's turn to take a long drink. "That puts you in one hell of a situation."

"I don't need you to state the blasted obvious, Gib."

"I'm assuming you've checked with all the pertinent people who might know where she went. Servants, family, and friends. Mail."

The old man's attempt at humor didn't get past Morgan but he was in no mood to be coddled. "Her servants and Constance are the only people who know her, and none of them have any idea where she went."

Gibby got up and poured more wine into Morgan's glass. "All right, let's go backward and see if we can come up with something. Where did she come from?"

Morgan's stomach rumbled, and his chest tightened. "India, and I sure as hell don't want to think she's gone back there."

"First thing in the morning, I'll have someone checking to see if any ships left for India today."

"Blast it, Gib! I don't know what I'll do if she boarded a ship today."

"Does she want or need to hide for any reason?"

Not now. Not with Rajaratnum dead and Warburton on his way to Newgate.

"Hide? No."

"If she's in any kind of trouble, or if she was frightened of anything, is India where she would feel safe?"

"I don't know. I remember she told me one time that she felt safe at Valleydale." Morgan jumped to his feet. "That's it! She's gone to Valleydale! That should have been the first place I thought of. Gib, you are a genius."

The old man puffed out his chest and smiled. "I'm glad you finally realized that."

Morgan emptied his glass, placed it on the desk, and headed toward the door.

Gibby rose. "Wait a minute, don't you want to hear why I came over here and waited over an hour for you?"

Morgan stopped. "Oh, sorry, Gib, but I don't have time to listen right now."

"This is a first. You don't want to hear about my conversation with the viscount?"

"Of course I do."

"Well, he wanted to—"

"But not right now, Gib. I must get to Valleydale. Arianna is already a full day ahead of me. We'll talk when I return."

"When will that be?"

"I don't know, but I promise we'll talk when I do."

❧

Arianna sat in a chair by Post's bed and laid a cold, wet cloth on his forehead. His jaw was badly swollen on one side, and he had bruises, welts, and cuts on his hands and arms.

"You shouldn't be doing this, Miss Sweet," he said, his voice weak and whispery.

"Nonsense. This is one of the reasons why I came to Valleydale. To see if I could be of help to you with some of my father's tonics and elixirs. Not that I don't trust the doctor that Lord Morgandale sent to care for you. I'm sure he's quite knowledgeable and that he helped you greatly. It's a blessing that horrible man who was beating you with the board thought you were dead and stopped when he did."

Post nodded.

"This cold cloth will help keep the fever down. The tonic I gave you to drink will help, too."

"Was it supposed to taste like dead leaves in dirty water?"

"Yes it was."

At the sound of Morgan's voice, Arianna jerked around and saw him standing in the doorway of Post's room. Their eyes met and held for what seemed like forever. All the love she felt for him bubbled up in her throat. An expectant rush sizzled through her, and she wanted to run to him and throw her arms around him. And she would have sworn that he looked as if he was happy to see her, too.

Walking up to Post's bed, Morgan said, "I know how bad it tastes, because I had to drink it myself a few times. I can attest to the fact that it will help you feel better."

Arianna rose and stepped away from the bed.

Post tried to raise himself up on his elbows. "My lord, you shouldn't have come."

"Don't try to get up, Post." Morgan took hold of the man's hand and said, "Lie back down before you hurt yourself. You look better than I thought you would. I'm glad."

"I'm much better today, my lord. You didn't have to come to Valleydale to check on me."

Morgan smiled at the man. "Of course I did." He took the cloth off Post's forehead, dipped it in the basin, wrung the water out of it, and replaced it on his brow.

"I'll be back to my duties before you know it."

"I have no doubt about that. You're a strong man, but I'll make sure Mrs. Post knows you are not to come back to work until she says you are ready."

"Excuse me, my lord, Post," Arianna said, rising from the chair. "I'll leave now and give the two of you time to talk."

Morgan looked at her. His gaze was so intense she felt a chill on her arms. Had she just imagined earlier that he looked as if he were glad to see her, too?

"Arianna, wait in the drawing room for me."

"I had planned to see Jessup's family and pay my respects."

"Do not ignore me on this, Arianna. Wait for me in the drawing room."

As she walked past him, he grabbed her arm and stopped her. She silently gasped.

"Do not even think about leaving this house," he whispered. "I rode like the devil all night to get here, and I'm in no mood for your impulsive behavior. I do not want to have to go looking for you again." He let go of her as quickly as he'd grabbed her, and she hurried from the room.

Arianna walked into the drawing room, her stomach shaking. It was clear that Morgan was furious with her over something, and that caused a deep ache in her heart. Was he angry that she had come to Valleydale? Surely he knew she had to check on Post and visit Jessup's family. It was her fault that Rajaratnum had come to Valleydale.

After she had left Mr. Warburton's house, she went home and fell on her bed. Morgan had told her not to let Mr. Rajaratnum make her cry, and she hadn't, but that night she cried herself to sleep for failing her father. She had let him down because she hadn't found his formula. But in the light of day, she had realized she could help Post with her father's satchel of medicines, so she had left immediately for Valleydale.

The first thing Arianna saw upon entering the drawing room was the life-size portrait of Lady Elder. How did a woman learn to become as commanding as that lady looked? Arianna feared she would never be as strong or as disciplined as Morgan's grandmother.

Arianna walked over and looked out the window at the gorgeous tree-lined drive. She had missed this place. She absolutely loved it here. As deeply hurt as she was by Morgan's anger toward her, she felt at home here in this house.

"You left me."

She whirled. "What?"

Morgan walked further into the room with a piercing gaze directed at her. "You left London without telling me or anyone else where you were going."

"You are right. I should have asked permission before coming to your house. I apologize, but at the time, all I could think was that I just needed to get here and check on Post. I knew I had some remedies in my father's satchel that would help him."

"Just three days ago, I took your innocence on the settee in your drawing room, Arianna. Just two days ago, there was a madman who had his hands around your throat. You have the bruises on your cheek and neck to remind you." He walked closer to her. "Did you not stop to think I might be a little worried about you when I found out that you had left town without telling me or anyone of your whereabouts?"

"No, I didn't think," she said softly.

His eyes narrowed, and his lips formed a crease of frustration. She hadn't meant to worry him, and it broke her heart to know that he was angry with her about it.

"Explain to me why, because I do not understand your reasoning."

"I was no longer in danger from Mr. Rajaratnum or anyone else, and as for what happened on that settee, I told you I would not require anything from you, and have no fear, my lord, I intend to hold to my word on that."

He looked incredulous. "You require nothing from me?"

"Correct. You are in no way responsible for me. I have now seen Post, but I would like to visit Jessup's family for a little while, and if you would be so kind as to allow me to stay long enough to visit Master Brute, I'll be on my way."

Morgan folded his arms across his chest and drummed his fingers on his arms. "Will you?"

Fighting tears of sorrow that threatened to invade her eyes, and much as it hurt her to say it, she whispered, "Yes."

Morgan turned and walked back to the double doors that led into the drawing room. He closed first one door and latched it at the floor to hold it steady. He then closed the other and turned the key under the doorknob until it clicked.

"What are you doing?" Arianna asked, feeling a little unsettled.

"Locking the door."

"Why?"

His gaze steady on hers, he walked toward her. "Because I don't want to be interrupted. I have something to show you and plenty to tell you." He reached into his coat pocket and pulled out the empty bottle of perfumed water her father had made for her.

She smiled and gasped. "I thought I had lost that. I couldn't find it when I got to London. Beabe swore she'd packed it, but we couldn't find it anywhere."

"It was left here. Mrs. Post gave it to me."

"I realize it's almost empty, but thank you for not

throwing it away." She reached for it, but he drew it back and covered it with his hand.

"Not so fast."

Perplexed, she lowered her hand. "Surely you don't want a lady's perfumed water bottle."

"Oh, no, I do want this one."

He wanted it? "All right. As much as I would love to keep it, after all you have done for me, I certainly can't deny you. It's yours."

Morgan held the bottle up and looked at it. "Have you ever really looked at this bottle, Arianna?"

"Certainly."

"What's on it?"

"The ingredients. My father told me he wrote the ingredients on it so that it would be easy for me to have more made, if for whatever reason he wasn't available to make it for me."

"You didn't question why he didn't write them in English?"

She smiled. "Of course not. We lived in India. Why not write it in Hindi?"

Morgan shook his head and smiled.

Arianna was confused. He went from being angry at her to smiling. What did that mean?

"This is not written in Hindi. It's another little-known Indian language, and my apothecary had a hell of a time finding anyone who could translate it."

"Your apothecary?"

"I was going to have more made for you before I returned it, but I couldn't. My apothecary assures me this is not a formula for perfumed water, as you call it, but it's a eucalyptus-based formula that could quite possibly be a healing tonic for the lungs."

A chill shook her body. "No."

"Yes. You've been looking everywhere for your father's formula to cure consumption, and it was written right here on your bottle."

Arianna covered her face with her hands. Sweet relief washed over her. "I don't believe it."

He took hold of her wrists and brought her hands down from her face. He looked deeply into her eyes. "I have never lied to you, Arianna."

It felt like her heart was bursting with love. "I know that." She wanted to hug him so desperately but was afraid to make a move for fear he would think she was making demands on him. So she said, "I must get this to the Royal Apothecary Scientific Academy."

She reached for the bottle a second time.

He pulled it back just short of her grasp again. "Too late."

Her breath stalled in her throat. "Too late?"

"When you were not home for me to talk with you about this, I took matters into my own hands. I've already had my apothecary take it to the Academy under your father's name. I'm sure their testing has already begun."

"Oh, Morgan." She threw herself into his arms so fast and hard that he stumbled backward, and they fell on the settee together.

Her lips found his, and she kissed him with all the love she was feeling. He responded eagerly to her advances and pulled her into his arms.

"Those better be tears of joy I'm kissing from your cheeks."

She leaned away from him and dried her face with the back of her hands. She had no idea the tears had fallen, but she answered, "They are. Morgan, how can I ever repay you for what you've done for my father?"

He looked down into her eyes and smiled. "You could marry me."

Her heart lurched, and she pushed away from him. "Marry you? No, no. I promised you I would not ask anything of you."

"You aren't asking, I am. Marry me, Arianna."

"Morgan, this is not the time to tease me about this. My emotions are already on the brink. I am so filled with love for you, I can't keep from telling you any longer, but I don't want you to feel you have to marry me because of what happened between us."

Morgan brushed a strand of hair from her face and wiped the last of the dampness from her skin, careful not to hurt her bruised cheek. "I don't. I've not wanted to admit it before, but I think I fell in love with you the night you arrived at my door."

"No, I remember that night clearly. You thought me the biggest nuisance you had ever encountered, and you just wanted to be done with me."

He grinned. "That's true, too, but it didn't mean that you didn't put your mark on my heart. I finally admitted to myself that I love you. I don't want to live without you. I can't live without you, Arianna."

"Oh, Morgan," she whispered, throwing her arms around his neck and holding him as tightly as she could. "I never thought to hear you say those words."

"You had better say yes to my proposal, because I've developed one of your bad habits."

She leaned back and looked into his eyes with wonder. "What?"

"Quite unaccustomed for me, yesterday I impulsively applied for a license to marry you!"

Arianna laughed. "You didn't!"

"I swear it on Lady Elder's copy of Lord Chesterfield's letters. So don't you think you should put me out of my misery and say, 'Yes, Morgan, I will marry you'?"

She threw her arms around his neck and said, "Yes, yes, I love you, and yes I'll marry you."

They kissed sweetly, lingeringly, for a long time, with each enjoying the feel and taste of the other. When Morgan finally let her go, he said, "I'll send word to Jessup's family that we will both be over to pay our respects tomorrow. Right now we are going to see Master Brute, and from there, we are going to get on Redmond and ride to the coast."

As he took her hand and helped her rise, she smiled eagerly. "The coast?"

"Yes." Morgan pulled her into his arms. "We will be married as soon as we get back to London. But make no mistake, Arianna, you are already mine. All and completely mine." He turned her loose. "Now go and get your heaviest cape. I'm going to have Mrs. Post pack us a basket of food and wine. We're going to stay and watch twilight descend, and I'm going to love you the way I wanted to but couldn't the last time we were there."

Her heart felt so full she could hardly speak. "I don't know what to say. I'm so overwhelmed, Morgan."

He smiled. "Must I teach you everything? Say you

love me and you can't wait to be alone with me on the coast."

Arianna laughed and threw herself into his arms again. "I love you, Morgan, and I can't wait any longer to be alone with you."

He kissed her hungrily for a brief moment and then turned her loose and said, "Good. Now go, and I'll meet you at the front door in a few minutes."

Less than an hour later, Arianna and Morgan made it to the coast. He helped her slide down from Redmond, and he then handed her the basket. While he hobbled the horse, she spread a thick blanket on the ground. The sky was gray but not threatening rain. When she took off her bonnet and let it fall to the ground, a brisk breeze fluttered a wisp of hair. She looked out over the dark blue water—the water that had brought her to Dorset, to Valleydale, and to Morgan. And now because of Morgan, her father's work would be recognized.

Morgan's arms slipped around her waist from behind, drew her back against his chest, and bent down and kissed the back of her neck.

"Mmm, you always smell so good," he whispered.

She turned her head toward him and kissed his cheek. "Did I tell you how happy you've made me?"

He laid his chin on the top of her shoulder. "Yes, but you can tell me again if you want to."

She turned in his arms to face him and slipped her arms around his neck. "My heart is so full of love for you."

He grinned, stepped away from her, took off his cloak, and spread it on top of the blanket. "I like the sound of that. Tell me more."

"I can never repay you for what you have done for my father."

An overexaggerated wrinkle formed in his brow. "Is that how I made you happy? I thought it was by telling you that I loved you and because I filed the necessary papers to marry you before I even asked if you would consent."

She smiled when she saw he was teasing her. "That, too, of course."

He reached up and untied the bow that held her cape on her shoulders and laid it on top of his cloak. "Good, because when I found out yesterday that you had left London, I almost went mad."

"I didn't mean to cause you such worry. I think I have loved you since you carried me to the drawing room and plopped me down on your settee like a sack of grain."

He laughed and pulled her to him. "Did I do that?"

She reached up and untied the bow of his neck-cloth and gently unwound it from around his neck. "Without an ounce of remorse afterward."

Morgan started unbuttoning his waistcoat. "That was a heartless thing to do. I insist on making it up to you for being such an inconsiderate beast."

She helped him shove his coat and waistcoat off his shoulders. "What do you suggest?"

His blue eyes pierced hers with love. "Lie with me, Arianna, and let me love you."

A thrill of excitement and expectancy spiraled through her. She turned her back to him and said, "Unfasten me." He quickly opened the buttons and helped slip the bodice over her head. Arianna slid the straps of her shift down her arms, and Morgan started pulling on the strings of her stays.

"I'm beginning to understand why you like to wear the sari, Arianna," Morgan grumbled.

"Does that mean you will allow me to wear them once we are married?" she asked while unfastening the waistband of her skirt.

"In our bedroom, yes; anywhere else, hell no. Also—" As he pulled the stays from around her and threw them aside, he stopped speaking.

Arianna turned and faced him, holding her shift up to cover her chest. "Also what?"

Morgan ripped off his collar and pulled his shirt over his head. "You can dance for me anytime you want to."

She gave him a teasing smile. "Perhaps I should do that for you on our wedding night."

"Oh, yes," he said, working the buttons on his breeches. "I think that would be a fitting wedding gift." He lifted one foot and started tugging on his boot. "And what would you like from me?"

"For a wedding gift?" she asked, stepping out of her skirt.

"Yes," he said, tossing one boot aside and starting on the other.

Arianna thought for a moment. "You have already given me everything I want."

"Have I?" He threw the other boot aside. "I think there is something else you want and you are afraid to ask for it."

"No. There's nothing." She smiled and let her shift fall to her feet, leaving her clothed only in her plain drawers. "I have you. What else could I possibly want?"

"Come here, beautiful." He pulled her into the circle of his arms and wrapped her tightly to him.

His naked chest was warm against her skin, and his embrace immediately covered her against the coolness of the air. "Master Brute will be your wedding gift."

She gasped. "Morgan! I can't take your horse."

"He's already yours." Morgan kissed the tip of nose. "You're cold. Let me warm you."

Morgan bent his head and slanted his lips over hers in a slow, tender kiss. Her lips parted, and with her tongue, she entered his mouth, tasting him, wanting there to be no part of him she didn't know. He moaned his agreement and pulled her tighter against him. Her breasts flattened against his chest, and his hardness rubbed against the soft womanly part of her.

He breathed in deeply. "Did I ever tell you that I love the smell of you, the taste of you, and the feel of you in my arms?"

She smiled, kissing his cheek, his chin and his neck. "Mmm. Yes, but tell me again. I'll never grow tired of hearing it."

With slow movements, he shoved her drawers down her legs and then did the same with his breeches and kicked them both aside.

She watched his gaze sweep down her face to her breasts, her stomach, and lower, before scanning back up to her face with appreciation shining in his eyes.

"You are beautiful, Arianna. I am a lucky man because you are mine."

"Thank you. It pleases me that you think so."

"I do."

She looked at his fine masculine body with the same loving tenderness he gave her and said, "You are a magnificent man, and I am blessed to have you."

He laughed shyly for the first time. "I hope you always think that."

They lowered first to their knees and then stretched their bodies out on the soft pallet he had made from the blanket, her cape, and his cloak. She turned willingly, eagerly, into his arms. Their bodies entwined, and their lips met. He pulled the sides of his cloak around them and kissed her fiercely. His hands stroked along her spine to her waist, over her hip, and down her thigh, sending chills of expectancy pulsing through her.

He lifted, stroked, and molded her breast with his hands. He sought and found her nipple and rubbed it gently between his thumb and finger, causing her to gasp with delight. Soaring hunger filled her. She spread her hands over his wide shoulders, strong back, and down to the flat firmness of his stomach, loving the feel, the firm texture of his bare skin. She didn't know how long they kissed and touched, becoming familiar with each other, soothing each other, enticing each other.

Morgan reached over and gently touched her bruised cheek with his fingertips before letting his hand slide down her jaw to the base of her throat. Arianna saw Morgan swallow hard.

"You know I could kill Rajaratnum all over again for touching you," he said in a gravelly voice.

She placed her fingers to his lips. "I took you at

your word when you said we never had to think about that man again."

He nodded and rolled her over on her back and rose up over her. He looked deeply into her eyes and said, "I almost went insane yesterday when I heard you had fled London with your trunks. I was ready to tear England apart or sail to India if I must to find you."

"It was an impulsive thing to do."

"A weakness you have?"

She smiled and nodded.

"Don't do it again. You are mine, and I never want to be without you."

She tilted her head up to meet his eyes. "Does that mean even when you think of me as Miss Tart rather than Miss Sweet?"

"I especially love it when you are Miss Tart."

He kissed her sweetly, longingly, before letting his lips leave hers and kiss their way down her chin, along the column of her throat to the valley between her breasts. His tongue traced a hot, moist trail down to her nipple, where he caught it up in his mouth and sucked gently. He caressed each breast before moving his hand down to her waist, over her stomach to the most womanly part of her, where he let his hand linger.

Arianna moaned and sighed at the waves of pleasure tightening her stomach and her core. His hands caressed her waist, her hip, and her inner thigh. Sensation after sensation flowed through her body. His touch was gentle, strong, and sure.

Something deep and wanton stirred inside Arianna. She felt the way she had on the coast when Morgan had taken her breath away with what he had done to her with his hands. She wanted to please him that way but still knew so little about how to do it. Her hands left the broad sprawl of his shoulders to the small of his back and lower to the firmness of his buttocks. She loved the feel of his taut skin, and she kneaded his flesh. She smiled when he moaned his approval. When her hand touched his hardness, he gasped, and she quickly moved her hand.

"No, Arianna, it's all right. I want your touch."

And so she did, exploring his member, feeling its weight in her hand for the first time.

Morgan moved on top of her, his body stretching the length of hers. His lower body settled between her legs, and he fitted his hardness against her. A slow spreading of delicious, languorous warmth spread through her, and she lifted her hips toward his. With a gentle push, he entered her and started an easy rocking motion that was pure pleasure. She joined his movement, her arms circling his back and pressing him closer, harder and deeper into her.

Their hips moved slowly at first, and as their passions soared, so did their movements, until Arianna once again felt as if she was going to burst with pleasure. Suddenly she cried out his name, and her body once again gave itself up to ecstasy.

Moments later Morgan whispered, "I love you," sank deeply into her, and then collapsed on top of her with a satisfied sigh.

For a long time Arianna lay breathless, fully contented, enjoying the comfort of his body on her.

"Morgan, will it always feel this good? Will you

always take my breath away and make me feel like I'm soaring?"

He raised his head, and with his arms, took his weight off her. He smiled confidently. "I will."

"Then may I feel it again right now?"

He laughed and rolled her over on top of him.

Arianna gasped in surprise and looked down at him. "What do I do?"

Morgan rose up, slid his arms around her back, and cupped her to him. "Anything you want to, my love. When you are on top, you are in control."

Her eyes brightened. "I might like that."

"I have a feeling you will," he said and then covered her lips with his.

Arianna thrilled to his touch.

Epilogue

My Dear Grandson Lucas,

I have no doubts that you Lucas, Lucien, and Alex are all better gentlemen and more set for life's pleasantries and foibles because of the knowledge you've gained from my dear friend Lord Chesterfield. Here are more wise words from him that come straight from my heart to yours: "Be wiser and better than your contemporaries, but seem to take the world as it is and men as they are. I have been young, and a great deal too young. Idle dissipation and innumerable indiscretions, which I am now heartily ashamed and repent of, characterized my youth. But if my advice can make you wiser and better than I was at your age, I hope it may be some little atonement. God bless you!"

Your loving Grandmother,
Lady Elder

WHEN IT WAS DECKED OUT FOR A PARTY AND ALL THE side doors were thrown wide, no room was as grand as the Great Hall. Morgan looked across the candlelit ballroom and among the crowd until he found Arianna. She was talking to his cousins' wives Henrietta and Susannah. The three ladies hadn't had long to get to know each other, but so far, he was glad Arianna seemed to fit in well with the duchess and the marchioness.

Arianna held her father's award of recognition tightly in her hand, a rolled sheet of parchment tied with a black ribbon. Morgan was glad he'd suggested they have a reception in her father's memory after the ceremony at the Royal Apothecary Scientific Academy. She was very pleased. And nothing gave him more pleasure than pleasing his wife.

"You are still a jackal of the highest order," Race said, clapping Morgan on the back.

Morgan turned to Race and to Blake, who stood beside him. "Me? Why?"

"Because you had the gall to marry while we were still out of Town."

"What was I supposed to do? Wait until you two decided you wanted to grace London with your presence again?"

"You could have sent a messenger, and we would have come right away."

"I could have," Morgan said with a slight grin, "but I didn't want to wait."

"I suppose we can understand that, can't we, Race?"

After clearing his throat, Race said, "I can, for sure."

"I was just watching Arianna, Henrietta, and Susannah," Morgan said. "They seem well suited as friends, don't you think?"

His cousins looked at the three women and nodded.

"Isn't that Lord Snellingly standing with them?" Race asked.

"Yes," Morgan said, "but I think those three ladies can handle him."

"I know Henrietta can," Blake said.

As Morgan looked at their wives, he turned thoughtful and said, "I remember when Henrietta first arrived at your house, Blake, and declared you were her guardian."

"Yes," Race added. "And she was haunted by a curse or something. What has happened with that?"

"Nothing," Blake said. "Thankfully she never even thinks about that any more. The best thing I did was take her to see the woman Gibby told me about. I worried if it was the right thing to do at the time, but now I know it was. After her meeting with Mrs. Fortune, Henrietta's never had another moment's thought about being cursed."

"That's good to hear," Morgan said.

"And, Race," Blake added, "I remember that it was just months ago that Susannah came to your house, hoping to talk you into giving her our Grandmother's pearls."

"Oh, I was there," Morgan said. "I remember that day very well."

"So do I," Race said. "I still get angry with myself when I think that for a short time, I thought Susannah had stolen the pearls."

"Did you ever do anything to Gibby for his part in that?" Morgan asked.

"No, I figured his boxing match with Prattle had beaten him up enough. And now he has the issue of the twins to keep him the center of attention for a while."

"Did either of you ever find out what happened when he met with Viscount Brentwood?" Morgan asked.

Both his cousins shook their heads. "I suppose one of us should try to find out," Race offered. "Looks like Brent and his brothers are in London to stay."

Morgan and Blake nodded, and then Blake said, "And, Morgan, remind me again, what was the reason Arianna came to Valleydale?"

"To see our Grandmother," Morgan said innocently. "Remember, she wanted help from Lady Elder."

Race started smiling, and then Blake smiled. Race's smiled turned to a wide, mischievous grin, and so did Blake's.

"You bloody blackguards," Morgan mumbled. "I know what you're thinking."

"Morgan, we—"

"Don't say it, Race," Morgan warned.

"I have to."

"Let him say it," Blake encouraged.

Morgan held up his hands. "All right, all right, you don't have to beg me. I promise to ask Arianna if she can teach Henrietta and Susannah some of her dancing moves."

Morgan, Blake, and Race laughed heartily.

Suddenly Arianna, Henrietta, and Susannah surrounded the cousins.

"You gentlemen seem to be having a good time," Arianna said.

"What is the cause of your merriment?" Susannah asked Race.

For the first time in his life, Morgan thought he saw Race and Blake blush, and that delighted him.

Race slipped his arm around Susannah's waist and said. "We were just talking about how lucky we are to be very happily married."

Henrietta smiled at Blake and said, "We don't believe that, do we ladies?"

"Not for a moment," Arianna agreed.

Morgan slipped his arm around his wife's waist and said, "Arianna and I are honored that you joined us in celebrating her father's accomplishment and his posthumous honor."

"Yes, thank you all." Arianna looked up at Morgan and smiled. "Of course, I'm disappointed that while his eucalyptus mixture wasn't a cure, I'm elated that it is a tonic that helps clear the lungs and brings temporary relief to those suffering with consumption."

"That's a step forward to finding a cure," Morgan added.

"I don't know if I told all of you," Arianna said, "but if it hadn't been for Lord Chesterfield, we never would have found my father's formula."

Morgan looked incredulously at his wife while his cousins looked astounded at him. "Arianna," he said, "what exactly do you mean?"

"Yes, we'd like to hear that," Blake added.

"When I saw Mr. Rajaratnum draw a pistol from his pocket and point it at Morgan, I hit the man over the head with the copy of Lord Chesterfield's letters Morgan had given me, causing Mr. Rajaratnum's aim to miss when he fired at Morgan."

"You gave her a copy of Chesterfield's letters?" Race asked.

"Whatever for?" Blake added.

"She had never heard of the man," Morgan said.

"And Morgan constantly talked about him," Arianna said with a smile.

"What?" his cousins asked in unison.

"It's a long story, cousins," Morgan said, "and best told over a glass of wine some stormy evening."

"We'll hold you to that," Race said and then suddenly added, "Over here." Race motioned for a waiter to bring the tray of champagne to them. He handed everyone a glass and then said, "To Mr. Albert Sweet for his great accomplishment and contribution to the world."

Cheers were exchanged all around, and then Arianna said, "Thank you for that on behalf of my father, and now I would like to offer a toast." As she lifted her glass, she looked up at Morgan, smiled, and said, "To the three rogues by our sides. May their dynasty live long."

The End

THE ROGUES' DYNASTY

A  TO

A *Marquis* TO
Marry

AN *Earl* TO
Enchant

Available from Sourcebooks Casablanca

Dear Readers,

I hope you enjoyed Arianna and Morgan's story as much as I enjoyed writing it. For me, it isn't difficult at all to write about a heroine who is eager to learn about love, but it was a bit of a challenge to write about a hero who is a conservative, reluctant lover, and still make him strong and sexy. But by the time I had finished the book, I was totally in love with Morgan.

All quotes from Lord Chesterfield at the start of each chapter are taken verbatim from his letters. However, throughout the book I attributed quotes to him he didn't say. I do this for entertainment, not to give credit where it isn't due.

While finishing *An Earl to Enchant*, I had a germ of an idea that would add three more breathtaking gentlemen to The Rogues' Dynasty Series. I shared this idea with my editor, and she loved it. I want all of you to join me in looking forward to Viscount Brentwood and his twin brothers' stories.

If you missed the first two books in The Rogues' Dynasty Series, you can still get copies of *A Duke to Die For* and *A Marquis to Marry* from your favorite local or online bookstore. And watch for the reprint of one of my previous books, *Never a Bride*, coming October 2010.

I love to hear from readers. Please visit me at ameliagrey.com or e-mail me at ameliagrey@comcast.net.

Happy reading,
Amelia Grey

About the Author

Amelia Grey grew up in a small town in the Florida Panhandle. She has been happily married to her high school sweetheart for more than twenty-five years.

Amelia has won the Booksellers Best Award and Aspen Gold Award for writing as Amelia Grey. Writing as Gloria Dale Skinner, she has won the coveted Romantic Times Award for Love and Laughter, the Maggie Award, and the Affaire de Coeur Award. Her books have been sold in many countries in Europe, in Russia, and in China, and they have also been featured in Doubleday and Rhapsody Book Clubs.

Amelia loves flowers, candlelight, sweet smiles, gentle laughter, and sunshine.